Grayslake Area Public Library District
Grayslake, Illinois

1. A fine will be charged on each book which is not returned when it is due.

2. All injuries to books beyond reasonable wear and all losses shall be made good to the satisfaction of the Librarian.

3. Each borrower is held responsible for all books drawn on his card and for all fines accruing on the same.

CRIES OF THE LOST

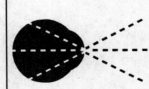

CRIES OF THE LOST

CHRIS KNOPF

THORNDIKE PRESS
A part of Gale, Cengage Learning

GALE
CENGAGE Learning·

Farmington Hills, Mich • San Francisco • New York • Waterville, Maine
Meriden, Conn • Mason, Ohio • Chicago

Copyright © 2013 by Chris Knopf.
Thorndike Press, a part of Gale, Cengage Learning.

LIBRARY OF CONGRESS CATALOGING-IN-PUBLICATION DATA

Knopf, Chris.
  Cries of the lost / by Chris Knopf. — Large print edition.
    pages ; cm. — (Thorndike Press large print crime scene)
  ISBN 978-1-4104-6666-2 (hardcover) — ISBN 1-4104-6666-3 (hardcover)
  1. Murder—Fiction. 2. Loss (Psychology)—Fiction. 3. Grief—Fiction. 4.
Revenge—Fiction. 5. Large type books. I. Title.
  PS3611.N66C75 2014
  813'.6—dc23
                                           2013042910

Published in 2014 by arrangement with The Permanent Press

Printed in the United States of America
1 2 3 4 5 6 7 18 17 16 15 14

ACKNOWLEDGEMENTS

This is a work of fiction inspired by the experiences of my son's Basque grandmother, Juana Maria Guruceta Iglesias. She and her family left Spain during the Spanish Civil War, and subsequently settled in Nicaragua. They were compelled to leave that country as well because of the threatening behavior of the dictator Anastasio Somoza Garcia, and his son, the future dictator Anastasio Somoza Debayle.

All the characters are made up, and while much is based on historical events, the story is completely fictitious.

Spanish translations were the work of Ellen Willemin and Randy Costello. Gracias. For French, staff translator Paige Goettel did her usual stellar work — with additional contributions by Mark Bonnot. All things Italian were guided by Gelsomina-Lolaluna (nom de plume), a Milanese friend who has a family home in the Lake Como region.

5

Andrew Wood, Birmingham lad, consulted on East End vernacular.

Digital technology assistance was provided by Bob Rooney and Mark Bonnot at Mintz & Hoke. Frank Gomes told me about all the crazy things you can do these days with telecommunications technology. Al Hershner set me straight on microphone capabilities. Any technological errors, omissions or oversimplifications are my responsibility.

Fritz McPherson at the Royal Bank of Canada, Grand Cayman, provided insight into the Caymanian banking system, some of which I messed with in the service of storytelling. Duane at the Turtle Nest Inn on Grand Cayman chipped in with local intelligence.

Dave Newell, president of the Wills Agency in Bennington, Vermont kept the facts straight on the insurance biz; Sean Cronin continued as staff weapons expert; Henry Ciccone captured the essence of Albany's municipal architecture; and my son James Gyre threw me the names of a few dubstep luminaries.

Readers this round included veterans of the Wesleyan Writers Conference, Lucille Blanchard, Marjorie Drake and Jill Fletcher. Thanks as always to veteran readers Randy Costello, Bob Willemin, Sean Cronin and

Mary Jack Wald. All indispensable.

Abiding thanks to Judy and Marty Shepard and their team — Susan Ahlquist, Joslyn Pine and Lon Kirschner — for bringing the book into the world.

Thanks, of course, to Mary Farrell for her enduring patience, and Jack and Charlie for saving me from the burden of excessive concentration.

CHAPTER 1

The tropical sun hung hugely over Grand Cayman Island. We were inadequately shaded by a wind-rustled palm tree overhead. We sat in our rented Suzuki Swift in a remote corner of a parking lot that served the First Australia Bank. The car was small enough to nearly hide below a trimmed hedge. I had a foolish urge to crouch down in my seat.

"What could go wrong?" I asked.

"Is that a rhetorical question?" Natsumi asked back.

"Sort of. Though I'd like your opinion."

"Nothing and everything."

"Talk about rhetorical."

"Philosophical. Remember, I'm a child of the East."

"We don't have to do this," I said.

"You're right. We could leave the safe-deposit box where it is and never learn what's inside."

"What's the likelihood of that?"

"For you? Less than zero. Was there ever a more curious person?"

"Or paranoid," I said.

I'd recently discovered that my late Chilean wife Florencia had a secret bank account at First Australia in George Town — the capital of the Cayman Islands — swollen with money and unanswered questions. Armed with the proper codes, IDs and verifications, and without leaving my computer in America, I'd been able to scoop out and secure most of the liquid assets. Not so with the damn box. They wanted me there when it was opened. I understood why, but handling transactions in person was counter to proper clandestine behavior. Behavior that had thus far kept me and Natsumi Fitzgerald alive, out of jail and fully operational.

"Fair enough," said Natsumi. "Which is why we're still debating this and not zooming forward like we normally do."

"Sometimes we debate as we zoom."

"I'm not used to seeing you conflicted, Arthur. It's not that endearing."

It was good she couldn't hear all the conflict raging in my head, perceptive woman that she was. The decision to stop off in the Caymans on the way to Chile —

where most of the withdrawals from Florencia's secret account had been routed — probably seemed last minute to her, but I'd been chewing on the idea the whole time we'd been in New York preparing for the trip.

While thoroughly absorbed in securing false passports and drivers' licenses, opening bank accounts in strategic places around the world, setting up international phone coverage and web access and winnowing electronic gear, clothes and other essentials down to single carry-on bags, there was always room in my brain for a little obsessive deliberation.

To be fair to myself, having learned that my wife had a secret offshore account — stuffed with millions of dollars — the safe-deposit box seemed inconsequential at the time. It was only when I tried to extract the contents, and was refused, that my hyper-curiosity kicked into gear.

"How did Florencia get whatever's in there, in there in the first place?" asked Natsumi. "You said she rarely traveled."

"You can send the bank anything you want and they'll stick it in a box. It's the getting out part that's hard. You got to be there in person."

"We're wearing disguises. Does that help?"

11

It amazed me how easy it was to change your appearance with simple, off-the-shelf theatrical cosmetics. It just took patience and decent hand skills, which Natsumi had in abundance. Yet I never trusted it. Maybe to fool third-grade mobsters and private citizens, even regular cops. But I held us to higher standards.

The hunted could only survive by outwitting the best of the hunters.

"It does," I said. "Though I like you better as a girl."

She pulled aside the rearview mirror to check her handiwork. "I thought it was easier to switch gender than race. The sport coat isn't the best choice for the climate, but I needed something baggy."

I cleverly chose a black wig, moustache and some basic prosthetic enlargement of my nose — not a small thing to begin with, now a commanding presence.

"So what's the plan?" she asked.

"We walk in and ask for the safe-deposit manager. He, or she, takes down all the account information, pulls the file and asks for the passport and driver's license of the person whose name is attached to the account. This is verified by the account manager within the bank, who will accompany us. Assuming everything's in order, we're

12

taken into the vault and given access to the box."

"Surely someone knows it's Florencia's box. Someone higher up, or people in the back office who manage the vault."

"They think it belongs to Kirk Tazman, an imaginary senior vice president of Deer Park Underwriters, the shell corporation Florencia used to manage the account. I have Kirk's passport and driver's license in my pocket. The Caymanians have gotten a lot stricter on verifications since I pulled the liquid assets, but they can't probe every transaction, not when all the paperwork looks legit."

"This is feeling really sketchy," said Natsumi.

"Indeed. Should we abort?"

She looked over at me, questions flickering in her eyes. "That's not up to me."

"It has to be partly up to you if you're going in there with me."

"I've never asked that of you," she said.

"I know. But you should have a vote. It's only fair."

"Oh, great. A monumental interpersonal issue to sort out on top of everything else. And me dressed like a boy."

I just sat there and waited her out. It didn't take long.

"Okay, then this is easy. Let's go," she said, getting out of the Suzuki. I had to walk briskly to catch up to her. Not a simple thing for me, old bullet wounds in my head and leg still asserting their influence. I was getting there, but it was frustratingly slow.

"Why easy?" I asked.

"I'm not going to prevent you from doing what you know you'd do for sure if you were on your own. Not taking that on, thank you very much."

We walked in silence until we were nearly at the front door of the bank.

"I guess I put you in a bad spot," I said.

"Don't feel bad," she said, swinging open the door, "the good intentions are noted. Smile for the security cameras."

The bank's lobby expressed all the scrupulous professionalism of any big city bank, though in a more cheerful color palette. The tellers and people at desks along the periphery were all Caymanians of African/European descent, in a variety of shades — young, crisp and earnest. We picked a short line behind a small flock of Dutch tourists. Only one entered into a transaction. Maybe he felt more secure running in a pack.

When we got to the counter, I slid a piece of paper in front of the teller and said, "We'd like to access the safe-deposit box

14

under this account number, please."

She picked up the paper with two hands and studied the number. Then she looked at us, one at a time.

"Have you spoken to Mr. Etherton?"

"We haven't," I said. "I was told to make my presence known at the bank and you'd direct me from there."

"Mr. Etherton manages the safe deposits," she said, picking up her phone. "I'll get him for you."

I nodded agreeably. Natsumi nodded along with me.

"That would be splendid," I said.

Mr. Etherton was a tall, light-skinned black man with a bald head and movie-star looks, only slightly marred by the severe cast of his face. I'd call it a scowl with a bit of curiosity mixed in.

"You are the people who presented this account number?" he asked us from the teller side of the counter. Far more nervous than curious, the young woman teller nodded, looking from us to Mr. Etherton.

"We are," I said. "Is there a problem?"

He looked from the slip of paper to our faces and back again, as if searching for a family resemblance. I felt my heart rate begin to ramp up, with intimations of fight/flight tickling at my nerves.

"Please wait," he said.

I looked around for security guards and found two near the front door, one on either side. They were smiling and chatting with each other in Jamaican patois. Their service weapons were in modern, quick-draw mesh holsters. I didn't look for cameras. No point in delivering a full facial when we knew they were all around, and now likely trained on where we stood at the teller's counter.

Mr. Etherton gestured for us to follow him into a cubicle office off the lobby. We sat in the two chairs facing his desk and presented him with our ID and paperwork. His scowl stayed in place as he read through the material, turning occasionally to his computer, typing in some command, then comparing what he saw on the screen with the paper in his hand.

"There have been significant withdrawals from the asset portion of this account."

I'd kept a small amount at the bank to keep the account intact. Just as a precaution.

"Temporary," I said. "We expect to refresh the account in the near future."

Mr. Etherton finally had something he could feel mildly pleased about. He nodded and left with all our stuff, closing the door behind him. Knowing he needed the original account manager to sign off on the IDs didn't make me feel any less vulnerable.

An excruciating half hour later, a young woman popped her head in the cubicle and asked us to follow her. We walked down a wide hall and came out into a large area with rows of desks filled with Caymanians working the phones. Mr. Etherton waved to us from the other side of a stainless steel gate at the back of the room. When we arrived, he swung open the gate and gestured for us to follow him down a passageway toward the open vault at the back of the bank. A Japanese man was waiting for us. His hands, folded in front, dropped as we approached. He bowed. We stopped and returned the gesture.

"Welcome to First Australia. I am Mr. Sato," he said to both of us, as if that explained everything. Then he said something in Japanese to Natsumi. She pointed to her throat and croaked out a response. She sounded like a Japanese guy with a bad cold. The man bowed again sympathetically, adding a few more words that Natsumi answered with a curt nod.

Without shedding his severity, Mr. Etherton used a key to open a tall gate made of the same stainless steel piping as the little gate. He directed us to go first, and then

17

followed, Mr. Sato taking up the rear.

We stopped at a desk from which Mr. Etherton pulled out a five-by-eight-inch piece of printed card stock covered with disclaimers and provisos. At the bottom was a line for me to write Kirk Tazman's signature. I signed and handed the card to him. He compared it to another card drawn, with some flourish, from the inside of his suit jacket.

He nodded at Mr. Sato, who nodded back, and we passed through the final gate and moved into the vault. It was lined floor-to-ceiling with safe-deposit boxes, technically long drawers with a single handle operated by yet another key. Mr. Etherton glanced at the card he'd taken from his pocket, then located our box. Before extracting it from the wall, he asked that we make ourselves comfortable at the table and chairs in the center of the room, a utilitarian arrangement with comfort the least of its attractions.

Mr. Sato stood by and watched Mr. Etherton withdraw the box and place it on the table. The box was secured by a lid you opened with a simple latch. Before doing so, Mr. Etherton placed his card in front of us and pointed to a section labeled CONTENTS. It was a large space filled in with only two words: COMPUTER DEVICE.

Mr. Etherton and Mr. Sato seemed to expect a reaction, and when they didn't get one, Mr. Etherton opened the lid.

Inside the box was a small manila envelope addressed to the bank. Inside the envelope was a flash drive taped to a tattered postcard promoting a hotel on Saint-Jean-Cap-Ferrat, a peninsula on the Côte d'Azur in the South of France.

I put the drive and postcard in my pocket and said, "I'm taking it. Where do I sign?"

Mr. Etherton, having stood at a respectful distance, leaned into the table and stabbed a thick finger at the bottom of his card where a British version of "The authorized holder of the account number has agreed to the full transfer of liability for the possession of, etc., etc." was printed. I signed with Mr. Etherton's pen and stood up.

"Thank you," I said. "Shall we go?"

Natsumi led the way back through the series of gates. Mr. Sato walked behind me. I could hear him making little huh-huh sounds as he walked. Mr. Etherton locked up the gates as we went.

No one looked up from their work areas as we passed through the bank lobby. All seemed normally, industrially engaged. Messrs. Etherton and Sato dropped off partway through the walk. I turned back and thanked them. Mr. Etherton thanked me back; Sato had already disappeared.

The security guards ignored us as we walked through the middle of their friendly, indecipherable banter, and out the front door into the hot wind of the easterly trades. We walked at a brisk pace across the parking lot, Natsumi staying close to my bad leg in a gesture of ready support.

I started the Suzuki and drove out of the parking lot with the same barely contained urgency. Natsumi slumped down in her seat and let out a breath with a "whoof" attached to it. I concentrated on moving through the busy, but casual Caribbean traffic, dealing with the strange sensation of right-hand drive, the standard practice on islands under the protection of the Queen.

We were staying at a resort hotel on Seven Mile Beach, not far from the center of George Town. We'd checked in as husband and wife, so as we made the transition from the denser parts of the city, Natsumi was busy freeing her long black hair from the boy wig and stripping off the tie and voluminous sport coat. She wriggled out of her black pants, revealing a pair of yellow short-shorts, thus completing the transition.

All I had to do was rip off the wig and

moustache and pinch off the extra meat around my nose. Natsumi helped me rub off the remaining flecks of adhesive.

"Feeling better now?" she asked.

Before I had a chance to answer, an SUV rammed into the back of the Suzuki. The little car leaped forward and twisted to the right. I fought to regain control. Then the truck hit us again, with greater force. The Suzuki slid nearly sideways and I threw the wheel away from the spin, forcing us into a barely controlled left turn into the parking lot of a hotel. The SUV shot by and slammed on its brakes. I couldn't see it as I raced through the lot looking for an exit, but I could hear the SUV screaming back in reverse. Natsumi gripped a safety handle overhead and wedged herself into her seat. I was almost to the hotel entry before I saw a way out — a narrow cut in a tall hedge, good enough for the tiny Suzuki, though way too narrow for a full-size American SUV. A group of potbellied businessmen had barely made it across the lane when I roared by, clipping a rolling suitcase, which in turn spun its startled owner onto his ample ass.

At the exit, the only real option was the main road. I made the turn, then slipped into another parking lot, this one serving a restaurant and a low row of tidy shops. I slowed to a slightly less homicidal speed and looked in the rearview mirror in time to see the SUV pass behind me on the main road. I gunned it again and got back to the main road, heading in the opposite direction.

I pushed my way as hard as I could through the loping traffic, with a greater eye in the rearview than the road ahead of me. With good reason, as I saw the SUV re-appear, many cars back, but gaining rapidly.

"Shit, shit," I said.

"You never say shit," said Natsumi.

"Have to start sometime. I wish this car was a little faster."

"I think we wanted good gas mileage," said Natsumi, through clenched teeth. "I'm getting seasick."

In what felt like a few milliseconds, the SUV was back behind our Suzuki, bearing down like an enraged colossus. Soon the only thing in my rearview was a chrome grill flanked by giant headlights. I tried to push the accelerator through the floorboards, with little increase in speed.

We bent around a gentle corner and came up behind a dusty pickup with an open bed bearing bundles tied down with straining bungee cords. I whipped around to his left, managing to put the pickup between me and the SUV. Horns blared as the SUV tried to follow me along the curb, the now incensed pickup driver doing his best to block the maneuver.

I downshifted and pushed the Suzuki's engine to its outer limits. The road in my rearview opened up, so I refocused my attention on the road ahead, swerving around cars and trucks, doing everything I could to put air between me and the SUV.

About a mile from our hotel, I thought I could let down, relax my tense shoulders and plan the next few moves, when there it was again, coming on impossibly fast. The gigantic chrome grill, the blacked-out windows, the relentless pursuit of hell's own sport-utility vehicle.

I can't outrun, I thought to myself, but maybe I can out-stop. There was a narrow shoulder to my left. I let off the gas and let the SUV come within a few feet of my bumper, then I jerked the wheel onto the shoulder and slammed on the brakes.

Natsumi yelped as the SUV shot by, trying to restrain all that ballistic energy. The result was a loud squeal from the tires, a lot of smoke, and a symphony of angry horns from the startled drivers caught in the moment.

I slid back on the main road, and at the

first opportunity swung right and shot down another side street, heading east away from the beach. Two blocks later, I was on the Esterley Tibbetts Highway that paralleled the crowded Seven Mile Beach area, where I could open up the Suzuki as much as I dared.

I craved a run to a safe place, but what was safe? We knew no one, had no legitimacy, even to the American diplomatic corps, since America had me officially categorized as a dead man. Having been in a coma for several months after surviving the attack that killed Florencia, it was relatively easy for my sister, a doctor, to declare me dead, after which I sneaked off the grid and lost myself in a crowd of fake identities.

Technically, Natsumi was merely missing. I frantically tried to invent a reason why. Eventually, an all-out car chase in broad daylight would attract the attention of the vigilant and well-equipped Royal Cayman Islands Police Service. Even if they saved us from the SUV, bad things would surely follow.

I tossed Natsumi my iPhone.

"Find the U.S. consular agent. I'm taking you there."

"What about you?"

"You have to figure out a reason why you disappeared in Connecticut and ended up here. I'm too busy right now to come up with anything."

"What about you?" she said again.

"I'll come get you. Then we'll pick up where we left off."

"Just like that?" she asked.

"I'll figure it out."

"What's going on?"

"I don't know."

Natsumi found the address of the consulate, which was in George Town as I'd hoped, having headed back that way. It was little more than an office buried inside a complex of restaurants and jewelry stores, but it was all we had.

"We shouldn't have gone to that bank," she said.

"Too early for postmortems. When we get to the consulate, I'm going to stop and you're going to run in the door."

"I'm not happy about this."

"Please trust me."

"I trust you, Arthur. I'd rather not leave you."

I kept up my speed, working hard to avoid killing pedestrians or colliding with the unhurried islanders, some in top-heavy panel trucks, others in gleaming European status symbols. If I were pulled over, I theorized, I could toss Natsumi to the cops and then make a getaway in the confusion. A very poor theory, but deliberation time was at a minimum.

For whatever reason, I managed to fly the Suzuki tight against the curb through the narrow streets of George Town unapprehended, following the iPhone's GPS directly to the front door of the U.S. consulate to the Cayman Islands. I pulled up to the curb.

"Leave your identification and cell phone. Try to avoid getting photographed or fingerprinted. They can probably make you, but stall for time."

"This is not what I want."

"Me neither. But it's our only way. Go."

She turned away, opened the car door and jumped out. She was halfway to the consulate door when two large men tackled her at a full run. She disappeared beneath a rolling mound of dark skin, white shirts with epaulets and blue slacks with a wide red stripe down the leg. Another man appeared at the passenger side window. He stuck a gun into the Suzuki and yelled something I didn't understand. I yelled back, words I don't remember. Over all the noise I could hear Natsumi screaming invectives in Japanese.

I stomped on the gas and raised the passenger side window as the car accelerated. The man with the gun ran alongside, holding his position, only to find himself suddenly clipped to a speeding car. He fired off a few rounds, but his aim was compromised by the angle of his captured arm.

Before the guy could lose his footing, I jammed my foot on the brake pedal, rolled down the window, and opened the passenger side door with the help of a sharp kick. The guy disappeared, leaving his gun on the passenger seat. I floored it again, causing the door to slam shut, and the little Japanese car — in sole possession of all my well-laid, thwarted plans — sprang aimless into the sultry, imperturbable streets of Grand Cayman Island.

CHAPTER 2

The first time I met Natsumi, she dealt me a bad hand. She was a blackjack dealer at one of the giant casinos in Connecticut. Blackjack was a good game for me before I'd been shot. I was born with a knack for numbers, so card counting came naturally. The math part of my brain had been smashed into sauce by a bullet, so it should have eliminated all complex calculating ability. And yet I was still pretty good at blackjack.

A neuroscientist could maybe figure this out, if I ever stopped running long enough to have the necessary brain scans and evaluations.

So as my luck at Natsumi's table quickly turned to the good, and even better, so did my luck with Natsumi. Her luck you could question, since knowing me put her in mortal danger, resulting in a spontaneous partnership that turned into love and a more devoted connection, and led to the current catastrophe in the Cayman Islands.

Together we'd uncovered and dispensed with Florencia's killers, in a decidedly extra-legal fashion. But far more questions than answers still lingered, leading us to the safe-deposit box in the First Australia Bank in George Town.

Florencia had owned an insurance agency in Connecticut. A bland, but highly profitable little operation that she'd used to embezzle millions of dollars from unwitting insurance companies. The wrong people discovered the scam before I did, which is what got her killed. What I didn't know was, why embezzle all that money in the first place? We sure didn't need it. Her company threw off plenty of legitimate revenue. And I did fine in my research business. It made no sense.

My success in market research had been fueled by an irresistible curiosity. As Natsumi liked to point out, I had a very hard time sharing the same planet with an unanswered question, especially one as big as this.

The very definition of a blessing and a curse.

Unless we'd been tailed since arriving in

29

the Caymans, there was no reason the people who snatched Natsumi would know where we were staying. We'd used different names, different passports, different appearances. So I took a calculated risk and went back there to retrieve our belongings, which included some electronic gear that would be difficult to replace on short notice.

I parked the Suzuki, wiped it down and left the key in the driver's side visor. In the room, I consolidated our stuff as well as I could, checked out and called a cab. He took me to another car rental place where I upgraded to an SUV of my own, a Ford Expedition. What it lacked in agility was made up for by a false sense of indestructibility.

Soon after, I had another hotel room closer to downtown George Town, with a view of the harbor and city beaches; though its main appeal was high-speed Internet access and lots of standard North American electrical outlets for my equipment.

I went online and immediately confirmed the obvious. The people who captured Natsumi were the Royal Cayman Islands Police Service. I had to assume, with no other data, that the SUV belonged to another group altogether, since there was no reason for the cops to take such radical action.

30

They had regular Crown Vic and Charger cop cars with lights and sirens, and no good reason to rear-end suspicious characters.

I thought, for now, I'd have to ignore the SUV and focus on the RCIPS, since they were the ones who had Natsumi.

And getting her back was the only worthwhile goal in the known universe.

I only had to wait a day to get the package from my favorite theatrical makeup supplier. I'd learned over time how to alter my appearance very quickly with a minimum of effort. I didn't know how well these improvised adjustments could fool emerging facial recognition software, though it seemed a risk worth taking.

So I chose one of my regular looks — a long grey-haired guy with my real nose, bushy eyebrows and round sunglasses. And baseball cap. Essentially a combination of John Lennon and Bernie Madoff on his way in and out of court.

I drove to the Central Police Station, in a dense area of central George Town. It was a three-story, reasonably nice-looking building of recent vintage with a tropical hip roof and friendly facade. To proceed, if my farfetched operating theory was correct, I just needed the right manhole.

It looked as if regular traffic, like cops changing shifts, moved in and out of a parking lot in the front of the building. The rear was invisible behind a tall blue wall topped by closely coiled razor wire. My heart sank at that, assuming my objective was well guarded on the other side.

The area was way too congested and exposed to survey by car, so I parked a block away and did a ground level reconnoiter.

I strolled along the front of the building hoping to look like a witless, meandering tourist. Moving on foot, I could easily see that the back of the police station was a minor fortress bristling with radio towers, huge transformers and windowless sheds. There were a lot of important things back there the peaceful Caymanians went to a lot of trouble to protect. Surely phone service was one of them.

I kept walking, passing a grassy area between the HQ and another government building. Right next to the sidewalk were two large, temporary black and yellow signs. They read TELEPHONE LINES and FIBRE OPTIC CABLE, respectively. Narrow, freshly filled-in trenches connected the signs to a half dozen raised-access hatches loosely arrayed around the lawn.

I stopped and looked up at the sky wondering if there really were Greek Gods and if they were up there playing a practical joke on me.

With nothing visible saying I couldn't, I strode across the grass, and holding my smartphone to give me an excuse for looking at the ground, checked out the access hatches. They were elegant things cast in bronze, with an embossed design depicting a seabird, the words George Town, and a description of the function of the hole underneath. I read "sewer," "drain water" and "electrical." The two trenches terminated at the hatch labeled "communication."

With nothing else to do but draw unwanted attention, I continued over the grass to a twisty little George Town side street, and after stopping for some more supplies and retrieving my truck, went back to my room to wait for nightfall.

I waited until two in the morning. Then I dressed all in black, including a black knit cap, and drove back to the police station. I brought a small flashlight wrapped in black duct tape so I could hold it with my teeth, and a long metal rod, one end of which I'd bent into a hook.

The sidewalk and parking lot in front of the building were well lit, but the grassy lawn next door was in deep shadow. Even so, I predicted about thirty seconds of profoundly dangerous exposure, though that couldn't be helped. I had come to accept there was no such thing as absolute security, if your intention was to function in the world. Even the world's shadowlands.

I used the metal hook to lift the hatch cover — a very heavy thing — and guided by the flashlight in my mouth, climbed the ladder down into the hole. I stopped partway to slide the hatch into place, then stepped down to the cool concrete floor.

As I'd hoped, I found myself in a small box that acted as an access closet for all the telecom lines running beneath the street. I'd been in similar places before, long ago, when I was doing field research for a company that made heavy-duty cable connectors for the phone business. Technology had changed a lot in the intervening years, but I thought it unlikely the government of the Cayman Islands would see any purpose in replacing those hardy, static couplers with modern electronic circuitry.

I was half right.

A bundle of standard copper cables, each

with a familiar connector, ran parallel to a pair of digital lines, capable of handling both voice and data. I used wire cutters to cut the plastic bands that held the bundles together, and counted twelve separate cables. I disconnected one of the connectors to confirm they were in fact standard 50-pair cable, and they were. The digital T1s were joined by connectors I'd never seen before. I took a dozen pictures from all angles with my phone.

Then I climbed the ladder, pushed up the hatch cover and slid it clear enough to push my way through. The sound of the heavy bronze cover dragging across the cement base seemed horribly loud. My whole body clenched as I braced for the yell of a cop, a bright light in my face, the blow of a nightstick. But none of that happened, and a few moments later I was in the rented Ford heading back to the hotel, breathing heavily and wordlessly thanking those potential Greek Gods for saving my life, and possibly Natsumi's, one far more deserving than mine.

Despite very strategic packing, I had almost nothing else I needed for the mission at hand. In my defense, there was no way I could have known any of it would be needed. I sat down at the computer and began to order, thinking through the various stages in the process, striving to consider every detail, to visualize every contingency. I was familiar with some of the necessary technology, another byproduct of the research I did for the telecommunications people. And though things had advanced considerably since then, the basics were still there.

As the sun was coming up, I downloaded the last application and hit the last submit button for the hardware order. The nightlong effort had done its job of keeping the waves of anxiety I was feeling from overwhelming me. Now, thoroughly depleted, I was able to fall asleep, visions of the big cops piling on Natsumi only briefly flickering across my mind.

By midafternoon I was back out on the street, walking the neighborhood around the police station in a fresh outfit and hairdo, memorizing what I was afraid to record with the camera on my smartphone. There was little purpose to this, other than giving me something to do that kept my mind off my galloping fears.

Before Natsumi, I'd been in plenty of mortal peril of a type that would fill anyone with dread, even a person as indifferent to his own safety as I'd become. But this was another thing. It was about a person who trusted me, who had thrown her lot in with mine, foolishly no doubt. In ways more existential than purely physical, she'd saved my life. Losing her was a prospect beyond unbearable, beyond unthinkable.

So I didn't think about it, and instead concentrated on the task at hand.

That night I called my sister Evelyn. The last time she'd heard from me we were in New York preparing to launch our trip to Chile, before getting sidetracked to the Caymans. Evelyn had been a co-conspirator in getting me declared dead and providing vital logistical support as I worked my way through solving Florencia's murder. This had exposed her to a variety of potential prosecutions, which continued to be of concern. If things eventually blew up, it would be hard to contain the collateral damage, the primary victims being Evelyn and Natsumi.

So there were good reasons to limit what I told her, with the likely deluded assumption that I could limit her culpability. Running counter to this was Evelyn's insistence I keep her informed of every single, solitary thing I did, on a daily basis. I knew why. She'd been more involved in my upbringing than my parents. Not that they were neglectful or abusive in any way, they just didn't have the life skills to deal with their kids. My mother was a receptionist and data entry clerk at a community health center; and my father worked at whatever he could with a fifth grade education, including fork lift operator, cashier at a public parking lot, dishwasher, cab driver, home healthcare worker for the state-run hospice, and probably dozens of other part-time, put-together ways to keep the family fed and in our apartment above the dry cleaners in downtown Stamford, Connecticut.

What these resumes didn't reveal were my mother's goofball sense of humor and unrelenting optimism, and my dad's sweetness and unconditional support for anything and everything we wanted to do.

My sister used to say, "I think if I wanted to be an axe murderer, Dad would say, that's fine, sweetie. Just be the very best axe murderer you can be."

So it was left to her, ten years older, to shepherd me through the thickets of scholarships, academic achievement and the vagaries of professional life. This made her something of a busybody, and I owed her too much to completely deny her that prerogative.

"Arthur, where the hell are you?"

"Grand Cayman Island."

"Vacation! That's wonderful, you really need it."

"Not exactly. We came down to empty out the safe-deposit box attached to Florencia's Caymans account."

"Oh," she said, a bit deflated. "What was in there?"

"I don't know yet. It's in code."

"Really."

"So what's been happening up there? The last time we talked they hadn't traced Florencia's laundering operation."

"We turned over all the agency's internal records, but apparently, vital pieces of information that could have led to the missing money had been thoroughly scrubbed. I wonder how that happened."

"Gee, I don't know. Heck of a thing," I said.

"They aren't even sure how much was embezzled. That creep who stumbled on the scam said it was millions, but who knows? Since none of the insureds ever had a loss she couldn't cover, how do you assess damages? Bruce Finger, who's back running the place, told me it was a dead issue. And even if it was worth their trouble to pursue further, our own liability insurance would cover any loss."

Not likely, I thought, knowing the actual tab.

"Bruce did say there was one guy, a retired FBI agent, who still has a bug up his ass about the whole thing and pesters him on a regular basis. But it hasn't come to anything."

"Shelly Gross. We haven't heard the last of him."

We exchanged the usual back and forth — her telling me to be careful and take care of myself, me assuring her with no success that I would. Before I hung up, she said, "You got the guys who killed Florencia. Why take all these crazy risks now?"

"I don't know why she did the things that got her killed."

"And you have to know."

"Bullet through the brain or no bullet through the brain, I have to know."

The boxes arrived at the hotel the next morning. I met the delivery truck at the hotel loading dock. I showed the driver my ID, and then offered him a hundred dollars to hand the boxes over to me directly instead of going through the concierge.

"I probably woulda done it for free," he said, "but since you're offerin'."

I took the service elevator up to my floor, and once inside my room, put the DO NOT DISTURB sign on the doorknob and locked the door.

I slit open all the boxes and laid the equipment out on the bed, relieved that everything I'd ordered was there. I spent the day reading through instruction manuals and running demonstration programs, testing, configuring and integrating the components. Always agreeable work for me, even under extreme circumstances.

Out of their bulky packaging, I was able to carefully fit the field equipment into a large backpack. As darkness fell outside, I put on my black clothes and lay down on the bed to preserve my strength and calm my mind. I folded my arms across my chest and visualized the equipment configuration as a schematic diagram, with boxes and arrows, switches and connectors. For no good reason, this put me to sleep, delivering me five hours later to the chosen launch time.

I dragged myself out of bed, stuck my head in a sink full of water, toweled off, put on my black beanie, and struck out into the soft, hot air that perpetually caressed the summertime Caribbean archipelago.

At the police station, I repeated the prior operation, without hesitation. The hatch cover lifted off with less effort and minimum clamor. I wiggled out of the backpack and dropped it down the hole. Then I followed, sliding the heavy metal plate over my head when I was halfway down the ladder. I hooked two LED lanterns on the cable trays overhead, which lit up the crowded space like a birthday party.

The first task was to decouple the 50-pair cables and reattach the connectors to a switch block that gave me access to the voice information flowing through the lines. This caused the telephones served by each of the 50-pair cables to go dead for a few seconds, but I was reasonably sure no one would notice, even the cops.

Back when I last studied similar switch blocks — used to set up large temporary phone banks for things like conventions and fund raising events — a row of little red lights indicated which lines were operating at any given time. And that's all you knew. Now, a wireless interface sent a signal to an application on my laptop that displayed the phone activity on a dynamic graph. I could see which lines were in use, by 50-pair cable, and by individual line. And then with a click of the mouse, I could hear any conversation I wanted to.

Decoupling the two data cables was more problematic. Any interruption in service would likely trigger analytic software to trace the break to the source, in this case, my hatch. My hope was I could plug in the phone-tapping devices quickly enough to have it show up as a simple blip in the network.

The devices were designed to be installed in a rack system with other telephonic gear in a closet somewhere inside a building. So it took extra care handling the exposed circuitry, and sharp aluminum edges, though in less than twenty seconds I had both units securely linked into the T1 lines. If the operating manual was to be believed, no one would be the wiser.

I had to use a separate wireless unit to feed the T1 voice and data into my laptop, but it was simple enough to toggle back and forth between the legacy phone lines and the ultra-modern.

That was good, but just a start. Once I was sure I was capturing all the information from all the cables, I booted up another application, called a voice analyzer. Legal and freely available like the switch block and tapping gear, voice analyzers were programs used by call centers to direct incoming calls and determine the mood of the callers. It could judge subtle nuances in the caller's tone of voice, as well as home in on key phrases, like, "fuck you and all your robot operators."

I'd spent much of the day programming in cop language and words relevant to Natsumi, like "Japanese," "American," "casino," "First Australia Bank" and "safe-deposit box." The voice analyzer would look for these words, analyze the tone with which they were delivered, and through the wireless connection, beam it all into my laptop.

Once I identified whatever cables were associated with the police station, I'd kill the other feeds to preserve bandwidth and processing capacity.

It didn't take long.

Apparently the Colonial governing authorities believed the Royal Cayman Islands Police Service was worthy of the most up-to-date communications technology, and had dedicated a pair of T1 cables to that purpose.

I felt a little wistful unplugging the big old 50-pair switch block, as if mourning another part of my life that had become obsolete.

I watched the computer screen for another hour for keywords related directly to Natsumi, though for naught. So I packed whatever gear couldn't be left behind, including the brilliant LEDs, and climbed back up the ladder.

Probably because I was so tired, or because of all the pent-up nervous energy, I pushed the hatch cover with too much force, causing it to clang against the cement mount. I whispered a curse at myself as I lunged up through the hole, and this time far more carefully, dragged the big metal disc into place.

I'd just made it to the side street where I'd parked the SUV when floodlights snapped on behind me. I continued to curse myself in silence as I started the truck and argued in my mind over what to do next. Then I stopped arguing, and drove around the corner and down the street directly in front of the police station.

Better to know.

The area surrounding the building and the grassy lawn next door was lit up like a night game at Shea Stadium, and a pair of RCIPS cops were out with flashlights and hands resting on the butt ends of the billy clubs stuffed in their belts. I drove by, and they barely looked at me, until I stopped and rolled down my window.

"Hey, sorry," I said, "could you tell me how to get back to Seven Mile Beach?"

They seemed a little conflicted, looking both at me and up and down the street. Then one of the cops tapped the other on the shoulder and walked away, his flashlight scanning the sidewalk across the street from the station. His partner stayed with me to give directions.

I thanked him, then said, "What the hell's going on here anyway? You guys are looking really intense."

"Routine police business, sir," he said, his speech graced with an Island lilt. "Best for you to just move along."

"Yeah, yeah, sure. No problem. Can I turn around?"

He nodded, so I moved slowly up the street, made a very careful and leisurely three-point turn, and drove past them. They waved as they went back into the police station, their equanimity restored and my hatch left behind, undisturbed.

I drove back to my hotel, filled with relief and the residue of nervous tension, defiant in the face of the capricious and unforgiving night.

CHAPTER 3

I was in my hotel room in the company of all the phone traffic going in and out of the RCIPS HQ. If I hadn't had the voice analyzer, I'd have to listen to conversations one at a time, in real time, to uncover useful information. With the analyzer, it was more productive to let a few hours go by so the application could search for keywords, and subtleties, such as standard American versus Caymanian inflections.

Not that this was easy. It took every ounce of self-control to keep my suppressed anxiety from exploding out the top of my head. I ran a mantra in parallel with my regular inner monologue. Something like, "Stay calm. Don't panic. Don't get hyper. Concentrate."

And stay occupied. So while the program ran in the background, I did a search of local news outlets for any hint of Natsumi's capture, though nothing came up. That told me something, though I wasn't sure what. I went to the American consulate's website and read up on what to do in the event of arrest by local authorities. Since the first instruction was to alert the American consulate, which I couldn't do, the rest was of little value.

To the best of my knowledge, no one knew I'd survived the bullet that was supposed to take me along with Florencia. Any revelation to the contrary would start a process that would likely end with me in jail for the rest of my life.

After an agonizing wait, I went back to my monitoring program.

There were three hits: "Japanese," "American woman" and "American consulate" — all within the same phone call. I clicked on the recording.

"Status," was the first word spoken, in a tone the analyzer described as abrupt.

"We talkin' to the Japanese girl, inspector, but she not talkin' back."

"Nothing?"

"Just demandin' to be turned over to the American consulate. We try to explain that we scoop her up before goin' in there. Why should we turn her over now?"

"No questions about that?"

"No, sir. She just keep telling us to call

48

the consulate, and all this nonsense about how kidnapping an American woman was going to spark an international incident."

The line was quiet for a moment. Then the inspector said, "So she's American. You know that."

"She talk like an American and why else the American consulate? You told us to ID her, but she don't touch nothing and won't take food or water. This girl know from fingerprints and DNA. Maybe if we can bring her into the station . . ."

"No," the boss said, cutting him off. "Can't take that risk. Stay in the house and keep your heads down. We're bargaining with the Americans now. Need to keep the merchandise safe. She has to eat and drink eventually. Give it another couple hours, then print her and swab her mouth whether she like it or not."

When they broke the connection, I searched for more hits, adding a few new keywords like "swab" and "DNA." A new list, sorted chronologically, appeared on the screen. I clicked on the first conversation:

"Inspector Josephson," said the boss, answering the phone.

"We did like you say with the prints and swab. Man, that little Jap girl, she's a tiger," said the other man. He was breathing hard.

"Get that stuff over here."

"On the way, inspector. Georgie bring it after he drop Antonio off at hospital. Girl near opened up his face with those claws."

"Just get it over here."

"He's coming."

The next call was an hour later, initiated by Josephson.

"Okay, Officer Brick, the girl's name is Natsumi Fitzgerald. That's all our American friends are giving up. They seriously want this person. You didn't hurt her any?"

The other guy let out a sharp laugh. "All the hurtin' was done to our side. You try swabbin' a wild dog."

"Tell her we now know everything about her. Tell her she's in big trouble with the Americans, so she doesn't want to go to that consulate. Tell her we can keep her in George Town long as she wants. Just need a little cooperation."

"But we know nothing but her name."

The inspector sighed.

"She doesn't know that. We got her name, that's good enough. You never interrogate anybody? Do I got to come over there?"

"No, sir. I'll call back in an hour."

He was true to his word.

"She don't care about our story, inspector. She still demanding to go to the consulate. She say her name's Zelda, not Nat-sumi. And she drank a lot out of the bathroom faucet when she went to take a piss. I think it gave her a boost."

I could hear the thoughts of the inspector as he absorbed that last bit.

"Brilliant, officer. Just brilliant."

"Can't be watchin' a woman take a piss, sir."

"You like your job?"

"Yes, inspector."

"Watch her take a piss. Just don't look like you're enjoying it."

"Yes, inspector."

The next calls were innocuous and incon-clusive. Natsumi was holding firm and there was no movement on the negotiations with the Americans, whose exact identity was never revealed. Near the bottom of the list, things took a bad turn.

"Time to move the Japanese girl," said the inspector.

"We bringin' her in?"

"No, need a new place to be keeping her. The Americans getting hostile. Say they send the SEALs, bust up the place, put on the diplomatic pressure. This thing's startin' to get ahead of my pay grade."

"They don't know we're here," the officer said, in a plaintive way.

51

"Brick, you don't know these people. They got ways of knowing shit we never dream of. Get out of there and come see me when you're secure."

Damn it all to hell, I said to myself. I clicked on the last call on the list, placed only an hour before. The incoming call to HQ was from a new number, a different cell was my guess.

"We all settlin' down and comfy, inspector. I be by to discuss."

"No. Meet me at Henrique's. At the bar. No uniforms."

"Aye, sir. Understood."

The second they clicked off, I jumped over to Google and searched for bars or restaurants called Henrique's. Nothing. Then I searched the name and got more than I could sift through in short order. I went back to restaurants and bars and searched each site for anyone named Henrique. I tried not to look at the time as I felt the opportunity drain away.

I went back to Henrique the name, and tried coupling it to anything bar related.

Then bingo. Henrique Fox, Bartender of the Year 2007. Still holding court at the Crazy Parrot Caribbean Grill and Saloon. I clicked over to their site. One block from my hotel.

I ran into the bathroom and stared at myself in the mirror. For comfort, I'd removed the Bernie Madoff disguise, and there was no time to put it back on. Under the hat and wig was my shiny bald head. I put on a pair of black-framed glasses and a loud tropical shirt over a white T-shirt and white linen pants. I also brought along a dark blue lightweight blazer and a different baseball cap.

It would have to do.

The Crazy Parrot was easy to spot, a giant neon sign depicting its namesake hanging above the door of a tattered, Colonial-era stucco building. Inside was a clean, brightly lit if well-worn space, painted in the usual array of brilliant Caribbean colors. Most of the floor space was taken up by the bar, with maybe a dozen tables lining the opposite wall. I sat at the bar, ignoring the other guests as I looked expectantly at the bartender.

Once I had a beer in hand, I looked around the place. It was thinly patronized, mostly by small groups of men and women. Five men sat at the bar, one solo and two pairs engaged with each other in conversation.

There's an old trope in books about cops and robbers that the cops are always easy to pick out of a crowd, even in civilian clothes. It sounds sort of believable, but it's not exactly true. Normal, non-narcissistic cops look and act like everyone else when they're off duty. So either pair at the bar could have been my quarry.

I first concentrated on the two with the greater age difference. The older man was doing most of the talking. He was bigger than the younger man, who showed a hint of deference in the way he actively listened. There was a TV above the bar showing a soccer game. I moved behind them, ostensibly to watch, which half worked. I would have been close enough to overhear them speak, if it hadn't been for the TV.

So I stared at the TV, sipped my beer and tried to will their voices into the auditory range. Unsuccessfully.

The solitary drinker got up and left, so I took his seat next to the other pair of guys. It only took a few minutes to eliminate them from consideration. I fought the impulse to look down the bar as I finished my beer and sauntered back out to the street. I climbed into the Ford, from which I had a good view of the entrance under the giant parrot, and waited.

The older man, I assumed the inspector, came out first with a cell phone held to his head. He continued talking as he climbed into a stripped-down Honda Accord and drove away. His officer was another half hour, likely taking the opportunity to get in a few extra beers. He crossed the street and got into a white, nondescript coupe of likely European origin. I pulled out of my spot and did an unhurried three-point turn a dozen feet down the street, coming around just in time to see the white car turn left at the end of the block. I turned on red, and again, caught the rear of the white car just as it made another left. This brought him out to a wider avenue that ran parallel to the waterfront. I was able to settle into a reasonable distance behind, and even allow a vehicle or two to get between us without losing sight of my quarry.

The avenue followed the coast to the south, through an affluent, gate-heavy residential area, then around to the east, where traffic thinned and the white car picked up the pace. I felt the strain as competing impulses — close in or drop back — fought in my chest. I picked the wiser competitor and let some more air open up between us.

We were well clear of George Town by this time, zooming toward Bodden Town, the second largest municipality on Grand Cayman. We almost got there. With little warning, the white car took a fast right down a narrow road paved in crazed macadam festooned with sprouts of ragged grass. It looked too confining and too exposed at the same time, so I slid by and pulled off to the side of the road. I punched up the maps function on my smartphone and located my position. The sandy road led south toward the coast, where a cluster of streets hugged the beach.

It was the only way in and the only way out.

I drove back and slunk down the road. The white car was out of view, which was favorable to a point. I moved slowly, scanning for taillights, or the colorless gleam of moonlight off white car paint.

I made it all the way to the sea with no results. I'd passed a few side streets along the way, so I backtracked and toured a pair of tiny neighborhoods of single-storey cottages with colorful stucco walls and tile roofs, but no white coupe.

I went back down to the coast and explored the last option, another settlement, with some of the homes directly on the sea, which I could hear after lowering the window of the SUV.

And there it was. A white car parked next

to a large van, behind a house that faced the beach. Inside the house, with a high degree of probability, was Natsumi Fitzgerald. Hungry, thirsty, likely frightened, yet doggedly determined.

I sped back to the hotel and emptied the room, loading everything into the rented SUV. Then I drove south toward the airport through the windy Caribbean night. I felt my chest start to tighten as I played my mind forward to the next few moves.

What I needed first was a place, a hotel or motel, as close to the airport as possible. And it had to possess a few key qualities. So I forced myself to concentrate on that task, ignoring the escalating stress reactions as I circled my destination with no viable candidates in place.

I'd just begun to fashion alternative strategies when I saw the sign, FIRST AND LAST RESORT, outside a forlorn cluster of tiny bungalows guarded by an office building with a shiny tin roof, lit by a powerful floodlight mounted on a nearby telephone pole.

I pulled in.

The guy at the desk inside the office had been on this earth a very long time. His skin was the color and texture of weathered leather. His thick, flat nose covered most of his face, and I could see his eyes, despite the low light, were black marbles set inside golden ponds. A cigarette was tucked between his fingers, and a small glass, filled with dark rum, was close at hand.

"I need a room," I said.

He thought about that for moment. "No other reason to be here, I reckon," he said, his voice more British than island lilt, and all coarse grit sandpaper, wetted down.

"You got one?" I asked.

"You got money?"

"I do."

"Then we got one. Our best, near the back. Quieter." He pointed his finger at the sky and moved it back and forth. "Lots of planes up there."

"That's perfect," I said, handing him my credit card.

I waited as patiently as I could through the laborious check-in process. His hands were steady, but achingly deliberate, dedicating equal time to running through the paperwork, pulling on the long filter-less cigarette and sipping from the small, rum-filled glass.

He put a big brass key tied to a thick plastic tag with the address of the motel on the counter. He tapped his fingers on the key before sliding it across to me. "Number's on the side of the building, but I can show you. If you're feeling confused."

I assured him I was fine navigating on my own, and thanked him again for accommodating me.

He shrugged the longest shrug I'd ever seen. About two minutes up, and twice that down. "No matter," he said. "You get lost bad enough, we got the authorities to do the retrievin'. Got to do something with all those taxes, right then?"

Though I'd never done it before, booking a chartered plane was ridiculously easy. The plan was to hop over to Tortola in the British Virgin Islands, logistically easier since the trip was between British Overseas Territories. That was my assumption, anyway. I called on the way and asked if I could load all our stuff ahead of time, and have the jet wait until the moment we were ready to take off. This was not a problem. It didn't appear anything would be a problem as long as adequate funds were available to cover the cost.

I reminded myself that this was Grand Cayman Island, a place where some of the richest people in the world stashed their money, and would often want to get in and out of town in a hurry.

I asked a cabbie waiting at curbside for directions to the Luxflite hangar.

"You mean de VIP con-van-ience center. Luxflite don't have anyt'ing so dodgy as a hangar."

"My apologies."

He pointed to an area to the left of the A-frame main terminal. "Just follow dat road 'round to de end of de runway. De're signs."

"That's convenient."

There it was, as promised. A single-story, hip-roofed building surrounded by lush tropical foliage and a parking lot filled with confident European and American sedans. Inside, two fashion model-perfect young women, prime examples of the robust Caymanian genetics, rose from their mahogany desks to greet me. I didn't know which one to address.

"I'm Jonathan Lembert," I said, casting my eyes from left to right. "I called about a jet?"

"You have luggage to leave with us, no?" said the beauty on the right.

"I do. Luggage and gear. Out in the parking lot."

Without losing eye contact, she held up a tiny pager and pushed the button.

A few seconds later a large white guy in a dark suit appeared, smiled and shook my hand. "I will handle that for you, Mr. Lembert," he said, with a hard-to-place British Commonwealth accent.

"Would you care for tea? A cocktail?" the woman on the left asked.

"I'm all set. Thanks."

The large man seemed slightly offended that I wanted to stay with him through the loading process, which was too bad, but I couldn't allow anything to be left behind, unlikely as that was. I distracted him with contrived American banalities.

"I'm really starting to dig soccer. You know, what you call football? You have a national team. I bet you watch the World Series. I mean, this is still North America. The Dominicans are nuts about baseball, and they're Caribbeans, right? There's been like a thousand of them in the majors. Can I help you with that? It's pretty heavy."

He cast a gaze that was equal parts appreciation and disdain, and with one hand, lifted the bag into the cargo hold of a Cessna Citation 525B jet airplane.

Back inside the building, one of the women gave me a leather folder with the photos and resumes of six pilots on call for our flight, four men and two women, all

61

with military and major airline experience.

"Call us when you leave George Town. We'll be waiting."

These were the moments when I thanked the ambition of my dead insurance agent wife, who bilked millions out of her carriers and clients instead of an easier and safer few hundred thousand. It meant that of all the worries a person could have living under assumed names and identities, for me, money was not one of them. As long as I was a careful steward of my illicit resources. This was an extravagant splurge, though well warranted by the importance of the next several hours.

With a critical link in the escape route secured, with any luck, I walked mentally through the next phase as I drove back to the bungalow motel near the airport. I hoped all the data I needed was living on my little laptop, with no essential scrap now loaded on the small jet. I was normally diligent in my preparations to the point of obsessive compulsion, and yet somehow I always seemed to overlook some obvious detail. Maybe that was the problem. Too obvious.

Back in the room, I booted up the laptop and a voice synthesizer — another call center application — this one capable of replicating anyone's recorded voice, in this case Inspector Josephson's. I'd built a menu of about two dozen statements, some declarative, others innocuous to cover the unexpected. I probably needed more than that, but I had to consider the time it would take to toggle through potential responses versus normal conversational back and forth, where there's little or no lag time between speakers.

I clicked on the cell phone number of the RCIPS officer I'd intercepted. My first line identified his boss as the caller.

"We good here," said the cop. "Nothing to report."

I clicked on my next line. "There's been a change of plans. We need to move her again."

"What's that?"

I stuck to my script. "It can't be helped. I have the place. You don't have to worry about that."

"New place?" asked the cop.

I searched my neutral lines. "Can't discuss that now. We need to move fast."

"We in trouble over this?" he asked.

I clicked on a good answer, but took a little too long getting there. "I'll tell you later."

"We got a delay here," said the cop.

"Maybe somebody listening in."

"We need to move fast," was the best I could do.

"Okay, okay. Tell us where to go."

I gave him the address and room number at the motel. I had him repeat it back to me. I told him it would be waiting for them, the door unlocked with the key inside. I asked him when he could get there.

"Twenty minutes, as long as that Jap girl not fight us over every little thing."

Good luck with that, I thought.

"I'll see you there," my inspector robot said, signing off.

Unfortunately, it was time to put the gun dropped into the Suzuki to good use. I hate guns. They frighten me. They're nasty to look at, hard to get without risk and prone to unplanned firings.

I'd never actually shot anyone, at least not directly with my own trigger finger. Didn't mean they weren't just as dead. But there were times when only a gun in your own hand will do. And this was one of them.

I dressed up in my black outfit, including a black ski mask. Then I packed the SUV with my remaining belongings and parked it in front of the unoccupied bungalow next door. It was more than a half hour before the white car and the van from the safe house arrived. I slid down in my seat, keeping the vehicles in view. The van backed into the parking space, the rear door only a few feet from the bungalow. The driver of the white car got out and met the man from the van at the rear door. They opened the van and climbed inside. Soon after they brought out Natsumi, handcuffed. Each cop held one of her arms, and they half lifted, half pulled her to the bungalow.

I jumped out of the SUV and followed them through the door, shoving both men into the room before they realized I was there. I flicked on the ceiling light, and with the gun pointed at the startled guy to the left, said, "Get on the floor, face down, hands on the back of your head."

When they hesitated, I leveled the gun at the other cop's face. "Get down now, or I start shooting. Easier for me."

When they complied, I dropped to my knees and shoved the gun into the first cop's neck. I pulled his service pistol from the holster and stuck it in the rear waist band of my pants. Then I said, "The key to the cuffs."

He rolled up on his left side and used his right hand to dig the key out of his pocket. He moved his other hand away from his head, with fingers spread as if to signal eagerness to go along. Once I had the key, and both of his hands back on his head, I moved to the other cop and freed him of his gun. For a dangerous moment, I had to take my eyes off them so I could get the cuffs off Natsumi, but they both stayed put on the floor.

As Natsumi rubbed her wrists, I moved her around behind me.

"Here's what happens next," I said. "You blokes are going to stand up very slowly, and with your hands back behind your head, walk to the bathroom."

They did as told and I followed them into the bathroom. I turned on the light and told them to sit on the floor to either side of the toilet. One had to squeeze in next to the wall, never quite making it; but after confirming that they could clasp hands below the tank, I had Natsumi click on the handcuffs.

As a final touch, I told her to cover their mouths with duct tape. It was only then they probably realized I really wasn't going to shoot them, and anger began to take the place of fear in their eyes.

"You Americans think you own the world," said Officer Brick, the one who'd been on the line with the inspector. I reached out and held Natsumi's hand before she could finish sealing the tape across his mouth. "But this girl and people like her are gonna take it away from you. One day at a time. They never gonna give up."

At the airport, we spent about twenty minutes wiping fingerprints off the Ford Expedition. I pressed my finger to my lips before leaving the vehicle and Natsumi nodded with understanding. Soon after that, we boarded the Cessna and the young lady pilot and her copilot shot the little jet into the sky. It wasn't until we'd landed at Beef Island on Tortola, passed through customs and shut the door of another rental car, that it felt safe to speak openly.

"You saved my life again," said Natsumi. "You keep doing that."

"I keep putting your life in danger."

"It's a funny way to impress a girl."

"It's not on purpose."

"All you have to do is tell me you love me," she said.

"I love you."

"See how much easier that is?"

Later on, she asked, "What happened?"

"The bank dropped a dime on us."

"To whom?"

67

"That's the hard part. I count two, maybe three possibilities. Did you learn anything from Officer Brick?" I asked her.

"He said the Americans were after me and my partner. Later on, he called you my boyfriend, but never said your name. They had mine after taking my prints and DNA. The casino prints us and takes a swab as part of their security clearance. Never knew they shared it with the Feds."

"I imagine that DNA was dearly acquired."

"They were trying to use me as leverage with people they simply called the Americans, so FBI, CIA, embassy people, who knows."

"What did they want to trade you for?" I asked.

She shook her head. "Don't know. But they really wanted me to tell them what was on the flash drive we took out of the safe-deposit box."

She looked away and then added, "There's not much else I can tell you. They mostly asked questions and I mostly told them to let me go. Pretty tedious all in all."

I gave my opinion that the SUV was separate from the cops, and she agreed. Neither of us wanted to believe the people in the SUV were our countrymen. Too sloppy and murderous. And we didn't want to believe our own government would try to run us off the road, naïve as that might have been.

"So we have three lunatic groups after us," she said. "The cops, American foreign agents, and who-knows-what in killer SUVs."

"That's my count."

"Maybe that visit to the bank wasn't such a great idea."

"Maybe not," I said. "But at least it taught us something."

"What?"

"Lots of people really care about what's on this flash drive. They knew it was there and were waiting to pounce on whoever dropped by to pick it up. It's important enough that these Caymanian bankers are willing to compromise their legendary confidentiality. Whether through bribery or coercion, that's a really big thing."

"So you're happy about this," she said.

"Very. Now that you're sitting next to me and we're safely out of harm's way."

"As far as you know."

"As far as I know."

We checked into a small resort hotel on Tortola just south of Road Town, capital of the

British Virgin Islands. Our room faced Sir Francis Drake Channel, the blustery little sea around which most of the archipelago gathered. The night was clear, and even with a feathery palm tree in the way, we could see speckles of light from neighboring islands, and even the ghostly white shape of a sailboat running downwind toward the southeast tip of Tortola, and then maybe on to the U.S. Virgins and beyond.

"Now what, chief," said Natsumi.

"I find postcards from the South of France irresistible."

"C'est bon," was all she said, pulling me over to the big bed under the lazy ceiling fan, where we found a way to put aside all conflicting impulses and obsessions by focusing on the one area where full agreement was a sure thing.

CHAPTER 4

At sunrise I was on my computer, where I spent a few hours burning down and wiping out all the evidence I could find of Florencia's money laundering activities. There was no such thing as permanently destroying data, but I could slow down any investigation considerably.

Of course, the best way to stay hidden was for no one to be looking for you. I'd relied on that from the beginning. But things had now changed irrevocably. If pursuers had the safe-deposit box, they likely had some or all of the fraud scheme, which could well lead back to Florencia despite my best efforts.

Though not necessarily to me. There were other players entangled in her underground operations who could draw attention, create diversions. But there was no way for me to know that, so I always had to assume the worst.

At least I had a distraction: the content on the flash drive taken from the bank on Grand Cayman. It was a Word document, a single page filled with numbers set within little boxes.

Code.

Before being smashed by a bullet, my brain was uniquely suited to code-breaking, something I did as a hobby, though sometimes it came in handy in my professional pursuits. The brain injury caused a thing called dyscalculia, which is a technical way of saying I'd lost most of my math skills.

As it turned out I was able, through persistent practice, to rewire my neural circuitry well enough to regain basic arithmetic, and even get a grasp on certain algebraic formulas, but that was about it. Looking at that sea of numbers on the computer screen caused a surge of loss that was almost nauseating. But it passed in a moment, as I realized I didn't have to be a great code breaker. I simply needed someone, or something, that was.

As in all things today, the solution began with the Internet. I searched for "codes and cyphers" and settled in for a lot of reading.

Natsumi woke an hour later and made us coffee while I explained the situation. She looked over my shoulder at the code and said, "Reminds me of roulette, only with more numbers."

"Indeed. Though a spinning wheel isn't going to help us here."

"What will?" she asked.

"I think it's some sort of substitution technique. Presumably, the numbers stand for letters, though it's not a simple 1 = A formula. Different combinations of numbers, running forward or in reverse, or diagonally, form part of the process. I've downloaded some off-the-shelf code-breaking software, which is running in the background, but I don't have much hope."

"How come?"

"There's probably a key, something that generates the numbers, but not inherent in them. In her scam, Florencia had used the phone number from the apartment she rented during grad school. If I hadn't guessed that, it would have taken a powerful computer to crunch all the possibilities within a string of ten numbers."

"But it's doable," she said.

"I think."

I spent the rest of the day on the code, pausing for about a half hour to arrange the trip to Europe. Which is all it took, online booking being the easiest code in the world to crack. The next morning, the guy at the front desk whistled at a cluster of cabs and their drivers, who were playing some sort of board game under a big shade tree. Through an unspoken selection process, one of them took us to the ferry in Road Town, which roared across the whitecaps and swells to St. Thomas in the U.S. Virgin Islands. We made it to the airport and boarded a plane that flew us, our bags and boxes of gear to Miami.

I spent most of the hop across the Caribbean quelling anxious thoughts about U.S. customs. My experience with international travel was thin, but even before the shooting, handing my passport to the American agents and watching them rummage through my belongings was decidedly creepy and ominous.

In the end, the female agent barely looked at us before scanning our passports, secured with stolen identities, and waving us through. The same was true at baggage search, which was literally nothing, the agents without a flicker of suspicion buying my story of being a telecommunications distributor on a selling tour of the Caribbean.

"Well, that was easy," said Natsumi when we were well out of earshot.

"I used the force."

I'd planned a day layover to go through everything, consolidating down to two carry-ons by stripping out excess gear, sending some of it to a storage facility I maintained in Connecticut, and a bit more to our final destination in France — the Villa Egretta Garzetta, pictured on the postcard in the safe-deposit box.

Feeling that our good fortune getting into the country reduced the odds of an easy trip out, I was moderately tense until we were aloft in the Iberia Airbus A340 heading for our connection in Madrid. Over the Atlantic, Natsumi slept while I played around with the code, with no success.

Still, I was convinced it was based on numeric substitution. Florencia was an MBA, a few courses shy of earning an actuarial degree, and her facility with numbers was nearly as good as mine. Maybe not with the more esoteric formulas, but she could usually see the significance of a complex spreadsheet at a single glance, absorbing the calculations in chunks, the way speed readers absorb whole paragraphs. It was more pattern recognition than anything, so it was likely she'd settled on some type of visual pattern, limiting the possible complexities.

It was also possible she'd designed it with

me specifically in mind, a thought that caused a little twist in my heart. She may have never wanted to reveal her deeply buried secrets, but knew realistically, if something happened to her, I'd find out anyway. She knew me, knew my predilections and persistence. I'd uncover the fraud and embezzlement, trace the money and secure the safe-deposit box. And she would have been right — only she couldn't know that the message sent beyond the grave, if it was indeed a message, would be received by a very different Arthur Cathcart.

I eventually exhausted myself, and managed to sleep the last hour of the flight to Madrid; and after a brief stay at the Madrid airport, we took the last leg of the trip to the Côte d'Azur.

The best way to imagine Saint-Jean-Cap-Ferrat is to picture a right hand, fingers together, with thumb out, jutting into the Mediterranean Sea from the southern coast of France. To the west, Nice is a fifteen-minute car ride. Monaco is about a half hour to the east.

St. Jean is the thumb to Cap Ferrat's hand. Contained within the two peninsulas is some of the most beautiful and expensive real estate in the world, a fleet of super yachts extensive enough to mount a major invasion, and wealth beyond measure (partly because a lot of it resides in banks on Grand Cayman Island).

We landed in Nice an hour before sunrise. By the time we secured our bags and checked through customs, the sun was beginning to light the sky from behind the southern reaches of the Alps. Though I usually strived for anonymity in rental cars, I'd chosen a 5-Series BMW, the roads of the Côte d'Azur notoriously serpentine, providing frequent opportunities for the ill-equipped and inexperienced to plunge down sharp embankments.

Anyway, given how common BMWs were in that part of the world, there was little danger of standing out.

Leaving the airport in Nice, we drove along the Promenade des Anglais, traveling east parallel to the crescent-shaped beach. Apparently the nightclubs in and around the old hotels lining the Promenade were disgorging the last of the night's club-goers, bleary-eyed, but still beautiful. A black-haired young woman in a painted-on, shiny green dress and impossibly high heels stuck out her thumb. I flashed by without hesitation, though a peak in the rearview showed her teetering on the high heels, looking incredulous at the receding BMW.

"Good decision," said Natsumi.

"Security first," I said.

"Hm."

We followed the swoops and curves, the rise and fall of the coastal road, through the narrow confines of densely packed urban clusters, squeezing by colossal buses and dodging suicidal motorbikes. Yet in fairly short order we arrived, intact, at the Village of St. Jean. Not a village in the conventional sense, more a settlement of luxury homes surrounding a row of shops and restaurants set into the hillside, overlooking a harbor crammed with small watercraft, motor and sail, sheltered from the Mediterranean by a curvaceous concrete and stone breakwater.

With the harbor on our left, we drove halfway up the peninsula to where the red dot on my GPS pegged the location of the Villa Egretta Garzetta. I'd come to appreciate that the people of the Côte d'Azur had learned to live on the vertical, the hotel being a fine demonstration. You parked your car on the shoulder across the street, then climbed a steep masonry stairway to an iron gate, beyond which you continued the upward hike through thick, aromatic foliage over large, circular ceramic tiles.

The main entrance was to the far right of

the building. To the left was a patio that extended the length of the hotel, covered by a pergola supporting a hundred years of wisteria growth. Hotel guests, the early risers, sat at round tables with starched white tablecloths, pouring themselves café noir from china pots and spreading jelly on croissants and baguettes.

Above the pergola were three stories of rooms, each with a small balcony where sprays of bougainvillea climbed across canary yellow stucco walls.

The lobby was windowless and about the size of a utility closet. A small chandelier cast a dull, yellow light from above, and a brass lamp did what it could to illuminate the front desk. Behind it stood a very tall, slender bald-headed man in his late sixties or early seventies. He gave a little bow.

Natsumi had the better French, so I let her navigate the greeting and check-in process. Monsieur Lheureux either had no English or chose not to use it, though his demeanor was very warm and engaged. This was likely aided by my choice of rooms — actually a full penthouse suite, their best, perched on the top of the hotel. In fact, they called it *Le Petite Villa Perché.* As with the BMW, it was an unfamiliar extravagance, but the only thing available on such short notice.

The manually operated elevator had room enough for one person and one bag, so we took turns. Monsieur Lheureux hoofed it up the stairs and gave us a tour of the penthouse, which had full views in every direction, with tangled gardens to the west and the mountainous Mediterranean coastline to the east, where at night we'd be able to see the lights of Monte Carlo. Before he left, a round, white-haired woman he introduced as Madame Lheureux showed up with a tray loaded with coffee, pastries, fruit and a copy of *The International Herald Tribune.*

When they left, we took it all out to the balcony overlooking the wisteria-laden pergola, the front gardens of the hotel, and at water's edge the red tile roofs of an estate invisible from the street behind a twelve-foot, pink plastered wall.

I remember having a single cup of coffee, and maybe half a croissant, when the weight of jet lag and sleep deprivation suddenly crashed down, driving us back inside and into the overstuffed antique bed and the welcome embrace of absolute unconsciousness.

■ ■ ■ ■

"What do you know of Florencia's child-hood?" Natsumi asked me four hours later, back on the balcony with a fresh pot of coffee.

"That she wouldn't talk about it."

"And that was okay?"

"You never met Florencia. Never has a person's privacy been so exuberantly preserved. 'No, Arturo, eez such a beautiful day and I'm sooo tired. Let's bring fresh fruit and sausage to the park and drink some wine.' "

"You just sounded exactly like a Spanish woman."

"Heard it enough. And technically, she wasn't Spanish. She was Basque. Florencia Etxarte. Her parents, whom I never met, were born in the Basque region, but then moved to Chile where she was born. They were academics, and wanted her to have an American education, so they shipped her up to Philadelphia where she went to Swarthmore for undergrad, and the Wharton School at Penn after that. My postgrad was in mathematics, but Wharton let us in on their statistics courses. That's where I met her. That year, she got a letter saying her parents had both died. She cried nearly inconsolably for about a week, but we never went to a funeral, and she never went back to Chile. That's all I know."

"That's it?"

"I tried to learn more after she died, but according to every available database, there was no Florencia Etxarte, or couples named Etxarte who died in 1996, or any other year that would fit their age range. Her birth certificate and Chilean passport in that name notwithstanding."

"We have birth certificates and passports for people who don't exist," she said.

"Exactly."

"You never ask me about my childhood."

"You told me you were adopted by an American sailor named Fitzgerald who brought you and your mother to the U.S., who died when you were eighteen. Your mother moved back to Japan and you stayed. If you want to tell me more, that's up to you."

"So that's how that happened. Don't ask, don't tell."

"Basically."

There's a well-supported theory that the mind works better when thrust into unfamiliar surroundings. I spent the next few days testing that theory on Florencia's code, while Natsumi explored the exquisitely beautiful surroundings of the French Riviera both on foot and by BMW. It was a satisfying division of labor, made more so by the keen attentions of the Lheuruexs, whose kitchen provided a steady stream of delicious food served everywhere but inside.

They also let me use their printer to make a few dozen hard copies of the code, better to study in bright daylight and to keep track of possible patterns with pen and pencil. On the tech side, I exported the Word document into Excel to cut down on the manual counting. This is how I made the basic determination that the letter 'a,' the most commonly used letter in Spanish, appeared twenty percent less frequently than it should have. Likewise, the most common Spanish consonants, "d," "l" and "q," were grossly underrepresented. I did the same analysis against frequent English letters with the same disappointing results.

Knowing there were code breakers in the world using software that could crack this thing in minutes didn't help. It wasn't just feelings of inadequacy. Florencia had hidden the information for a reason, and until I knew what it was, I dared not share the secret with anyone else.

"So what's the big problem?" Natsumi asked me, after I showed her my progress.

"Not all letters have the same number all the time. After you get past nine, they have to start doubling up. And even if I knew which numbers corresponded with which letter, the order is jumbled — it could read backwards, forwards, diagonally, or a combination thereof — and there's no word spacing. And my Spanish could be better, though I think it's good enough if I could get the numbers right."

"So the code has a code."

"Something like that. A key that lives somewhere else."

"That lives here," she said. "At the Villa Egretta Garzetta. If, in fact, that's why the flash drive was taped to the postcard."

"Agreed. Florencia was a purposeful woman. There has to be a connection."

As far as I knew, she'd never been to St. Jean, but then again, what did I know? The hotel had been run by the Lheureux family continuously since the thirties. Do I dare ask if their register listed a girl named Florencia? And if so, what would that tell me?

"Go ahead, ask them," said Natsumi, after I gave voice to the thought. "Why not?"

"Seems like a security breach. Even if it was possible to do."

She used two fingers to stick me in the shoulder.

"The bank thing has you twitchy. Rationally, this is low risk, high potential reward. Like you say, the probabilities are on our side."

As is often the case, Natsumi had a really good point. Further proof that two brains were always better than one.

"Okay, you do the asking," I said. "French is impossible."

"Naturellement."

And so we asked Monsieur Lheureux at breakfast the next morning if it was remotely possible to see if a girl named Florencia Etxarte had checked into the Egretta Garzetta at any time in the last four decades.

"She's a friend of the family, and though we love her, we doubt this claim," said Natsumi in French. "She's such a fibber."

Monsieur Lheureux looked untroubled.

"Of course," he said, "we have all the hotel's records on a computer file beginning at the beginning. It is the work of our son. Traditional and modern. It is the way of the Egretta Garzetta."

Natsumi was culturally incapable of a good gloat, but the look she gave me as she translated was pretty close.

Before we finished the last plate of prosciutto and sliced cantaloupe he returned to our table. His expression didn't bode well.

"We have a Florencia in the registry, August 3rd, 1988. Though regrettably, her name is Florencia Zarandona, not Etxarte. She was registered with a Miguel and Sylvia Zarandona. My pardons."

We thanked him, and when he left, Natsumi bowed in contrition.

"Sorry," she said. "I raised your hopes."

"Never apologize for a smart move."

She looked up at me. "Why do you look so happy?"

She didn't press me when I led her back upstairs to the Petite Perché and booted up the computer. I brought up my research logs and clicked on a file titled "Zarandona."

"The name must have come up at least twice, for some reason, in my original research. You want to have at least three corroborating data points," I said, "but two is worth saving, in case number three pops up later on. Happens all the time."

"What now?" she asked.

"Down the rabbit hole."

The next time we spoke, it was nearly dinner time. She'd gone off on a journey into the foothills of the Alps and I'd traveled through trackless census and immigration data, news sources in English and Spanish, plumbing every legally available source of information on the Internet covering the prior half century.

She poured from a bottle of red wine purchased in Provence, I ordered up some tea. I tried to coax her into the day's travelogue, but she was insistent.

"I'm much more interested in what you learned."

"Everything or nothing."

"Which means?"

"If I have the right Florencia, I have a lot," I said.

"What are the odds?"

"Good. Miguel and Sylvia Zarandona were Basque professors at the University of Bilbao. And committed socialists. This was not a good thing in Franco's Spain. So in 1968, during a lot of upheaval there, the Zarandonas fled the country with their young son."

"And Florencia?"

"Florencia was born in '72."

"Both Florencias?"

"Yup. Same year, different days, so there's your shadow of a doubt. Though I used to do a lot of ancestry research for the rich and lazy, and conflicting birth dates are common."

"Wow."

"She also had a grandmother with an interesting name."

"Etxarte?"

"Lorena Etxarte DeAnzorena. Etxarte is the surname per Spanish custom."

"That nails it," she said.

"I think it does."

"Why'd they go to Chile?"

"They were invited by an extremely convenient distant relative of Sylvia's. Convenient in 1968. Not so much later on."

"Sorry. This I can't guess," she said.

"Salvador Allende. President of the Chilean Senate at the time, two years later, president of the country. A fellow Marxist, with Basque ancestry, from an upper crust family — like the Zarandonas, by the way — and clearly a hater of everything Franco represented, it was a natural fit. He got them both jobs at his alma mater, the University of Chile, and life was good."

Natsumi asked me to put it on pause so we could get ready for dinner. It wasn't until we were back down under the pergola, fresh and clean and in the kind embrace of the Lheureux family, that I was able to share the rest of the information.

"You said life was good," she said, picking up the story, "I'm guessing it didn't stay that way."

"I'm sure the Zarandonas had many fine qualities, but luck wasn't one of them. A year after Florencia is born, Allende is overthrown by the military and his socialist regime wiped out. Augusto Pinochet, sort of a tin-horn version of Franco, is now in charge, and the only thing that amounts to good fortune for the Zarandonas is that Pinochet is too busy purging government workers to spend much time on the academics classes. But that would come later, and the first school on the list was the biggest, the University of Chile."

"*Qué lástima.* What a shame. What happened to them?"

"I don't know. They made it for at least five years; the last botany course taught by Professor Zarandona — that would be Sylvia — was held in 1978, also the year their son died at eighteen of a brain tumor. After that, the public record goes silent."

"Public?"

"Anything available online. I'd need a few weeks going through the print stacks in libraries here and in Latin America to call it a dead search, but experience tells me I'm almost there."

"Though you have a theory."

"No. Just a common sense assumption

that they went underground, or fled the country under different identities, or both. If it wasn't for the hotel registry, I'd figure they'd been disappeared. People like the Zarandonas didn't just lose their jobs under Pinochet, they were killed. By the thousands. Often secretly. The proverbial knock on the door in the middle of the night."

"God."

"So we know that didn't happen, at least not as of 1988. By then, Pinochet was on his way out. The political killings were supposed to be a thing of the past. The Zarandonas were now free to travel. Did they sign in at the hotel under their real names because they only had their real passports? Otherwise, did they live under assumed names? Those are gross assumptions. Too little data."

The next day Natsumi coaxed me out of my lair atop the Egretta Garzetta and showed me as much of the Côte d'Azur as she could in a day and part of the night. We ended the trip with a scrotum-shrinking drive up a one-and-a-half-lane switchback road, in the dark, to a little city called Eze, that as far as I could tell hung off a cliff straight up from the Mediterranean.

"It's called a *village perché*," said Natsumi. "I assumed you were only comfortable in perched places."

Even an obsessive like me, with a head crammed full of data and boiling hypotheses, was easily distracted by the view from Eze — at night with the lights of Cap Ferrat to the right, and Monaco to the left; and in the day, the cliffs, peninsulas, grey-green flora of the Alpes-Maritimes, and the deep blue Mediterranean spread out to the horizon.

It was a sight I hadn't seen in many years. Florencia rarely traveled, and I got my fill tracking down missing people, one of the more engaging sidelines of my research business. Except for an occasional detour to Canada or Mexico, the journeys were restricted to the Continental U.S. Fortunately, I'd spent a year between undergrad and graduate school living in London and making frequent forays to the Continent, usually to Italy, France and Spain. It was a student pauper's existence, running on cheap rail passes and youth hostels, but I recalled the joyful exploration, both physical and intellectual.

As I stood on that balcony in Eze, it sank in that given my status as a dead man — a legal necessity — more updated experience with the world would not only be enriching, it might prove essential to survival. More places to hide, to disappear into.

As for Natsumi, her status had now changed from missing person to fugitive. That heightened the danger to both of us. If she were in custody in the U.S., it wouldn't take a committed investigator long to put together the pieces of our story. I knew one in particular, that retired FBI agent Shelly Gross, who had the skills, the knowledge of the case, and the contacts with the agency, to get there very quickly.

For all I knew, he already had. He had the time, and was very, very mad at me. Witnesses could link Natsumi to a person linked to a series of events leading up to some bloody killings. The larger question, have they identified that person as me, the real me? Presumed dead, but apparently very much alive?

The Caymanian cops knew from the start she was a valuable asset. That had to connect to the bank. It could be the contents of the safe-deposit box, but it could also be our immediate past. Maybe we'd already been caught and just didn't know it yet.

In the plus column, we had a lot of money tucked away in a lot of secure places, multiple identities with supporting documents and an increasing facility in the art of staying invisible.

Which included never lingering in any one place too long.

I looked down at the distant harbor of St. Jean and called in to Natsumi that I thought it was time to go.

Since Natsumi had the most experience driving over the lethal coastal terrain, she had the wheel of the BMW while I played with the onboard GPS, doing an A-B comparison with the one on my iPhone. Each had their positive and negative features, and separate opinions as to our exact location. Feeling that blue dots and red pins were too imprecise a measure, I went online and downloaded a marine navigation app that tracked location by the actual latitude and longitude.

This took some doing as we lurched and hurtled down the mountainside, but before we reached the Egretta Garzetta, I'd achieved the goal and had begun to toggle between the two GPS programs and the waypoint app.

When we pulled up on the shoulder across from the hotel, I had a winner. The car GPS's blue dot was floating in the sea several feet from the waterfront estate. The iPhone had the hotel firmly pinned to the earth, in both red and blue. I wrote down the full coordinates from the waypoint app as Natsumi patiently followed me into the hotel.

Somehow, it didn't surprise me that Monsieur Lheureux knew the precise latitude and longitude of his family's hotel, described in degrees, minutes and seconds. The app had tagged on a few more seconds, but that was it. The Monsieur was pleased to add the refined position to the family records.

Certain that Natsumi would find this equally engrossing, I showed her the coordinates when I met her upstairs in our rooms.

"This is fun for you?" she asked. "No wonder you love staring at numbers. Why are you looking at me like that?"

I went over to the breakfast table that had been serving as my desk and took out an unmarked copy of Florencia's code. There it was in the middle of the third row. First the degrees, separated by three other numbers. Then the minutes, separated by three different numbers, then the seconds, followed by three other numbers, only two of which were distinct.

"The number seven is the letter 'e,' " I said to Natsumi.

She walked over and I handed her the coordinates for the hotel. Then I pointed to the corresponding numbers in the code.

"It's a catalog of locations, beginning with the Villa Egretta Garzetta. And likely some text. I've only got the start of a key, but it's a good start."

"Brilliant," said Natsumi.

"No. Lucky. Even better."

CHAPTER 5

The Spottsworthy Mews, buried deep inside London's Kensington and Chelsea Royal Borough, was a quick cab ride away from the room we'd rented in a monstrous hotel on the eastern edge of Hyde Park.

Florencia's code was very precise, but not enough to pinpoint an exact location in the tightly compressed, mad tangle of ancient urban development that was London. So we were reasonably sure about the mews, but had no idea which of the thirteen residences within was the target.

Listed second on Florencia's code, after the hotel in St. Jean, the mews was our first choice. And convenient, as it not only got us out of town, it got us all the way out of France. It was a reasonably stress-free trip, the enormity of Heathrow somehow bestowing the illusion of impenetrable anonymity. Reality being quite the opposite, of course. As the global nexus of travel both illicit and benign, no airport had greater and more sophisticated security.

I dedicated the first few days at the London hotel translating the bulk of Florencia's code, determining there were nine designated locations, taking up three quarters of the content, with the rest normal text, or a different species of numeric expression, or a combination of both.

In addition to London, there were pinpoints in Venice, Madrid, Budapest, Switzerland, Lombardy, Edinburgh, Costa Rica and New York City.

"Do you know what's there?" Natsumi asked.

"No idea."

"But you have a theory."

"No. But I do have what's left of the code."

What I had were the numbers for d-e-g-m-i-n-s-c, all single digits. After 9, each letter was two digits each. I ran the letter frequency query through Excel, identifying the letter "a" as 23, and gaining some certainty the text was in Spanish. Thus the English-only code-breaking software was no help at all. I was facing the limit of my capabilities, and the frustration likely showed.

"I think you should find someone to help

you," said Natsumi. "The energy needed to succeed at this must be far greater than your need to come up with a good cover story."

She was right. My preoccupation with security was likely unfounded, since we had what should be the essence of the code. I just needed the words.

"And here we are in the UK, code breakers' paradise," I said. "Home to Bletchley Park, *The London Times* crossword puzzle, George Smiley."

"I don't know about any of those things."

"That's why we have Google."

In a few minutes I had a name that fit the bill nicely. Edwina Firth, a New Zealander, Professor of Cryptanalysis, University of London, winner of a recent code-breaking contest held by *The Daily Telegraph*. In the photo taken at her award ceremony, she looked like a pleasant, open-faced woman poised to agreeably enter middle age.

"She's cute," said Natsumi.

"Is that an observation or a warning?"

"I'll know better when I meet her."

After some discussion, we crafted an email to Ms. Firth:

Professor Firth:
I am an American businessman on holi-

day here in London. I stumbled upon the notice in the *Telegraph* of your success in the "Enigma 2012 Challenge." I have with me a much simpler cipher, created by a friend of mine with whom I've lost touch. It's partially solved, and it would be most gratifying to have the task completed. I would gladly compensate you for your time if you would be kind enough to give it a look.

Sincerely,
Gilbert Freeman

"Perfect," said Natsumi. "Just add in 'on holiday here in London with my wife.' "

"You don't really think . . ."

"Never trust a cryptanalyst. You want to talk crafty."

We had to wait a few days for a reply, which we spent casing the Spottsworthy Mews. This was difficult, since by definition, the flats and townhouses of a mews were off the main road, and grouped around an open, paved courtyard. There was no way to approach any of the dwellings without being exposed to all. And it would be no surprise if the area were well covered by security cameras. So my cleverest idea was to walk arm in arm with Natsumi right into the mews and look around like dumb tourists.

So we did, which turned out well, because in the window of one of the homes was a prominent sign that read TO LET. I pointed to the sign and we walked over to it. I pulled out my pocket notebook and wrote down the contact information. We were now dumb tourists hoping to spend an extended time in London.

The estate agent was a one-office firm a quick bus ride from the mews. I expected a quaint little Dickensian hole in the wall, but we got a modern office building with three floors and hundreds of agents manning phones and clattering away at computers.

"That would be Hunley's property," said the receptionist, dialing him up from her switchboard.

Hunley was a tall, sallow young man with sparse reddish hair, inadequate shoulders and a weak chin. Though his ready smile was sturdy enough.

"Well then, we've been to Spottsworthy, have we?" he asked, shaking our hands.

"Just now. It's sort of exactly what we've been looking for," I said.

"I can understand that," he said. "It's one of my favorites. It's a year's lease, of course."

"That's fine," I said.

"Could we have a look?" said Natsumi.

Hunley acted as if she'd snapped him out

of a reverie.

"Of course, yes. Let me get my jacket and the key."

A cab was waiting for us in front of the building. The cabbie nodded to Hunley like they knew each other. Hunley said "Spottsworthy" and we were off.

"So, have business in London?" Hunley asked.

"On sabbatical," I said. "Writing a book."

"What can you tell us about the neighborhood?" Natsumi asked. "How're the neighbors? We're looking for quiet."

"Then you're looking well. A mews is the favored place for people wanting quiet. All tidily tucked away and all."

"And all the flats are let but this one?" I asked.

"No flats. They're all proper houses," he said, "and mostly lived in by their owners. This one is owned by a couple on assignment in America, as it turns out. They rarely sell. Too desirable. Can't say I know if they're all fully occupied at the moment."

"Security?" she asked.

"Of course."

It took him a few tries before getting the door unlocked, an awkwardness he covered with increased chatter and feigned amusement. The door opened into the sitting room, which was dark, full of overstuffed furniture and lined with bookcases crammed with books and a variety of pottery, pictures, clocks and other knickknacks. The space opened up to a dining area, beyond which was a set of French doors leading to a tiny garden. It smelled freshly cleaned, in a pleasant way. The street noise was a distant swish and hum. I pulled aside the drapes and saw a clear view of the twelve other units.

"We'll take it," I said.

"You haven't seen the rest," said Hunley.

"No need."

"I'm seeing the rest," said Natsumi.

Hunley followed her up the stairs.

I went to my email immediately after getting settled into the mews. Edwina Firth had written back.

> Dear Mr. Freeman:
> I would be pleased to look at your code (no compensation necessary), though I can offer no assurances that the puzzle will be solved. I'm sure you are aware that unbreakable ciphers do exist.
> My office hours are nine to eleven A.M. Monday, Wednesday and Friday. Pick your day and I'll see you then.

She included the address and her phone number.

After setting up the appointment, I started browsing sites in the UK where I could source gear. An easy enough task — in less than an hour, I'd located a dozen distributors within Greater London that could provide what I needed.

I went over it with Natsumi.

"I've identified the cameras here in the mews. Not very well hidden. All we need to do is find where they converge and tap the feed. There should be a switch box, and with luck, a router that sends the images to home base via the Internet."

"Okay. And what do I do?"

"Meet the neighbors."

After a relatively brief cab ride, I had enough supplies to cover initial operations.

Later that day, I visited the offices of the building that sat between the mews and the street and asked if I could take a few snapshots of our new dwelling from above. The request was bizarre and homely enough that they readily agreed. I'd lived among Londoners. I knew their weakness for eccentricity.

"Hoping to inspire jealousy on the home front?" said the fellow who led me to the perfect window above the mews.

"Exactly," I said. "Especially my brother-in-law, who told my wife's parents I was an intellectual weenie who'd never amount to anything."

"Good for you, then."

I brought a telescoping pole to keep the camera still, and shot at the highest resolution the professional Canon could achieve. It was all done in a few minutes, which left ample time for shaking hands and trading quips with the cubicle denizens clearly in need of diversion from their official duties.

Back at the computer, I downloaded the images, and after some enlargement, identified the coaxial cables from each camera, tracking where they joined together and dove down a conduit behind the southeast corner of the mews.

Getting there involved several sorties down alleys and behind commercial buildings, and one risky clamber over a chain-link fence, but I eventually reached the spot. The conduit, strapped to the wall, ran into a grey metal box bolted to the side of the building. The box was secured by a type of simple keyed latch a child could pick. Pleased as I was by this, I felt a bit of resentment that the security company guarding my newly established home would be this sloppy.

"Wankers," I said under my breath, as I fiddled open the lock.

Inside I found the switch box, and to my delight, a wireless router. In a few minutes, using the gear brought along in a light backpack, I'd hooked into the feed, sending the signal through the secondary router I'd brought along, which beamed it via the Internet directly to my computer.

Back at my desk, I tested the connections and saw the five security cameras pop up on my screen. Using a network video recorder and surveillance software that allowed you to skip over long periods of inaction, I could efficiently track the comings and goings of the neighborhood.

"Our next door neighbors are George and Mirabella McPherson," said Natsumi. "He's a financial guy and she's an astronomer. How cool is that?"

"How did you meet them?"

"I knocked on the door and introduced myself. I didn't actually meet George, but Mirabella was very friendly and welcoming, and we ended up chatting for quite some time. She's French. I think I used up every bit of our backstory. You better study it again. How was your day?"

"We're now monitoring the complex. We'll

give it a few days and see what the software can tell us."

"We don't have to wait that long for the McPhersons. They'll be here in about an hour for tea. They've never been inside this house. Said the couple who owns it kept to themselves. Mirabella is beside herself with curiosity."

"Just don't let them in the spare bedroom."

"Right. The surveillance array might take some explaining."

George McPherson, about sixty-five, was much older than his wife. He had a large head lightly covered in very thin, white hair, and a thick neck — so at first he seemed overweight, but on closer inspection was reasonably trim. Mirabella was at the age, mid to late thirties, when the bloom of youth is still confidently in place. With high cheekbones, thick black hair contained by a headband and a flimsy knit dress over minimum underwear, sexual sparks flowed in with her and filled up the dowdy sitting room like a scattered handful of scintillations.

"At last, we are here," she proclaimed, with a big smile, as they entered the sitting room. "Ten years, but we finally made it."

George was less celebratory. "About what you'd expect, right?" he said, looking around. "Nothing all that amazing."

"Phooey to you," she said.

She began telling him about our situation, for which I was grateful, since — to support Natsumi's point — manufactured memories are a lot harder to keep track of than genuine. The gist of the story had me writing a book on cyber security and Natsumi taking a year off from her psychotherapy practice. Fortunately, the McPhersons were polite enough not to press us for too much detail, being satisfied to dominate the conversation talking about themselves.

"The chap who owns this place also works in the city," said George. "I'd see him on the tube. Never said hello."

"What about the other neighbors," said Natsumi. "Surely some are friendly?"

They competed with each other to assure us many were, and not to believe that all Brits were a stuffy, dismissive lot.

"We even have an Indian family," said George.

"The Malhotras," said Mirabella. "Very sweet people."

"Don't fancy the food. Smell it halfway down the block."

"But you never let it show," she said, part

compliment, part entreaty.

We shared what the estate agent Hunley had to say about the mews, stretching his views a bit.

"He said it was fully occupied," said Natsumi.

George turned in his chair and pointed toward the courtyard.

"Number eight, on the corner across the way," he said. "Haven't seen a soul in five years."

Tea time flowed into dinner, for which Natsumi was prepared, and the desultory conversation made its way skyward, with Mirabella as our eager guide. Though my knowledge was very limited, I always enjoyed hearing about the cosmos; and with Mirabella's French accent and extravagant use of superlatives and metaphors, we were thoroughly spellbound. I noticed she'd put away a full bottle of red wine, which likely added something to the presentation.

I kept to tonic and lime, since my tolerance of alcohol rarely extended beyond a couple of beers. So when Natsumi rose to clear the table, with George's help, I was able to provide Mirabella with a sturdy arm when she insisted I escort her to the courtyard for a quick look at the stars.

"Of course, there is so much light pollution from London, but even so, the brighter stars and planets you can see."

She pointed out at least two little pin-pricks that had played a role in her previous narrative, and emphasized how stars in a constellation had actually nothing in common.

"They are so far away from one another, am I right?" she said.

"I guess you are."

"So, quickly, I just want to tell you something," she said, squeezing my arm. "You ask about friendly neighbors. George and I can be more than friendly with the right people. Never here in Spottsworthy, but you can be the first. It will be fun."

To say I lacked sophistication in these matters was a gross understatement. A full-out geek from birth, my friends were all geeks, with social skills at best non-irritating. Until Florencia, I'd hardly had a date and knew nothing about women, much less the type of libertinism suggested here. So it took nearly a minute for what she was getting at to sink in. Then I started to babble something, but she saved me by giving my arm another squeeze.

"Don't say anything now. Just think about it."

"Okay. Hey, let's see how they're doing

with the cleanup."

It was another hour before the McPhersons journeyed back to their house next door, awash in wine, beer and cognac, though hardly showing it.

"Well, that was a lot more than I expected, but pleasant," said Natsumi. "He's a nice enough guy, but she couldn't be more interesting."

"Oh yes, she could," I said.

"I mean all that wonderful astronomy."

"They're swingers."

"Of course, they are. This is swinging London after all."

"No, I mean they're actually swingers, you know, like, in the somewhat indiscriminate carnal sense."

She stared at me. I quickly described my conversation with Mirabella out in the courtyard under the stars. When I explained how long it took me to catch on, mirth lit up her face.

"And you were worried about Edwina Firth, the cryptanalyst," I said, squeezing a laugh out of her.

"You know I'm willing to do anything for the cause, but honestly, George McPherson?" said Natsumi.

The comparison with beautiful Mirabella being immediately obvious, I launched a string of reassurances, which she made me stop.

"I don't doubt you at all, Arthur, not one tiny little bit, about anything. I never have, and never will, and I'm sorry I teased you about Edwina Firth. It was unbecoming."

I was the last person to attribute the sort of good fortune that tossed Natsumi into my life — literally at a moment of life or death, in the middle of the night — to anything more than the mindless confluence of haphazard circumstances; but at moments like that, I wondered.

We rode the tube to Tottenham Court Road station and walked from there to Edwina's office on the campus of the University of London. It was in one of the mid-twentieth-century buildings the school surely regretted for their blocky, Soviet motif blandness, now made worse by an unflattering aging process. When I lived in London, I spent a lot of time hanging around the university, its libraries, little study cubbies and giant bookstore. It felt a bit like a homecoming.

"I used to sit on that bench and eat peanuts and Cadbury Bournville Dark for lunch. I walked down here every day from Camden Town, which used to be a dump, but all I could afford. I was the thinnest I'd ever been. Until now," I remarked to Natsumi as we neared the cryptanalyst's office.

Edwina was also on the thin side. Her very thick, dirty blond hair was pulled up away from her face and her eyes were round and bird-like, as if in a constant state of surprise. She was cordial, but wasted little time getting down to business.

"Let's see what you have," she said, in her nasally Kiwi accent.

I gave her the string of numbers absent the navigational bearings. And the letters I'd already been able to decipher.

"I'm reasonably sure the text is in Spanish," I said.

She looked up at that and smiled.

"¿Está tratando de hacer esto más difícil?" she asked.

"Sí, Señora. Me han dicho que usted adora un desafío."

Natsumi looked at me inquiringly.

"She thinks the Spanish was an attempt to amp up the challenge," I said.

Edwina was back studying the numbers, her long fingernails tapping out an arrhythmic beat on her desk.

She drew in a deep breath and brought the paper up closer to her face.

"Do you have this in digital form?" she asked.

I gave her a flash drive. "Excel."

She spun around in her chair, after taking the drive, which she inserted into a slot on the side of a Mac laptop. I could see the screen, but nothing on it made any sense to me.

"I'm thinking the Henniger-Rosen Table Cascade," she said, after about twenty minutes of study.

"Underwriters and actuaries are big on tables," I said.

"They are."

"My friend was one of those."

She went back to her screen, frowning. "It's simply a matter of getting the rhythm of the cascade. Otherwise, the constantly shifting relationships can tie you up in knots. Very interesting."

We waited while Edwina worked for about a half hour at her computer, hunched over the keyboard as if she needed her body weight to control the calculations.

"I have about a million if/then scenarios loaded in this little laptop, but it'll take a solid day or more to run all of them," she said, reluctantly looking away from her screen. "Not including about four hours of programming, so we're sure we're asking the right ifs and thens."

"That's quite an imposition," said Natsumi, breaking her silence.

"No, dear," said Edwina. "It's what people like me do for fun. Which is why I'll never be married. Unless you know someone of the male species who suffers from the same condition."

"I heard of one once, but I'm afraid he's lost the facility," said Natsumi.

"Pity."

When I had two workdays of video-recorded traffic within the mews under my belt, I called up the surveillance application and assessed the results. As the McPhersons would have predicted, no one arrived at or left number eight. Although the same was true for five and eleven. I did notice that after the man of the house at number six left for work, another bloke stopped by for a couple hours. I wondered what Mrs. McPherson might have thought of that.

The only other thing I had to do was wait for Edwina's results, so I spent the time searching for a post-1978 mention of the Zarandona family, with no success. I wondered how the only evidence of their existence at the time was the paper trail left by a hotel registry. Yet I reminded myself that as omniscient as the World Wide Web often seemed to be, it only held a fraction of total human knowledge. If only because there were lots of things humans didn't want other humans to know.

I also spent time fretting over, and cleaning up, the various digital trails I'd forged, nurtured, then sought to abandon. The bank and investment accounts, identities, credit cards, online purchases, hotel check-ins, airline tickets, car rentals, passports, drivers' licenses, rental agreements, IP addresses, browsing histories, cell phone numbers — the list was a mile long and getting harder and harder to keep track of. I'd tossed enough breadcrumbs out there to open a bakery, which might have been the right strategy. Dazzle the opposition with complexity, with data paths so tangled they'd never be sorted out. But maybe this was now in the realm of offshore, national security operations, clandestine and untouchable.

In which case, all bets were off.

Mr. Freeman:
I have your answer. Quite an interesting little project. Would you mind coming by tomorrow so we can discuss it?

Edwina

Natsumi and I had to wait a while in the

hallway since one of Edwina's students had gotten in ahead of us. We sat on the floor and talked about everything but the remaining contents of the code. When the door opened, a young woman was a little taken aback that we were sitting there, and Edwina somewhat charmed.

She waved us in.

"It had nothing to do with linear regressions. Just a nice simple substitution code my computer here particularly enjoys sorting out." We settled into our places in the office and she slid a piece of paper across her desk. "The words are correct, and the sentiments quite clear."

Out of politeness, I held it so we could both read it, though I knew Natsumi's Spanish wasn't up to the task.

"Es imposible describirte cuánto me llena el corazón cada vez que pienso en ti. Siempre apreciaré cada momento que hemos pasado juntos . . . te amaré siempre y nunca me olvidaré de todo lo que has significado para mi."

"Can you make it out?" I asked her.

She shook her head. I wrote out the translation: "It is impossible to describe how full my heart is whenever I think of you. I

116

will always treasure every moment we have spent together."

Then the string of coordinates, then the close: "I will always love you and will never forget what you have meant to me."

"Oh."

CHAPTER 6

After recording another week's activity within the Spottsworthy Mews, we confirmed that number eight was the only house apparently uninhabited. So that seemed like the easiest place to snoop. We played a game of Frisbee out in the courtyard, which offered ample opportunity for running up to the façade and sneaking a look through the windows. All Natsumi or I could see were closed curtains.

I told Natsumi I was going to break in and have a look around.

"Okay," she said. "That's mildly frightening."

"By all appearances, it's empty. Nothing to be frightened about."

"Everything is a reason to be frightened. What do I do if you don't come back?"

I didn't have a ready answer, not having considered that possibility.

"If I'm not back by three A.M., check into

the Hilton next door to the place where we stayed on Hyde Park. Use a fresh ID. Bring along my laptop and backpack. Leave everything else. If I contact you and it's a setup, I'll ask you how your mother's doing. Give it a couple weeks, then turn yourself into the American embassy. You can probably bargain your way out of a prison sentence by giving up the story. Just be careful how you meter it out. Save the best till last."

"Now I wish I hadn't asked."

"No, you were right," I said. "Foolish of me to leave you unprepared."

I waited until midnight, then dressed in my favored blacks and headed back to where I'd tapped into the video feed, which was attached to number nine, right next door.

Between the two houses was a wall, which I hadn't noticed before, having come in from the other direction. I dragged over a piece of garden furniture, which gave me just enough height to heave myself over.

I was in the garden, which was about the same size as ours, and though untended, it felt bigger. As with ours, it backed up to a large building that faced the street. The building had a big double-hung window, locked. Instead of a set of French doors, this mews house had a single, glass-paned door, curtained off. The lock looked sturdy, and it was, resisting all my efforts to effect a breach. So I picked a loose brick off the ground, and after wrapping it in my jacket, busted out a pane of glass.

I reached inside and opened the door, guiding my way with a small flashlight.

Inside, the room was naked but for two cots, a TV on a small stand, and a card table with two folding chairs. On the table sat a lamp and two partially full ashtrays. The kitchen next door was equally spare, with lightly equipped cabinets, a coffeemaker on the counter and an open waste basket against one wall. The freezer held a few frozen meals, and the fridge was mostly filled with beer, along with some cheese, salami, fruit juice and a cantaloupe that felt and smelled reasonably fresh.

The sitting room at the front of the house was empty. The curtains, made of heavy material, were pulled tightly across the windows. I went upstairs and found the bedrooms also empty, though the bathroom was well stocked with towels, toothbrushes and toothpaste, shampoo and antacids. The floor of the shower enclosure was moist.

I started down the stairs, but only made it halfway before what felt like a metal rod smashed into my back.

Losing my footing, I pitched forward, then fell down the stairs facedown, bouncing on my chest, my hands flailing around for a way to slow my fall. I hit the landing at the same time a heavy body fell on me, grabbing the collar of my jacket and slamming my face into the floor. I grunted, I think, but the only sound from my assailant was heavy breathing and partially formed Spanish words.

A kick in the stomach came from another direction. I doubled up and prepared for more of the same.

"I'm done, lads," I said in my best impersonation of an East End Londoner, hoping Spanish guys wouldn't pick up subtle telltales. "No reason to pile on."

I got one more kick, for good measure, but then things quieted down as they studied me in the dark.

One of them pulled something that felt like a T-shirt over my head, which was then secured with duct tape around my neck. I was led into the kitchen and dropped down into a kitchen chair.

"No offense, mate," I said. "Thought the place was abandoned. Just lookin' to cop a squat."

I heard the unmistakable sound of a shell being loaded into the chamber of a semi-automatic.

"No call for the artillery," I said, "I ain't seen you, and got no reason to care you were ever here. Movin' on soon as you let me go. With apologies. Wouldn't like it myself 'avin' some bloke disturbin' me tranquility."

One of them said in Spanish, "Tell us your name and who sent you."

I shook my head.

"Sorry, don't know what you just said. Italian is it? Been to Rome for a bit of football. Nice city." I felt the tip of a gun pressed against my temple.

"Pushin' that thing at me ain't teachin' me Italian. Shit, I can hardly talk English, me native tongue."

"Spanish," said one of the men. *"Hablamos español, estúpido."*

"Okay, sorry. Never been to Spain. You speak English? If not, we gotta find somebody who can."

The gun was pulled away from my head, and they were silent for a while. I strained to hear sounds of movement.

One said in Spanish, "What are we going to do with this idiot?"

"How do we know he's telling the truth?"

"We don't."

"Let's start cutting his balls off with a

steak knife. Maybe that will improve his Spanish."

"You're sure you don't know somebody who speaks English?" I said, slowly and loudly as if that might help them understand what I was saying.

"Call Rodrigo," one of them said. "We need instruction."

After a pause, I heard the other man say, "Rodrigo, we got a guy here who broke into the house. Anglo. Says he's a squatter. No, he walked around, but didn't see us. What do you want us to do?" After another pause, he said, "Okay. I know the place."

I felt two sets of hands pull me to my feet and direct me through the rear door. We crossed the garden, went through the big window of the building next door, then down two flights of stairs. At the bottom, we moved along what sounded and smelled like a rough, basement corridor. I asked them where we were going, but got nothing back.

We climbed up another set of stairs. At the top, one of them held on to me with the gun stuck in my kidney while the other opened a door. A few minutes later they pulled me through into a space with a different acoustic signature — a bigger space. A car started.

They both had me again, and with firm grips, taped my hands behind my back, then shoved me into the trunk of the car. It wasn't hard to affect alarm.

"Whoa, what's this? You don't have to worry about me. Just let me go."

"Shut up," one said, and cracked me on the side of the head with the gun barrel.

"Foockin' 'ell."

The trunk lid slammed shut.

Fear erupted in my mind and my heart tightened in my chest. I tested the tape restraints. My wrists were held firmly together, but I could partially move my hands and fingers. I thought furiously through several scenarios, none of them good, until I remembered the Swiss Army Knife in my left front pants pocket.

The car moved aggressively as it left the parking garage and began maneuvering the Chelsea labyrinth; though after about ten minutes, it slowed to a halt, then moved slowly after that. London traffic.

I twisted around until my hand touched the top of the pocket. I was able to pull out the fabric about a quarter inch at a time, bringing the knife along with it. This worked until the knife itself began to clog the hole, forcing its way back down again. So then I had to use a combination of pulling and holding that reduced progress to a tiny fraction every few minutes.

The car took off again after a long delay, but soon after it braked, and the driver stood on the horn in obvious frustration. We crept forward again.

My hand was nearly cramped into paralysis when I finally got the butt end of the knife between my thumb and index finger. The slick plastic and chromed metal surfaces caused the knife to squirt out of that tenuous grip, and I nearly lost it to my pocket again. I felt around the duct tape until I found some exposed adhesive, which I feebly tried to transfer to my fingertips. After several tries, they got sticky enough to allow me to gain a purchase on the end of the knife and pull it all the way out of my pocket.

I rolled over on my back, as far as my twisted position allowed, and wedged the knife against the trunk floor. Then I paused to catch my breath, wiggle my hands to get the circulation going again, and think about the next step.

The knife had one large and one small blade, and a pair of sharp little scissors, all neatly tucked away. I felt the exposed metal parts as I imagined how I could use a single hand to pull each into the open position. I started with the large blade, achieving little result beyond ripping off a piece of thumbnail.

The car got underway again, accelerating briskly, making a slow turn, and then maintaining a straight course at far greater speed. We were on an M road, one of the UK's four-lane highways.

I transferred the knife from my right hand to my left, and using my left thumb, pried the scissors out of the slot. I turned the scissors toward my wrists and snipped my way through the duct tape at about a millimeter per snip. Once the tape was sliced through, it took only moments to wrench my wrists free.

Life is a lot easier when you have your hands.

I cut the T-shirt off my head, breathing deeply of the dank air in the trunk. With improved leverage, I was able to force myself over on my right side so I faced the back of the car. I put away the scissors and opened the small blade, which I rarely used so I'd always have one razor-sharp edge.

Then the only thing to do was wait and try to visualize what could happen next.

It took another half hour to find out. First the car slowed and curved down an exit ramp. At the stop, it turned right and moved at a slower pace. The sound of the tires moving over the road surface changed, rougher and noisier. Minutes more passed, along with several turns, both left and right.

We left the road and jostled over a bumpy surface. I was doubly grateful to have my hands to reduce the battering inside the trunk.

And then the car stopped.

I arranged the T-shirt so it still loosely covered my head. I heard both car doors open and close, then the sound of the trunk lock opening via remote control. The lid lifted, introducing a blast of cool air.

A single hand grabbed a handful of my jacket and started to pull. I yanked the T-shirt away and slashed across the man's wrist with the small knife blade. He screamed *"Madre"* and let go, pressing at his wrist with his other hand, which held the gun. I grabbed the barrel and it went off, the bullet taking a piece of my cheek on its way. I stuck the little blade all the way into the back of the hand holding the gun, and pulled him toward the trunk. The gun came free, and still holding the barrel, I used it to club the guy in the face. He tucked in his chin as he pulled the knife out of his hand. His partner by now had a good hold on the back of the guy's jacket, and when he yanked hard, they both stumbled back a few feet.

I sat up in the trunk and started shooting. They spun away from me and went down hard, both screaming in Spanish. I got out of the trunk with the gun pointing at the writhing figures, barely visible in the soft light of the waxing moon. There were no other lights in view, and it looked as if we were in the middle of a grassy field.

The one who first grabbed me had at least one bullet in the thigh. He was trying to press his palm over the hole and stem the bleeding from his wrist at the same time. The other was shot in the gut. I stuck the gun barrel to his forehead and frisked him, finding a cell phone and a little snub-nosed revolver in his jacket pocket. The two men begged me to call an ambulance.

"What were you going to do with me?" I asked in Spanish, picking up a shovel that was lying on the ground.

"Just scare you. You don't have to shoot."

"Scare me you did," I said.

"You are from Domingo Angel. You lied to us."

"Spare me the moral relativity, boys," I said. "Who is Domingo Angel?"

"We need a doctor."

"Tell me who he is or I'll be happy to

stand here and watch you bleed out."

That might have already happened to the guy with the gut wound. He'd stopped speaking and was lying still on the ground.

"Domingo Angel. He is the VG, *Los Vengadores del Guardia*. Or they are him. But I'm telling you what you already know."

The Guard's Avengers.

"Where is he?" I asked.

The man laughed.

"You really don't know, eh Anglo? So who the hell are you?"

"Who is Rodrigo?"

"Go ahead and kill me. I tell you that and there's no point in having a life."

"What does Rodrigo have to do with Domingo Angel and the VG?"

"Go to hell. Back where you belong."

I traded car keys for the cell phone. Before handing it over, I dialed 999, the UK equivalent of 911. I listened to him tell her where they were. While the memory was fresh, I put the name of the town into my smartphone's GPS. Then I drove away in their Alfa diesel, noting to myself that I could no longer claim to have never shot anyone with my own hand.

I didn't know whether they'd survive, or how I'd feel about the ultimate outcome, either way. They'd clearly meant to kill me, and deserved what they got. I could have finished them off, but decided to let fate sort it out.

"Oh, thank God," said Natsumi, when she answered the phone.

"Sorry about that," I said. "The plan had a catch."

"What?"

"Two big Spanish guys. I'll give you the details when I get there."

She told me the name she'd registered under and the room number.

"You're not going to ask about my mother's welfare," she said.

"Nope," I said. "I'm sure she's fine."

"That's excellent," she said, and hung up.

The Hilton Hotel on Hyde Park had a lineage, via another hotel brand, which harkened back to a more confident Imperial time, and it looked it. I liked it for the location, which was about as central as you could get.

I parked the Alfa in the parking garage, and once up in the lobby, called Natsumi's cell number for a second time to be sure everything was still okay. Then I went up.

When she opened the door, her hand went up to my cheek, dressed in gauze and white tape picked up along the way. I told her it was wide, but shallow. She pulled me into the room and shut the door. Then she held on to me for several minutes.

"I'm sorry for what I keep putting you through," I said.

She shook her head, her face still pressed against my chest.

"It's what we are putting ourselves through. We're together. Tell me what happened."

So I sat on the edge of the bed and did just that, sparing no detail. She listened with Asian reserve firmly in place, though she did say, "I imagined something just like that happening. Or tried not to imagine, but instead assumed you'd simply lost track of time."

"Which I never do."

"Which you never do. Are you sorry you had to shoot those men?"

"No."

"Me neither. So what do you think?" she asked.

Before answering, I fell back on the bed, the ferocious physical and emotional strain of the last several hours finally starting to catch up.

"Impossible to know with so little data, but we know some things," I said, as Natsumi propped up my head with a pillow.

"The boys had a Castilian accent, like mine, sort of the Queen's English version of Spanish, which they probably noticed, and assumed I was from España. I can't say how that might relate to this guy Domingo Angel. The house at number eight is accessible from the back via a long corridor and parking garage of the building it backs up against. This is why the neighbors thought it was abandoned. Inside it was set up as a temporary, or part-time, residence."

"A secret temporary or part-time residence," said Natsumi.

"Correct."

"Isn't there a name for that kind of place?"

"A safe house. Like the one they kept you in on Grand Cayman. A hideout, or clandestine meeting place, or both." I propped myself up on my elbows. "Maybe they all are. All the coordinates. Safe houses distributed around the world."

"For whom?"

I dropped back down on the bed.

"Whom indeed, Florencia," I said to the ceiling, "who were you keeping safe?"

CHAPTER 7

There were six apartments above the Chinese restaurant that fronted on the nearly vertical Calle Dulcinea del Toboso in the Lavapiés barrio of Madrid. Each had two windows with tiny wrought-iron balconies that looked out on the street, which was so narrow you couldn't get back far enough to see if anyone could be standing there.

A bank of buzzers was just inside the unlocked door at the foot of the staircase leading to the apartments. The five names listed were Zhu, Chao, Saliba, El-Ghazzawy and Santillian. The sixth buzzer was blank. I buzzed Santillian, who didn't buzz back. So I went across the street and waited.

I wore a phony beard, sunglasses and a black beanie. Natsumi was back at the hotel doing research on the other coordinates and worrying. Given what happened in the Caymans and London, a little separation anxiety was understandable. But it made little sense to have both of us casing the apartments, doubling our exposure.

The trip from London was uneventful, which we made after holing up in the hotel room for a few days so I could search for news of two compadres with gun injuries found in a field in the middle of Surrey. With no success. I did a little better searching for Domingo Angel of *Los Vengadores del Guardia.* There was nothing on the VG, but there was a Domingo Angel who'd retired as a colonel about ten years before from the Guardia Civil, Spain's national police service. There was little public information on his career — aside from the official, praise-drenched announcement of his retirement — though his last posting was running a *comandancia,* or provincial headquarters, within the Basque Country.

I'd made one last visit to Spottsworthy Mews to retrieve whatever gear Natsumi had left behind, and to try to wipe the place clean of fingerprints and traces of DNA, probably a futile effort, depending on the skills and determination of anyone in pursuit.

And who would that be, and why? I didn't know, and it didn't matter. An excess of paranoia had served me well so far, and I saw no reason to abandon it now.

I left the router with the video feed from the security cameras, since it was accessible through the Internet from anywhere in the world. The monitoring software would be doing most of the bullwork, so I could check it once in a while without a big time investment. At that point, no one had come to or gone from either our house or the safe house.

Most of what I'd learned about video surveillance came from staking out another apartment, this one in New Britain, Connecticut. I wanted to replicate that approach on the Calle Dulcinea, but couldn't see how, since it required a secure spot across the street, and that was unavailable. So I was reduced to the time-honored, if primitive, hanging around doorways, sitting at café tables and strolling nonchalantly up and down the street for as long as I could without becoming absurdly obvious.

It took about two days, but I was rewarded one afternoon by the arrival of a Chinese gentleman, who helped the cause by pausing at the door leading to the apartments to take a call on his mobile. This gave me time to come up to him in a casual, non-threatening manner. What I hoped was non-threatening.

"Perdóneme, señor," I said, when he

snapped shut the phone. *"¿Le puedo pre-guntar algo?"* May I ask you a question?

He stood his ground, but his nod was anything but enthusiastic.

"Is the person Santillian who lives in your apartment complex a man or a woman?" I asked in Spanish.

Suspicion itched at his eyes, but he answered, *"Un hombre. Señor Nicho Santillian."*

I smiled as engagingly as I could.

"That's good news. I represent the estate of his Uncle Esteban who died last month in New York City. He has an inheritance coming. According to the family, Mr. Santillian didn't know of his uncle in the U.S. An old family squabble. With his will, Esteban hoped to make amends."

"Why are you telling me?"

"I've buzzed Mr. Santillian's apartment a number of times, but he hasn't answered. If you could get a message to him, the estate has authorized me to provide a nice reward. Do you ever see Mr. Santillian?" I asked him.

"Sometimes."

I handed him a card with my cell phone number.

"Have him give me a call. And your name?"

"Zhu," he said, after some hesitation.

"I'll make it worth your while," I said, putting out my hand.

He shook it, loosening up a little, and we parted ways.

Back in my old life, I had a sideline chasing down the beneficiaries of lawsuits, usually class actions, who were unaware of the successful proceedings. The law firms doling out the money could only hold unclaimed funds for a defined period, at the end of which they were turned over to the state. The lawyers hated to do this, so they paid me to accomplish the happy task of delivering windfalls to unsuspecting recipients.

I'd never had an occasion when one of my targets didn't at least agree to hear me out.

Our hotel in Lavapiés reflected the district's ragged economic status and chaotic diversity. We were on the top floor in one of the *residencial* units, with a galley kitchen and second bedroom where I could set up gear and cruise the Internet at any hour, day or night.

Natsumi could be just as restless, so it suited us both. Though after a week of this, we agreed that cabin fever was setting in.

"I need a glass of wine," she said early one evening. "In a bar, where there are people doing the same thing. I know this doesn't mean much to you, since you drink like a little old lady."

"You wouldn't say that if you'd met my Great Aunt Lucille."

So we went out and walked for a few hours through the streets of Madrid — the old narrow streets and broad boulevards, under the canopies of giant urban trees, across terrifying traffic circles and miniature parks — and finally making our way to the huge, open air Plaza Mayor, where Natsumi could have her wine and human proximity and I could have a clear view of potential threats.

We decided to stay and eat, and listen to an amplified guitarist and piano player on the other side of the plaza render what the waiter told us were the greatest hits of Isaac Albéniz.

"You seem to be enjoying the music," said Natsumi.

"I am."

"Though you never listen to music. Not meant as a criticism. Just an observation."

"I used to listen all day long while working at my desk. Strictly classical, though occasionally the Ramones. Or the Cars. If the work wasn't that demanding."

"But not anymore."

"The bullet took out most of my math skills, which are associated with music."

"The math is coming back," she said. "Why not the music?"

She had a point, though I knew a great deal of my former mind was irretrievable. The loss seemed less in actual intelligence than in the reserves of knowledge derived through experience and memory. There was so much I had to relearn, which I seemed to accomplish with some proficiency; yet I was left with a sense of incompleteness, that my original brain was a greater, more expansive thing.

I shared that with Natsumi.

"I like your brain fine as it is," she said. "Maybe I wouldn't have liked that other Arthur so much."

"He was fat and had a lot more hair."

"Then I definitely like you better. I'm way into rangy and bald."

As a kid I fit the stereotype inflicted on people like me — hyper-curious, socially awkward, idiosyncratic, completely disengaged from physical fitness unless coerced by sadistic gym teachers. As an adult, I'd led a vigorous life, though not enough to stay ahead of the calorie count. That was something else that changed after the shooting. Parts of me, like my left leg, would probably never regain full function. But the rest of me was far more able than ever. In the struggle of recovery, fueled by fury and maniacal impatience, I'd somewhat overshot the mark.

Whether Natsumi would have liked my original manifestation, mind or body, was an unanswerable question. And as consumed with love as I was for Florencia, would I have even noticed Natsumi?

She read my mind, as she often did.

"Who knows if we would have liked each other back then," she said. "What with Florencia and all."

"I was never big on ontological conundrums," I said.

"Good. Let's keep it that way."

Before returning to the hotel, we walked all four sides of the plaza's promenade, ignoring the shop windows filled with jewelry, shoes, glittering tchotchkes and sugary edibles, concentrating instead on the swarms of well-turned-out Spaniards, bedazzled tourists and nervous-looking immigrants and their families.

It was a night well spent, almost well enough to fool ourselves into feeling like normal people and not a pair of fugitives from forces known and unknown, for whom the joys and challenges felt by the throng around us were merely abstractions, attainable only in the imagination.

My cell phone rang the next day.

"Señor Felingham," said the man on the other end of the line, addressing the persona I'd chosen for the purpose. "This is Nicho Santillian. My neighbor tells me you've been trying to reach me," he said in Spanish.

"So he probably told you why."

"Something about a rich dead uncle wanting to give me money," he said in English, my Spanish not being the accent-free Castilian I thought it was.

"That's it, more or less," I said.

"What's the less part?"

"I just need to verify I'm speaking to the right Nicho Santillian."

"And how will you do that?"

"By asking a few questions. Can we meet?"

"Tell me where you're staying. I'll come see you."

"A neutral place would be better," I said, offering an outdoor café about a block from his apartment.

"How will I know you?" he asked.

"I'll know you," I said.

We arranged to meet the next morning for breakfast, early, before the office trade

141

filled up the seats.

Natsumi and I spent the intervening time going over the plan and discussing fallbacks and possible scenarios. And precautions, a subject that was taking on ever greater complexity.

Natsumi found this annoying. "You always say no matter how careful we try to be, we can't operate in the world without risk," she said.

"I know, but I'm afraid for you."

"My mother once told me fear attracts evil forces."

"She learn that from a Zen master?" I asked.

"Wes Craven."

"Okay, so we concentrate on the plan and let the rest take care of itself."

The next morning, I switched into a fresh disguise and settled in right after sunrise at the place across from Santillian's apartment. The morning crew was good enough to let me sit, ostensibly to work on my iPad, while they finished bringing out tables and chairs and preparing for the day. I asked for coffee as soon as it was available.

Mr. Zhu was the first to leave for work. That was lucky, because it gave me a chance to test raising the iPad, zooming in and snapping a string of photos. Most were soft, but at least one captured his profile and the clothes he wore.

The sun was still struggling to illuminate the narrow Calle Dulcinea when a Middle Eastern guy came out, presumably either Mr. Saliba or Mr. El-Ghazzawy. I shot off a few more photos, my performance improving slightly. By then I'd had two cups of coffee and a plateful of powdery churros, and the café staff graciously allowed me to continue sitting undisturbed.

At the expected time, a tall, middle-aged European man with dark grey hair, wearing a light jacket with the collar pulled up, emerged from the building. I shot off a half dozen photos, one of which showed nearly a full face along with the jacket and white shirt underneath.

I dropped the iPad to the table and sent a copy of the photo to Natsumi's smartphone. Then I left double the cost of the coffee and followed my quarry at a comfortable distance.

At the end of the block, he stopped, and was met by two other men. They shook hands, took out cigarettes and talked the way people do when they know each other well. The one I presumed to be Santillian cocked his head a few times in the general direction of our designated rendezvous point. The others nodded and one of them placed a call on his cell. After giving Santillian a friendly cuff on the shoulder, they moved off in separate directions.

When Santillian arrived at the café, he looked around for a few minutes, then sat at a table with a good view of the sidewalk. Natsumi walked past and dropped a cell phone on his table. Without pausing, she continued on down the sidewalk, moving rapidly, so all he could make out was a bulky jacket, blue jeans and a big, soft-fabric hat under which she'd stuffed her long, jet black hair.

I dialed the cell phone, and from a vantage point partway down the street, watched him answer.

"Hola."

"Good morning, Señor Santillian. How are you doing today?"

"I'm well, if a little confused. Why all the James Bond?"

"I could ask you the same thing," I said.

"I don't know what you mean."

"I'll hold while you give your friends a call to come join us. I don't mind the extra company, I just want everyone out where I can see them."

"I don't know what you're talking about."

"I saw you meet up at the corner."

144

He paused and looked up and down the street. Then he said, "This isn't about a rich uncle, is it?"

"No, but it could be just as profitable."

"What do you want?"

"Information."

"What makes you think I know anything?" he said. "I'm just a guy. I sell concrete. You from the competition?"

"Maybe I am."

I could see him looking around the street, as if trying to catch someone's eye.

"Sorry, Americano. I don't sell out my employers, even a putz like Andreas."

"So you've spent time in New York. Pretty good for a concrete salesman in a country that's more or less given up buying concrete."

He stopped looking around and frowned at the phone. When he put it back to his head, he said, "Okay, you've got me curious. I'll invite my friends. I assume you'll know when they get here."

"I will."

He hung up and pulled out a smartphone of his own. I watched him dial, converse, hang up and repeat the process. Then he put the phone down on the table and went back to surveying his surroundings.

I called Natsumi, who after a quick change

of clothes, had established a new position at the café across the street. I described to her what was supposed to happen next.

"I wouldn't be surprised if the other two guys called in reinforcements," I said. "Keep an eye on whoever sits down at your café. Snap a shot of anything suspicious and text it to me."

"Okay."

"And take a few shots of our table when we're all assembled. Make sure I'm in the picture."

"Documentation?"

"Evidence."

The other two men showed up soon after and sat down at the table. They looked a little unsettled as they addressed Santillian. He just shrugged. I gave it another minute, then approached, offering my hand to Santillian. He took it without getting out of his chair.

"Ed Felingham," I said.

"You know who I am," he said, and gestured toward his companions. "This is Jueventino and Anthony."

"Not Antonio?"

"My mother liked that guy in the psycho movie," he said in Spanish, obviously not for the first time.

"Are you guys in concrete, too?" I asked

them in Spanish.

They looked at Santillian, who kept a blank face, then nodded.

"Sure," said Anthony, "we do a lot of concrete."

"I thought you sold it."

"Yeah. We sell it, too," said Anthony, after a pause.

"So, Señor," said Santillian, "you said you want information."

He was studying me with some intensity. Seeing him up close, I guessed his age as early to mid-fifties. With even, finely crafted features, he was handsome at this age and probably movie-star stunning as a young man. In fact, I had the odd sense that I'd seen him on the big screen. Something black and white, a romantic comedy with subtitles.

Not something one equates with a concrete salesman.

"I'm interested in real estate," I said.

"I know nothing about real estate."

"You know about your apartment building."

"I do, of course," he said, "but I just live there."

"You sure do. According to the building owner, you rent out two apartments. Though apparently, you only live in one."

The force of his concentration kicked up a notch, then seemed to loosen as he sat back in his chair, nearly grinning.

"You're with him," he said.

It was my turn to be puzzled.

"Sorry?" I said.

"The guy hanging around Calle Dulcinea. Kept buzzing my apartment. Or maybe it was you. Shaved the beard?"

"Not me. I hate beards."

He didn't look convinced. "So, you're interested in that other apartment, is that it?"

"I am. It must be quite an added expense for you. I could help you out."

"I like the extra room."

"I'll bet you'll like the extra income even more. I'll double whatever they're paying you."

As we talked, Jueventino and Anthony continuously searched the buildings around us with their eyes, ignoring the conversation. There was no way to tell if they understood what we said.

"You seem very calm for a person playing such a dangerous game," said Santillian.

"I'm not playing," I said.

"Hm," said Santillian. "Then maybe we should get down to business. At the moment, there are a pair of crosshairs in the

148

middle of your forehead. I assume the same goes for me. What is it called, mutually assured destruction?"

I nodded.

"Your buddies might get away," I said, "but probably not."

The two of them looked at me.

"Ever been to London, Mr. Felingham?" Santillian asked.

I gave it some thought, then said, "I used to live there. Years ago."

"So not recently."

"That's right."

A waiter came over. Pleasantries were exchanged as they asked for coffee, juice and *pasteles.* Just a bunch of sales guys delaying the start of another humdrum day on the job.

"I'm all set," I said, when the waiter asked for my order. "Already had breakfast."

"I'm sure you have," said Santillian, after the waiter left us. "I can tell you what you ate after I watch the video."

I felt my smartphone vibrate. I looked at the screen.

Natsumi had texted me: "Green car across street to the west. 2 guys not getting out, looking."

I put the phone back in my pocket.

"Jueventino and Anthony can go join your

149

other *compañeros* in the Nissan over there," I said, nodding toward the green car. "No point in getting them killed just for keeping you company."

They looked at Santillian and he told them to go.

"All of you get the hell out of here," he said, which they did without much hesitation. "Can we start talking now?" he asked when they were gone.

"We can try," I said. "So how about that apartment?"

He took a sip of his coffee before answering.

"This interest you have, is it official or unofficial?"

"Define official."

He made a sound that could be interpreted as a light laugh. "I guess it doesn't matter anymore, does it?" he said. "It's all the same."

"It's just that official can mean a lot of different things."

He bought that. "True. So let me ask you, this interest, is it American?"

In a conversation filled with pauses, the next one was conspicuously long. It had to be as I played out a half dozen if/thens in my head. I finally gave it up and went with my first unexamined impulse.

"No," I said. "I'm an American, but that's the only connection."

He seemed to be processing that when he said, "And I'm not only a concrete salesman. I have a full line of building materials. Whatever you need, I can get it."

"Too bad I'm not building anything," I said. "Though what I could really use is a courier service."

He smiled a bloodless smile. "I have no use for such a service myself."

"Well, this might be a way to get into the business. All you have to do is find a man named Rodrigo and deliver a brief message."

Back when I fed my tuition payments by playing blackjack in Atlantic City, there was always a lot of talk among amateurs after a game about the "tell," the supposed giveaway gestures and facial tics that provided a look inside your opponent's mind. Never happened with the serious players, since they'd learned long ago how to keep those things in check no matter which way the cards were running. Santillian would have made a pretty good card player, though I'd have to coach him on that little flicker across the brow.

"This is Spain," he said. "We have a lot of Rodrigos."

"If you're as good as I think you are, you'll find the right one. When you do, here's the message: I'm not a threat. All I want is information. For me and for no one else, officially or unofficially. I seek conflict with no one."

"That's all well and good, but maybe this Rodrigo is seeking conflict with you."

I stood up. "Only if he doesn't understand, or has no respect for, the concept of self-defense."

I heard the sound of a car door close down the street behind me. Then the car started and moved in my direction. I kept my eyes on Santillian, who stayed in his seat, though I saw him steal a glance at the approaching car.

"What if I want to communicate with you?" he asked.

"Text," I said, reaching out to open the rear door of the cab as it pulled up to the curb. I wasted little time climbing in and slamming the door, and after sliding low in the seat, told the driver to take me to the first of several places I went that day before feeling safe enough to return to the hotel.

CHAPTER 8

While I was zigzagging around Madrid, getting in and out of taxis, walking in the front door of museums, shops and restaurants, then ducking out the back whenever possible, Natsumi was making friends with Spanish academics.

Where I would have detailed every conversation and led her through an exhaustive narrative, beginning with my initial findings, then a step-by-step description of each call and subsequent progress of the search leading to the final outcome, she simply said to me, "Raul Preciado-Cotto. Best in the business."

"At what?"

"The history of the Guardia Civil. The national police force of Spain. Kind of a CIA, FBI and National Guard balled up in one. Given Spain's past, not without its controversy."

"You've contacted Raul?"

"By email. He's a professor at the *Universidad Complutense de Madrid,* though forty years before that he was a journalist. A European stringer, funnily enough, for *The Philadelphia Inquirer.* Did that for thirty years."

"Thirty plus forty?"

"In the years before the *Inquirer* gig, he graduated from the Sorbonne, then kicked around a bunch of odd jobs and did a stint in Franco's Guardia Civil, which at the time was busy choking off the last of the resistance from the civil war."

"He's gotta be a million years old," I said.

"Ninety-eight. He has perspective."

"And we can talk to him?"

"Tomorrow at eight P.M. He said to bring Calvados. The quality of his commentary is apparently pegged to the vintage of the brandy, so you might think about selling some assets."

"What's our cover?" I asked.

"You're writing a book. Seemed to work okay last time."

"What are you doing?"

"Taking a sabbatical from my psychotherapy business. Why mess with a winning formula."

Before going to bed, I checked the video

feed from Spottsworthy Mews. At first I thought there was a glitch in the software, or an error in the log, since no activity had been registered for a few days. I called up the menu of thumbnails, listed chronologically, and started clicking through.

Not surprisingly, no one went in or out of the safe house. Our randy neighbors, on the other hand, knocked on our door every afternoon around cocktail hour, at least on one occasion with bottles in hand. I felt vaguely bad for them. It must be bloody difficult to drum up like-minded corespondents so conveniently close to home.

Other people moved in and out of security camera range, doors opened and closed — sometimes in great haste, goods and packages were signed for, hugs were followed by invitations, long conversations were held in the courtyard, a crew of blokes in white jumpsuits did maintenance work on the common area lighting, the guy boinking the housewife at number six made a nearly daily appearance (I committed myself once and for all to getting this information over to the McPhersons) and that was about it.

Until the facade of the safe house blew out into the courtyard.

Once the dust settled, the image showed people pouring out of their homes, a few stopping to stare at the flames raging out into the night air. Then the Fire Brigade appeared, pulling hoses through the courtyard, and blasting water into the ruined townhouse. Blue lights flickered from the smaller cop cars that could squeeze their way into the mews; bobbies, looking straight-backed and confident in caps and helmets and chartreuse slickers, hustled people back from the steamy, flame-lit chaos.

This all lasted until the feed suddenly winked out, likely because of the proximity of the junction box and router to the blistering heat of the fire.

It didn't matter. I got the point.

Professor Preciado-Cotto lived in the Salamanca district a block off Serrano Street in one of the most affluent neighborhoods in Madrid. His place was on the top floor of his apartment building, affording a generous view of the surrounding area, which included the American embassy.

As requested, we arrived at eight in the evening with a $300 bottle of Calvados. One of the security people at the front desk called up to him, and then the other escorted us to the apartment. He waited until Preciado-Cotto opened the door and we exchanged introductions. Then he left us and we were allowed in.

The furniture was massive and ornate, in a variety of natural wood tones. The rugs were Persian and several floor vases — big enough to bathe in — were focal points. A grand piano dominated part of the sitting area, the remaining space occupied by over-stuffed couches and chairs. Bookcases made of a woven reed-like material took up what wall space wasn't covered by art. At least two of the works were Picassos. I also identified a Chagall and a Kandinsky, which exhausted my knowledge of twentieth-century art. Large windows let in the bright lights of the city.

Preciado-Cotto himself was a bit less than five feet tall, with a straight back, bald head and fleshy face that seemed to make up a quarter of his body mass. He wore an embroidered smoking jacket over a silky white shirt, sharply pressed slacks and slip-on shoes, also embroidered with blue and gold medallions. His handshake was bone dry, but firm.

He took the Calvados and nodded appreciatively as he read the label. "You knew I was joking," he said, in lightly accented English. "But maybe I'm glad if you didn't."

"It's our pleasure," said Natsumi, as we followed him out to the sitting area. He stopped at a dry bar and retrieved three brandy glasses, into which he poured without hesitation generous helpings of the golden brown liquid. We sat, or rather were absorbed into the fluffy couch.

"We appreciate your willingness to speak with us, *profesor,*" said Natsumi.

"Emeritus at this point," he said. "Though they still drag me into the classroom now and again to guest lecture. I don't mind. You can't just write all day."

"If my research is correct, you've written nearly a hundred books," said Natsumi.

"Eighty-one. And over a thousand academic papers, newspaper and magazine articles and monographs."

"Hard to imagine," she said. "This is my first book."

"For some, writing is a disease. My father never understood." Seventy-eight years of professional accomplishment and a parent's disapproval is still the first thing that comes to mind. "Mostly I blame Hemingway," he added.

"You're not the first to find him an inspiration," I said.

Preciado-Cotto sniffed. "Not that. My father let him stay at our country house for a week just before Ebro, the battle that broke the back of *Los Republicanos.* I'm sorry, I know he is a famous American writer, but what a horse's ass."

"Your father was an arms merchant, supporting the Republicans," said Natsumi. "And yet you joined the Guardia Civil."

He pointed at her with a long, crooked finger. "If you know that, then you know why."

"Undercover work."

He dropped his hand back down on the arm of the chair. "Precisely. You need to go into the belly of the beast if you are going to understand his true nature."

He looked away and added, "Three years was all I could stand. Do you know Philadelphia?" He asked out of the blue, a clear signal that the subject needed to change.

"I went to graduate school at the University of Pennsylvania," I said, hoping they had a master's program in psychotherapy.

He was pleased by this. "I went there often to meet with my American editors. And to study hoagies and the Philadelphia Phillies. Connie Mack stadium. And the undergraduates of Bryn Mawr College."

"What happened to your father after the war?" Natsumi asked.

"He didn't like leaving Philadelphia, but took it well. He and my mother took a boat from Bilbao and landed in France. They made it to Geneva and eventually flew to Mexico City. He had to abandon his fortune, but not his business. That was all up here." He pointed to his head.

"And you stayed."

"Why do you want to write about all this?" he asked Natsumi.

"Because not enough has been written," she said.

He smiled. "So, my eighty books are not enough?"

Apparently won over, he spent the next two hours delivering a survey course on the history of the Guardia Civil, fueled by the expensive Calvados, which seemed to have no impact on Preciado-Cotto's clarity of thought or expression. Natsumi took careful notes and I stacked up the books he gave her as further reading on each area covered, not all written by him.

Throughout he dodged any effort, however subtle, to draw the story back to his own history with the notorious Franco-era version of the Guardia. On the other hand, he clearly enjoyed reminiscing over his time as a journalist, including one more encounter with Ernest Hemingway.

"It was sometime in the late fifties. He saw my byline on a reprinted article in the *Herald Tribune* and wrote me when he was passing through Madrid. We had drinks. Me a few, him more than a single person, even one as big as Papa, should be able to consume. We talked about our projects, and I could see him deflating when I described my daily production. For me, writing was breathing. A constant necessity. But I think for him it was very hard, especially by then, when he was so diminished by injury and drink and bad behavior. I thought, what a world we have here, the winner of the Nobel Prize in literature feeling defeated by a journeyman reporter."

Natsumi artfully indulged these finer, more romantic sidetracks without allowing the central story to drift out of view. She steadily, invisibly brought him back.

"After Franco, the Guardia returned to favor?" she asked.

His head sagged forward for a moment, making me think we'd finally tired him out, but it turned out he was simply framing his thoughts. "That's a matter of debate and interpretation. For some, the Guardia of the iron fist made for a better, safer society. You know they tried to take over parliament when the body of the Generalissimo finally decided to follow his brain. Our king saved us. After that, times changed, and things changed, especially when the Guardia had a new enemy to fight."

We must have looked at him blankly.

With a hint of disgust he said, "ETA. *Euskadi Ta Askatasuna.*"

"Basque terrorists?" I asked.

He nodded. "The filthy underground wars of modernity," he said. "All done under cover of moral darkness, shielded by innocents. Almost makes you long for big land armies and bombing raids."

As Natsumi gently guided him along this track, his speech gained momentum, as if the relative proximity of the last few decades energized the narrative.

"It didn't begin this way," he said. "ETA started as a bunch of academics, passionate debaters and pamphleteers, but nothing violent until that boy was killed, the guardia who stopped two of the ETA leaders trying to enter the country from France. One of the ETA people was chased down and killed, but the other escaped. That was the spark that lit decades of ugliness."

He talked about assassinations, and retaliations, on both sides. Bombings, kidnappings and bank robberies by ETA, disappearances and torture purportedly by the guardias. All in all, both filthy and entirely underground.

"I've only just started my research," said

Natsumi, when Preciado-Cotto reached a logical break in the story, "but I have a few names that have emerged. Do you mind if I ask you about them?"

He had no objection, so she brought up several people I'd never heard of, and a few I had through my own research. Then she asked, referring to her notes, "Did you ever meet Miguel and Sylvia Zarandona?"

His grip on the armrests of his chair tightened slightly. A tell, I thought to myself.

"They were socialists, certainly. But who wasn't in those days? Unless you were Francoist. I never understood why they left. Such beautiful people. I loved Sylvia. As a colleague," he added, looking at both of us to be sure we understood his meaning.

"I know they were exiled to Chile, though a few years after Allende died they seemed to have disappeared," she said.

He shrugged.

"I don't know. I was long retired when they left the country. We didn't correspond."

For the first time, I had an intimation that our welcome was beginning to fade. It seemed like a good time to kill the rest of the Calvados. A good strategy, as his mood seemed to right itself as the bottle emptied into his glass. Natsumi helped things along by returning the discussion to his reporting days, asking how he managed to transition from journalism into academia.

"My father finally had his way," he said. "His last act was to die and leave me his second fortune, safely tucked inside a conservative portfolio at a securities firm in New York. I didn't need to work, but I couldn't stop reading and writing, and I was ready for something different."

We heard about his return to school, his PhD and steady advancement up the academic ladder. Along the way, Natsumi managed to nudge him back into his study of the Guardia Civil.

"Everyone needs a life work," he said. "I swore the day I left the service that I would loyally chronicle the evils done in their name, understanding that not all guardias have been evil. Not by any stretch. Everyone has their heroes and villains. There is no black nor white."

By then it was after two in the morning, and even the bountiful reserves of Preciado-Cotto seemed to flag. After many thank you's, formal bows and gracious hopes for success with our project, we headed toward the door. That was when Natsumi acted as if she'd suddenly remembered to ask one more thing.

"Profesor," she said, again looking down at

her notes, "in all your studies, have you ever come across an organization called *Los Vengadores del Guardia*? Or the VG?"

This time a blind man could pick up the tell. He gripped her forearm, not to steady himself, but to give strength to his words.

"After Franco, not all guardias bent to the new order. It is always like this. Some thought the king would restore the monarchy to its former absolute splendor, and when he did the opposite, considered him a betrayer. For them, democracy was blasphemy. Socialism an abomination. Since Franco died they are diminished, but still endure. I believe certain forms of evil are immortal. I said there was no black or white, but that isn't true. Some things are pure black. I have no proof that *Los Vengadores* even exists, so I must avoid their mention in my writings. But, for some reason, the very name gives me a chill. Me, an old man inured to the fear of death."

Natsumi nodded solemnly, and without further comment, turned to leave. But Preciado-Cotto gripped her arm again.

"I don't want you to think I feel nothing for Miguel and Sylvia Zarandona. I do, deeply. But you don't understand how many brilliant, treasured lives have been taken from the Spanish-speaking peoples of the world. In the face of so much darkness, what else can a person do but bear witness, and pray he can sleep through all the cries of the lost?"

CHAPTER 9

The fire at the apartment house on Calle Dulcinea del Toboso only took an hour to consume all six apartments before collapsing into the shops on the first floor. Luckily, the ancient stone and brick main walls provided an adequate fire stop, so the buildings to either side were spared.

As were all the residents, according to the news report in the online version of *El País*. A Señor Chao reported that he was roused from bed by a neighbor pounding on his door, and he in turn, seeing smoke fill the hallway, got everyone else out in time.

I'd just finished the story when my smartphone chirped at me. I looked at the text message on the screen: "Rodrigo would like you to go to hell. I've been asked to arrange transport."

Natsumi and I had breakfast in that morning. A platter of meats, wheat toast, melons and eggs. As close as we could get to an American meal. Comfort food.

"Now what," she asked, blowing across the top of her freshly poured coffee.

"We go to the next set of coordinates."

"They'll be waiting for us."

"I know."

"Do you have a plan?"

"Not yet. This might be impossible," I added, after a pause.

"It might."

"Maybe we should give it up and go to ground. While we still can."

"Maybe we should."

"What do you think?" I asked.

"It's up to you."

"I thought we had that discussion. You deserve a vote."

"I vote to do what you want to do. You can never resent me for interfering with your impulses."

"What if my greatest impulse is to keep you safe?" I asked.

"It isn't. That doesn't mean you don't love me. I love you, too. This is what we have."

"This is why Westerners think you Easterners are so impossible to understand."

"Vice versa, buddy. Listen, what you're dealing with here is a war inside your own brain. You want to keep me safe, but you want to chase this rabbit, this unresolved question about Florencia, even more. It's eating you alive. Why, why, why, that little voice keeps screaming. It's the worst thing that could happen to you. A puzzle you can't crack, an enigma beyond interpretation. But I know that about you, better than you know it yourself. I've watched you, I've lived with your crazy determination. That's okay. Just stop trying to rescue me from yourself. It's too late. I want to be here. It's what I want to do."

I'd never heard Natsumi raise her voice, but she had other ways of adding weight to her words. I sighed and gave up the fight.

"We switch tactics," I said.

"Okay."

To me, a major data center that's been around for a while is like a vast, ancient ruin, wherein the fundamental structure is filled with tangled debris, crumbling walls and overgrowth. A fantastical painting of a 10,000-year-old city, beautiful yet decadent, equal parts order and chaos, and nearly infinite in scale. Nodes of gleaming contemporary design contained by primitive stone walls and supported by massive antediluvian foundations.

I don't consider myself a hacker, though I

understand the allure, the addictive nature of the pursuit. Though many do it solely for the money, and others to vandalize and wreak destruction for political reasons, or for its own sake, I'd be among those drawn to the challenge of cracking the code, penetrating the defenses, worming my way into private places arrogantly assumed to be safe and secure.

In my days as a researcher, the temptation to cut corners, or sneak in backdoors using illegal apps readily available to those who know where to look, was a daily thing. I just didn't do it. Partly as a matter of ethics, partly because if I started, I knew I wouldn't be able to stop.

I did often find myself drifting into grey areas, essentially wandering into files and databases that were left carelessly unsecured, or accessible through an unmonitored portal. I didn't break any locks, I just tried the doorknob, and if the door opened, I strolled on through.

Most of these skills and knowledge had been acquired during a long and involved assignment helping an insurance carrier design identity theft coverage. My job was to work with the underwriters and actuaries to define exposures. I did this by assessing the tactics of the identity thieves themselves.

In addition to becoming expert in stealing people's identities, I spent a lot of time with computer security people who gave me great insight into the vulnerabilities and breach points of even the most robust defense systems.

So even though I didn't have the chops that came from hours at the keyboard poking and prodding at security walls, I did understand the principles and best practices of your everyday successful hacker.

With these thoughts, I stood at the base of the data fortress that enclosed the *Dirección General de la Policía y de la Guardia Civil,* the governing authority of the Guardia Civil, and peeked in.

The first option was to select English translations, which I summarily rejected. Only the thinnest layer of information would be available in anything but Spanish. I moved through the outer layer quickly, arriving at the first guarded portal. Instead of testing the lock, I used standard commands to open up the hard code.

It was in a programming language I understood reasonably well, and the person who had written it was reasonably artful and efficient. This was good and bad, since a sloppier hand would have left more inefficiencies to exploit.

I settled in for several hours, studying every line of code and learning the rhythm of the program, searching for a way to get through the web-based layer and into the databases that lay behind.

It didn't happen that day, or that night, but eventually I stumbled over a string of code that delivered an administrative shortcut, and like throwing the switch on a teleporter, I flicked into a new server, a new database and a new reality. Then promptly hit a wall.

Where the layer I'd just pushed through was likely handled by an outsourced service, possibly offshore, the enterprise servers had been built up over years with the heavy hand of security clearly present. It made sense. It's what you'd find in any corporate database.

But at least I was partially in, and had access to the file structure, some of the directories, and other peripheral information. I could study that, which I did for another four days.

I apologized to Natsumi for disappearing so long into cyberspace, but she would have none of it.

"This is a big city. The Prada alone can take four days to explore. I have no complaints."

Another way I look at the current state of large-order IT is you have an enterprise system, usually with big data management capabilities, living at the core. I see this as the mother ship, around which swarm dozens, sometimes hundreds, of subsystems that are linked in through a variety of channels. I knew this to be the structural nightmare facing security people, charged with keeping the core impregnable, yet allowing all these motley websites, servers and applications, over which they had little control, to interconnect.

This was my next angle of attack. I started searching for pathways from the data center in Madrid out to the local command posts and their subsidiaries spread out across the country.

I assumed that interoffice communications would be the least secure, given the sadly false expectation that threats mostly come from outside. But not in this case. Somewhere on the IT staff sat a very clever, hard-nosed functionary responsible for internal security who took the job very seriously. I mentally tipped my hat, and shifted over to nodes less likely to fall under his domain.

And that's where I found the wormhole. Some enterprising tourist bureau in a small town in Valencia had teamed up with the community affairs director of the local Guardia Civil — who was looking to polish up the *comandancia*'s public image — to start a common website. You could go there and not only discover exciting tourist attractions, but also get pointers on safe driving and all the public services your hometown guardias provided.

The site used a content management system that allowed access by both the tourist bureau and the police via identical passwords. The first step was to crack into the tourist bureau's email server through a simple phishing exercise. That gave me the user name of the site's webmaster. I used this to ask the CMS to send me a new password. The second the email hit the admin's mailbox, I copied the new password and deleted the email. I entered the login information and dove into the administrative files.

As hoped for, the CMS had several directories through which I could connect with the operating system on the server that ran the *comandancia*'s management system. I found the screen where I could give myself full administrative privileges, which laid bare every file on the server, including personnel.

Of all the files, this was the one most likely

to be linked back to the core system, since a central operation would have to handle the bulk of the administrative requirements.

I was moving fast, driven both from the thrill of the chase and the fear that an alarm was about to go off on the desk of that wily internal security guy in Madrid, who could block me out in an instant, or shut the server down entirely.

Fortunately, that wasn't going to happen, though I didn't know that then, my nervous system crackling with a mixture of excitement and dread. Or disappointment, as when I reached a request form to obtain copies of personnel files. I requested the one belonging to Colonel Domingo Angel and was denied access. There was no getting around this one, and I shouldn't have been surprised. There was likely no more sacrosanct repository than a ranking officer's personnel file.

But I searched on, now several hours into the exploration, my eyes watering and my wrists and fingers literally cramping up. Natsumi came in the room a few times, bringing in tea and sandwiches and bottled water. If I'd asked her to, she would have pressed wet washcloths to my brow or massaged the kinks out of my shoulders and back. But a light hug was all I asked for and all she dispensed, and I was happy for that.

Then, as often happens, a mundane little function showed itself, at first so innocuous as to be invisible, but then it hit me like a bolt.

It was in a series of search links, along with things like Locate Post, Locate Communications Staff, Locate Regional Dispatch, Locate Animal Control, there was one simple link, Locate Retired Officer.

Two clicks later I had the P.O. Box, telephone number and email address of Colonel Domingo Angel.

"Pack your bag," I told Natsumi. "We're going back to France."

"The Côte d'Azur?"

"Close. Aix-en-Provence. A few hundred miles west of the Cap. Up in the hills."

"One of the coordinates?" she asked.

"No. Retirement home of Colonel Angel. I think."

"You cracked it."

"More or less. I couldn't get his file, but I have a P.O. Box in Aix, a cell phone number and an email address. It's a good start."

"Is there anything you don't know how to do?"

"You don't have to know. You just have to find."

176

■ ■ ■ ■

I decided to drive there from Madrid. My reasoning was complicated, and not wholly reasonable. After being cooped up for most of the month in that residential hotel room, I longed for fresh air and open spaces — not to be trapped in the confines of shuttle buses, waiting areas and passenger cabins.

And I couldn't take another gauntlet of security checks, with stern uniformed officials staring down at our passports, then over at us from behind bullet-proof glass; black-shoed sadists wielding electronic wands and shoving us through Orwellian X-ray machines; those tense moments before takeoff when a member of the ground crew comes aboard and whispers to a flight attendant.

Crossing the border by car wasn't nothing, but it wasn't the same.

For our car I chose an Opel Insignia, thinking it was a good size, comfortable, yet unassuming. I had no technical basis whatsoever for my assessment, but that was the mood I was in.

After cramming the car full of our luggage and gear, I checked out and we fought our way through the city traffic; and with Natsumi and her smartphone in navigation mode, we were soon soaring across the tawny, windswept plains of Castilla-La Mancha.

"Seems to be an appropriate part of the country to be driving through, given the odds of a successful venture," I said.

"Huh?"

"Don Quixote."

"Never read it."

"Just as well. You'd likely think the guy was an idiot."

"Do you read books, Arthur? I mean, did you?"

So much of our time together was spent demarcating our lives before and after I was shot, and before she was tossed unwittingly into the world that shooting had created.

"I read everything. Everything that kept my attention past the first page. No bias, no patterns. Fiction, nonfiction, coffee table books, newspapers, technical papers, magazine articles, cereal boxes, instruction manuals, pamphlets from the Jehovah's Witnesses. I was a professional researcher. Information was my stock in trade — and a lifelong obsession, which explains the profession."

"Is that still you?" she asked, in the guileless way she often did.

I looked at her so she could see my face

when I answered. "It is. I just haven't had the time to read."

How could I explain to her that the hurtling, bobsled run of our lives together bore no resemblance to the life I once led? She was a very smart woman. She got it intellectually. But her experience gave her no context for understanding.

"What about you?" I asked. "You haven't dealt a single hand of blackjack since I hid you out in my apartment in West Hartford. You don't get the urge?"

"Blackjack was my night job. By day I wrote research papers on Münchausen Syndrome by Proxy for my degree in psychology. That's when a mother, usually not a father, makes her kid sick so she can get lots of attention from medical professionals. I think I liked the subject because my mother always told everyone I was the perfect picture of health, even when I was hacking up my lungs with the flu."

"You revere your mother," I said.

"I do. She had to toughen me up for life, but she would never let anything really bad happen to me."

"My sister made all the health decisions in my family. From the time she was about eight."

"Quite a kid," she said.

"She's now a cardiologist, as you know. My parents were uneducated, but smart enough to listen to their kids, who were."

"My real father died before I had a chance to know him. He was working on a high-rise office building and fell off a scaffold. It takes over ten minutes to walk the distance he traveled in just a few seconds. My mother told me he was an honorable man, but nowhere near as fun as Chief Warrant Officer Jimmy Fitzgerald."

I looked over at her again. She had her head on the headrest and her eyes closed. A small, slim person, barely a hundred pounds soaking wet, she still managed to take up a lot of the cubic footage of whatever space she occupied.

"You miss him," I said.

"I do. He was a drunk, but a happy drunk. While other drinkers got nasty, he just wanted to give away his money, what little he had. And ya can't love people any more than Jimmy Fitzgerald loved me and me mum," she added, in a perfect Irish brogue.

The decision to drive was a good one for about two hundred miles. We were up on a plateau with nothing but high plains covered in grey green grass to either side, mountains in the distance and wind-roiled clouds

180

overhead, when from out of nowhere a black and white Nissan Patrol SUV with the bar of blue lights on the roof hysterically alight filled the rearview mirror.

I pulled over. Both guardias got out of the Nissan. One approached my door, the other stood behind the trunk of our car. Both men stood unsteadily in the fierce winds that blew across the plateau, their white shirts rippling like sea waves. The guy at our car door asked in Spanish for my driver's license. Then when I handed him the North Carolina version I'd used to rent the car, he asked in thickly accented English for our passports. He stood back from the car and studied the passports, holding his hat against the wind, then leaned into the window.

"Leave the vehicle, please," he said.

We stepped out into a warm wind blowing well over twenty knots. It made it hard to hear the cop's questions.

"Where is your destination?" he asked.

"Cerbère," I said. "We're traveling to France."

"For business?"

"And pleasure. We're touring Spain on our way to an academic conference," I said in Spanish.

He frowned at that, as if I'd given the

wrong answer. He was a tall man, with a doughy face and caved-in chest. His partner, standing several paces away, was shorter and thicker, and better looking. His gaze was fixed on Natsumi and he'd drawn his service weapon from its holster.

"What is in the car?" the tall guy asked.

"Luggage and electronic equipment. I'm a computer scientist guest-lecturing here in Europe."

The wind was making mischief with Natsumi's silk tank top, forcing her to clench her midsection. The short cop told her to take her hands away, waving at her with the barrel of his semi-automatic.

"Hey," I said, "what the hell."

Natsumi held her arms away from her body, allowing the tank top to flap around her torso and at brief moments expose her white bra.

"Why weren't you wearing your seat belt?" the tall guy asked me.

"I was. So was my wife."

"That's not what we observed. We can confiscate this vehicle and hold you at our post for questioning," he said in English.

"We're just traveling through," I answered in Spanish. "We will be sure to have our seat belts on for the rest of the trip."

"He should go and the woman should

come with us," said the short cop, throwing in the Spanish equivalent of "Chink."

"I'm not a Chink," said Natsumi. "I'm a Jap."

"I'm a scientist with associations throughout the global community. They know my travel plans. I'm expected in France tomorrow. If I don't show up, there will be international attention."

The tall cop didn't seem impressed, though a bit undecided.

"Let me see this equipment."

I opened the trunk and showed him the laptops, monitors, video cameras and various external devices. I gave a running commentary, much of it made up, that I hoped gave the regular gear an enhanced stature. I was fairly sure he had no idea what I was talking about.

He made me open our luggage, which he rummaged through until I couldn't re-zipper the bags. Along the way he pulled out a pair of Natsumi's panties, which he showed to his partner.

"See?" said the short cop, "I still think we should take the woman. She's suspicious. We need to talk to her in private."

Apparently satisfied with his search, the tall cop stuffed Natsumi's underwear back into her bag and slammed the trunk.

"You need to obey the laws of our country, Señor," he said. "That includes wearing your seat belt."

"We will."

He looked over at his partner, whose gaze seemed permanently fixed on Natsumi's midsection.

"He's young and far from home," he said to me in English. "They get over it."

"Just keep an eye on him," I answered, also in English. "Some day when you're not around, he's going to do something you'll regret."

"No lectures from you, Americano," he said. "Feel lucky you and the Señora get to go to France."

With that they got into the Nissan and roared back onto the highway, tires spinning on the gravel shoulder, then burning over the paved surface. Natsumi and I watched as it disappeared into the horizon.

"Well," she said, "that was interesting."

"Are you okay?"

"Assholes."

"I memorized the license plate."

"And?"

"And we'll see."

CHAPTER 10

The trip across the rest of Spain to Cerbère was smooth as silk. As soon as we crossed the border and sailed into the coastal zest of Languedoc — western Mediterranean France — I felt like an invisible weight had been lifted from my heart. A menace expunged.

With a bit of survivor's élan, we sped over hills and through fields and vineyards with the windows open and the radio playing music that would have been unrecognizable to me no matter where it played, though Natsumi had a different perspective.

"That's Eskmo in San Fran and Mala from London. Circa twenty eleven dubstep get-real-on-the-dance-floor music. Where you been, boy?" Natsumi asked, with just a touch of condescension.

"In a coma, okay?"

"Not the whole time. And it didn't make any difference anyway. You still wouldn't know anything."

"Okay, but I really was in a coma."

I purposely avoided the four-lane super-highway that could have rocketed us to the eastern side of the coast in favor of a circuitous ramble through the hills and verdant fields, endless vineyards and medieval villages — sometimes not much more than piles of organized stone with colorful modern signs — that graced our passage.

Driven by hunger and hopeful despite the late hour, we stopped at a hotel that promised fine food procured entirely from an area less than a mile in any direction from the hotel lobby. Of course it was closed. I rang the bell on the front desk anyway.

"Can we possibly buy some food?" I said in my lousy French to the old, bent woman who poked her head through the curtain behind the desk. "We are traveling and very hungry."

"Stay in the hotel and I'll get the old man up to give you anything you want," she said. "Otherwise, eat the trees."

Seemed like a reasonable arrangement.

The old man, Monsieur Prefontaine, was so delighted to have two hungry, culinarily unsophisticated Americans to shower with specialties of the house, that we nearly expired from overeating. It would have helped to know that the *bourride sètoise* — fish stew — followed by pan-seared *fois gras* set on caramelized arbutus berry *jus,* then by turbot roasted in a verbena infusion with crushed cooked apples and lemon, and a chicken baked in a basket of woven pine needles, represented only a partial sampling of a multi-course meal, most of which was on the house.

Monsieur Prefontaine stood at the table while we ate, giving us a comprehensive description of the contents, procurement, preparation and ideal presentation. We responded with relentless appreciation, for the flavors both novel and delicious, and for his generous attention.

The obvious occurred to me — food in France is truly an art form, not unlike drama. You can put everything you have into training as an actor, but your success is ultimately determined by applause from the audience. Monsieur Prefontaine had the exclusive focus of an audience of two, and he was determined to deliver his finest culinary performance.

The arrival of dessert was both a gigantic relief, and cause for horror, since it was composed of five large balls of ice cream, each flavored by plants and wildflowers harvested from the surrounding woodlands.

We sampled from each — lavender, *thym, rosmarin,* jasmine and marjoram. I was ready to beg off finishing the bowl, when Natsumi bravely dug in and rescued our family honor.

"Then perhaps we can now finish with our crème brûlée?"

It took all of Natsumi's considerable diplomatic skill to get us out of there with good will intact and up to our room, where we collapsed on the bed, hands resting on our bellies as if containing a potential explosion.

"I don't think I can take off my shoes," I said.

"I wonder what the crème brûlée tasted like."

"Local moss."

Having learned the benefits of apartment dwelling while staying in Madrid, we rented a pay-by-the-week tourist flat a few blocks from the Cours Mirabeau in the old town area of Aix-en-Provence. The rental agent was a very round woman with excess makeup and delusional body image, as demonstrated by the fuck-me high heels and form-fitting skirt.

The rooms were perfectly appointed, abundantly filled with light and fresh air by way of the classic French floor-to-ceiling casement windows, whitewashed rough plaster walls, the larder partially stocked with packaged meats, cheese and snack food, and a bottle of wine waiting on the counter with two glasses and a corkscrew.

The agent looked disappointed when we took it on the spot.

"But we have just begun to look," she said, her upsell strategy in ruins, assuaged when I offered to pay two weeks in advance.

We went through the unpacking and setup process like the regimented routine it had become, requiring very few words and little deviation from the settled division of labor. While I configured the electronics array, Natsumi went out to procure basic food-stuffs and necessities. Once the computers were up and online, I placed a few orders for gear I thought we might need for the next round, now that we had a fixed address to receive the goods.

I tested to see if my backdoor into the enterprise system at the *Dirección General de la Policía y de la Guardia Civil* was still unlocked. It was. I found the email address of the officer in charge of the *comandancia* that covered the eastern portion of *Castille-La Mancha*. By using my admin privileges, I was able to drop a note directly through the email server, thus disguising the origin of the message.

I wrote that I had witnessed two guardias (whom I described) driving an official vehicle — license number cited — buy the services of an underage prostitute with a small quantity of cocaine. It was rumored that this *pareja* — team — had also been using their authority to shake down small businesses in the remote rural areas they served.

I hit send and quietly sneaked out the way I came.

My packages started arriving a few days later. The largest was only about 2 × 4 × 3/4 inches. Inside was an AM/FM radio and flashlight that ran on batteries, solar power, or human power in the form of a hand crank. I unscrewed the housing and carefully extracted the electronics. Then I opened another box which held a micromini tracking device, which I also separated from its housing, disconnecting the AAA battery, the bulkiest part of the working system. Then I integrated the tracker into the power supply of the little radio, and managed to cram it all into the radio's green plastic case.

I downloaded the tracker's software and

ran a test, which it passed.

I moved on to InDesign and Photoshop, graphics programs that I used to create lurid new packaging for the radio and the shipping box. Also a selling pamphlet that announced to the unidentified recipient that he/she had been selected at random to receive this outstanding once-in-a-lifetime offer to visit a beautiful new condominium complex in Lloret del Mar on the Costa Brava, the resort region north of Barcelona. All travel and hospitality expenses for two people will be covered for three gorgeous days and exciting nights. All in return for just one hour touring the condominiums and watching an entertaining informational video.

All one needs to do is return the enclosed SASE with the quick and easy questionnaire filled out (please include all requested information) and you'll be sent the dates for your free fun vacation on Spain's glorious Costa Brava.

And the perfect-for-the-beach radio that never runs out of power? Keep it as a token of our appreciation for considering this unique and exceptional offer.

Natsumi had come home in the course of all this, just as I finished printing the material in high-res. While I showed it to her, I gave her the outlines of the plan.

"Okay, so we track the package back to his house," she said. "Then what?"

"I don't know yet. I'm too busy figuring this part out."

I printed out several test copies before producing packaging that looked legitimate enough. I'm fairly impervious to giveaways with a commercial purpose, but even I wouldn't throw out a little radio you can fire up with a hand crank.

At the post office, I told the woman behind the counter that my company was running a promotion wherein we picked a single number at every postal box location in France. That way, we could track the connection between the promotion and the successful sale of a condominium. If her P.O. Box came through, we'd publicize the event in the local newspaper. This was why it had to be hand-delivered.

"Give me the package," was all she said. I gave it to her and she disappeared into the back for a few moments, then returned and sat down at her station. "It's in the box," she said, and by her body language, told us we were dismissed.

"You gotta love the French bureaucracy," I said when we were back outside.

"All that nicey-nice doesn't get the mail

there any faster, Monsieur."

Then we went back to the flat and did something we'd also become accustomed to. Waiting.

"Arthur," said Natsumi, "why didn't we go to Chile?"

We were sitting on a balcony at our flat overlooking a small, lushly planted court-yard. She had a glass of wine, I was trying out cranberry juice and soda, with a slice of lime. I said the drink made me feel French, but Natsumi said I was confusing the Riviera with Cape Cod.

"The withdrawals from Florencia's Cay-man account mostly went to a bank down there, but none of the coordinates were in Chile. It seemed like a long way to go when far more fertile possibilities lay elsewhere."

"What do you think happened to the money?"

There was something about giving voice to the jumble of theoreticals churning around in my mind, often unarticulated, that felt uncomfortable. It was a type of superstition, that once out in the air before having a chance to mature, the suppositions would vaporize or turn into foolish fantasy.

Yet I owed Natsumi an explanation of where I thought things had been, and where they might be going. Especially if she felt moved to ask.

"It went into several different bank accounts in Chile which had been set up to redistribute the funds through another chain of financial institutions, some of which operated under questionable regulatory standards — essentially money laundering operations. From there, I think the money went to a person or persons connected to safe houses in Europe, Costa Rica, New York, et cetera."

"Which person or persons?"

"I don't know," I said.

"Since we turned up at two of those safe houses, you'd think the others would be on high alert, or already shut down, as a precaution."

"You would, except that would represent a pretty big financial loss. I'd leave them open, but closely monitored. As bait."

"That's what I was thinking," she said.

"I know. Which is why we're here."

We sat in silence for a while. I admired the little courtyard garden and the abiding beauty of the surrounding architecture. I didn't know what Natsumi was thinking, until she said it.

"That note built into the code was pretty suggestive. Does that bother you?"

I smiled at her.

"It does."

"Because you loved her so completely and can't imagine she'd also be in love with someone else."

"Also?"

"You can't love two people at the same time?" she asked.

"Not like that. Though I'm hardly an expert on these matters."

"You might be missing something."

"Really."

She poured some more wine, because she wanted to top off a nearly filled glass, or to kill time while she framed her thoughts.

"We assume because we found the post-card and flash drive in Florencia's safe-deposit box that she had composed the message. But what if it was the other way around? What if it had been sent to her, and she stashed it in the box? To me, that makes a lot more sense. She donated the money, someone else secured the properties. The code was a manifest, detailing how her investments had been deployed. Obviously something sensitive enough to put in code and for her to bury in an offshore safe-deposit box."

I hadn't thought of it that way, which Natsumi somehow knew. She was right, though.

It did make much more sense.

"So by that logic," I said, "the romantic words were written to her, not by her."

"Right. That makes a difference. Admit it."

"It does," I said, admitting it.

"We don't know if the same feelings were reciprocated," she said. "And in the absence of that insight, you'd be forgiven for thinking they weren't."

Even though Florencia and I were obviously mismatched in the physical attractiveness department, I never had a jealous feeling drift through my heart. Because nothing Florencia ever did suggested I should. At the few social events she was able to drag me to, she stayed by my side the entire time, and spent most of the evening showing everyone how devoted we were to each other.

"Thank you," I said to Natsumi. "Those are sublime and generous thoughts."

"You're welcome."

Two days later, the alarm went off on my smartphone. The little box on the screen told me the package was in motion. By prior agreement, Natsumi stayed at the flat and I ran for the car.

The tracking app on the phone was identical to Google maps, with the simple imposition of a bright green dot to distinguish the tracked from the tracker, represented by the standard blue dot. So there was no need to make visual contact, though I hoped that opportunity would arise.

It was in the early afternoon, so traffic in Aix was moving well. The green dot went from the post office directly to one of the city's main arteries, which took it to the four lane highway called La Provençale that ran south of the city; and if you went east, down to the Mediterranean, connecting the coastal cities all the way to the Italian border.

Which is where the green dot was headed. It was about a mile ahead of me, a distance which opened up quickly when we were on the highway. I sped up, slightly uneasy to be going almost 160 kilometers an hour, or about 100 mph. First data point: the package's owner had a lead foot. And less than adequate regard for the Gendarmerie, the French equivalent of the Guardia Civil, who patrolled the major highways.

Thus I was grateful when the green dot slowed to a more comfortable 128 kilometers an hour as the highway curved up the side of a steep hill. I considered keeping up the torrid pace, possibly identifying the vehicle, but settled on the mile gap I'd maintained so far. There was no point in thwarting the advantages afforded by the technology.

We had just begun to crest the big hill when the green dot exited the highway. I followed down a long exit ramp, turning left and driving down a rough country road with low hedges to either side. From there, the green dot made several turns onto ever more narrow roads, mostly through fields wild and cultivated, occasionally a tiny village as old and burnished over as the land itself.

And steadily we climbed, sometimes up easy grades, other times steep switchbacks that the green dot followed with the confidence of deep familiarity. It was more challenging for me to keep the car on the pavement and a steady eye on the tracker app.

After nearly a half hour of this, the green dot stopped. I slowed, zooming in on the dot to get a more precise fix on its location. According to Google maps, it was in the middle of a big field, but when I passed by I saw you reached that location by a long driveway closed off by a tall iron gate. I drove by and pulled over about a half mile away so I could fix the spot with a dropped pin, and used a navigational app to capture the latitude and longitude.

Then I drove back to Aix-en-Provence.

When I got there, an email to David Reinhart was waiting in his mailbox.

At any given time, I maintained about a half dozen fully-equipped false identities with associated drivers' licenses, passports, email addresses and other useful communications channels. And at least another half-dozen virtual identities acquired through a variety of means, none of which could be traced back to me. Since these were far simpler to set up, they were also easily discarded after serving the needs of a particular project.

I still kept many of them going when there was little reason not to, mostly to have a ready means of secure communications on an immediate basis. One of these online phantasms was David Reinhart. The last time he was deployed was to send a verification notice to First Australia Bank in Grand Cayman in support of Kirk Tazman's legitimacy.

Mr. Reinhart:
We would like to talk to you. It is possible that we can reach an accommodation that will both preserve your freedom

and protect the national security interests of the United States.

We understand your desire for anonymity. We are certain that a means for this can be established.

Our best intelligence suggests you are in a strong financial position. If this is not true, there is much we can do to alleviate your predicament.

Intelligence also indicates you are an American. We appeal to your love of country to help us come to a mutually satisfying conclusion to this matter.

Sincerely,
The Federal Bureau of Investigation

I read it three times as electric currents shot through my nervous system. Heat blossomed in my chest and spread to my abdomen. My breath caught in my throat and all the saliva in my mouth evaporated.

Shit.

I called to Natsumi. She must have heard something different in my voice, because she ran into the room. I let her read it.

"Shit."

"Indeed."

"How secure is this mailbox?" she asked.

"Secure enough that the FBI hasn't traced it back to me."

"Fucking bank."

My first impulse was to start moving money out of all my accounts, then stopped myself. The bank must have shared Florencia's account history, which would show the transfer of a lot of money, mostly into the Chilean bank, giving them a fair assumption of my financial well-being. I couldn't know if they'd tracked down where the rest of it went after I'd made my withdrawals; but after checking the accounts squirrelled away around the world, it was all still there. Now bait? I couldn't know that either.

Just to make myself feel better, I moved it all anyway. This took about three hours, but it was good therapy to be doing something.

Natsumi sat next to me the whole time, watching the computer screen and occasionally squeezing my leg or rubbing my shoulders. She listened to me muttering under my breath, but had the wisdom not to respond or ask me what I was saying. It was comforting, and despite the fury of the moment, I thanked her whenever I had a chance to do so.

"No prob, Arthur. You just keep doing whatever the hell you're doing."

Much of my strategy since being declared dead was to stay dead, and entirely under the radar. I believed the best way to avoid being caught was to avoid being pursued in the first place. I knew this was a little deluded, logic being that the more actively I operated, the greater the odds I'd draw the wrong kind of attention.

The email's existence said as much as the content of the message. If they'd known enough to track us down, I'd be upside down in a dark room somewhere at the tender mercies of an interrogation team. It was a big decision to rob themselves of the element of surprise, so their search must have stalled.

Writing to David Reinhart was also significant. He was clearly connected to the bank. Assuming they gave up everything they had, an interview with Mr. Etherton, the safe-deposit guy in Grand Cayman, would confirm my nationality. Yet David Reinhart lived in the outer precincts of my fabricated world of false identity. If they could have penetrated another layer or two, they would have.

It was also possible the reckoning with Florencia's killer had led to exposing her embezzlement scheme to the FBI. If I could grab an end of that string and pull it free, any forensic accountant could do the same. The trail led to the bank in the Caymans. They would have found it virtually empty, everything cleaned out but the safe-deposit box.

Easy enough to keep the box intact and wait to see who shows up to claim the contents.

"What a dope," I said to Natsumi, sharing my logic.

"Sort of," she said. "We did get the code. I bet they're thinking, what dopes *we are* for letting those tricky people grab the goods and make a clean getaway. With just a little stopover at the Royal Cayman Islands Police Service."

I said she had a good point. "Ramming our little car could be seen as an act of frustration. With no official jurisdiction, they took the crudest approach."

"They probably didn't expect the driver of the little car to take off like a jack rabbit on amphetamines."

"You're trying to make me feel better."

"You're hard on yourself, Arthur. Maybe that's what keeps you alive. Keeps us both alive, but I'm on your side, even when you're not."

I logged the return address from the FBI email.

Eloise.Harmon@fbi.internationalopera tionsdivision.gov.

I was almost disappointed by the simplicity of it all, though thinking the likelihood of there being a person named Eloise Harmon at the FBI was the same as having a crew of men in black chasing down aliens.

Then, with the exception of a single channel of communications, I killed off David Reinhart, without remorse.

CHAPTER 11

I called my sister Evelyn.

"I'm not even going to ask you where you are," she said.

"Provence. In Aix-en-Provence."

"Do you remember any of the French I taught you?"

"*Un peu.* Any change in the government's interest in Florencia's scam?" I asked.

"Not that I know of. Why?'

"Just asking. Has Shelly Gross been around?"

"Not as far as I know," she said. "Should he be?"

"Not necessarily."

"I might be able to help you more if you'd stop being so cryptic," she said.

"Florencia's account in Grand Cayman was being watched. We got the contents out of the box, but were nearly snatched in the process. It looked like the FBI was involved, but we can't be sure."

"Oh, dear."

"Evelyn, you probably were closer to Florencia than anyone but me. I want you to answer me honestly — did you ever suspect that she was having an affair?"

The phone was quiet a long time before she answered.

"Absolutely not. She loved you, Arthur, like crazy. I couldn't have been her friend if she hadn't."

"Did you suspect she was skimming and lapping, laundering money and hiding it in an offshore account?"

"No. But it's not the same."

The conversation drifted into far less significant waters after that. Before signing off, she had one more thought.

"I will say one thing. I always wondered if all that noisy vivaciousness was hiding something very different. Something quietly sad."

Psychologists will tell you that feelings are merely unarticulated thoughts. And possibly far more accurate. But only language can turn subconscious insight into serviceable ideas and concepts. And until Evelyn had spoken those words, I was unaware that I shared the same intuition.

Or was this a manufactured memory, empirical evidence in search of erstwhile intimation?

The radio with its embedded tracking device spent the next week in the house up in the hills. With its position pinpointed by the GPS, I was able to use Google Earth to fly overhead and eke out a description of the property.

The main house was in a U shape, shadows from the tiled roof indicating a variety of story heights. Judging by the size of neighboring houses, there was easily 5,000 square feet of living space. A swimming pool was tucked inside the U, which was contained by a curved stone wall. How much of the surrounding land belonged to the estate was hard to estimate, though large pine trees and wild Provençal flora dominated the landscape, with only a few acres nearby cleared for cultivation.

Not bad for a retired colonel in the Guardia Civil.

The alarm for the tracking device went off at nine o'clock at night. We'd gone to bed early, reflecting the oddball schedule we'd fallen into, with no outside forces on hand to shape more regular behavior. I grabbed the smartphone off the table and forced my eyes to focus. The green dot was out of the house and starting down the long driveway at a good clip.

At the end of the drive, it turned right, retracing the route it took on the way in. I carried the phone around with me while I got dressed, and made a bucket of coffee. Natsumi wandered into the kitchen rubbing her eyes and muttering, "What's going on?"

"Pure speculation, but I bet whoever picked up the radio at the post office left it in the car. Now it looks like he's heading back to Aix."

"Or she."

"Or she. If it looks like the green dot is actually coming to town, I'll go lie in wait."

"To do what?" she asked.

"Identify our target. I don't know after that. Depends on what I identify."

It did indeed look as if the possessor of the radio was following the path back into town. I pulled up the tracking program on the laptop and showed Natsumi how to zoom in and out on the green dot.

"You can get close enough to pat that dot on the head. I'll call you as soon as I know anything more."

I drove to an entrance ramp at La Provençale about a mile outside of Aix and waited. I zoomed in as far as the program would let me, and set the tracking to continuous, thus following the green dot as it raced down the highway.

As it closed in on the end of my ramp, I took off, timing my entry so I could fall in directly behind the pursued vehicle. As luck would have it, there was only one car within my headlights, a late model crossover SUV with what looked like a Volkswagen logo stuck on the rear hatch. It was moving along rapidly, but I no longer feared a car able to outrun my rented Opel.

As hoped, the Volkswagen exited onto a main artery that led to the broad Route de Galice, and subsequently into the heart of Aix-en-Provence. I followed the vehicle into the snarl of streets north of the Cours Mirabeau, which delineated the major districts of the city. It pulled down a narrow street lined with restaurants and outdoor cafés, then took a sharp right down an even narrower lane where it stopped and parked along the curb. I drove past into a tiny courtyard, where I turned around and went back toward the Volkswagen. I drove by in time to see a short man with a head of thick black hair, broad in both shoulder and waist, pointing the remote key at the SUV, whose lights flashed in response.

I had my man.

I had to park in a residents-only parking

zone in order to keep my eye on my quarry, who found his way to a street filled with nightlife, and subsequently disappeared into a dimly lit café. I waited for a few moments, then followed.

He sat by himself at a table along the wall, facing the door to the café. He was around forty and had a broad forehead and massive Gallic nose. He held a glass filled with an unidentifiable amber liquor with both hands, which were thick with short fingers showing the battering of hard manual labor. I looked around the place as if searching for someone, and then not finding her, turned and left.

I went across the street to an outdoor café and sat in a seat with a clear view of the man's hangout. I ordered a coffee and called Natsumi.

"Do you think you can flirt in French?" I asked her.

"C'est possible."

"How quickly can you doll yourself up and slip into something sexy?"

"Are you suggesting what I think you're suggesting?"

"He's drinking alone in a bar on the Rue de Pourcieux." I gave her the exact address. "Not a bad looking guy, though I doubt many exotic Asian women come on to him.

And by the way, he's way too young to be our colonel."

"I hope he's a leg man. I don't have much in the way of cleavage," she said.

"I'll be at the café across the street, so I'll see you go in. Then I'll follow and stand at the bar."

"There's no guarantee here, you know," she said. "Femme fatale wouldn't be high on my list of life skills."

"Nah, go on. You're a natural."

About twenty minutes later a cab pulled up and Natsumi got out, carefully I'm sure, given the startling shortness of her black skirt, nicely complemented by a pair of high black boots. She held a clutch to her white silk blouse and had a brilliant blue silk scarf around her neck, the only thing I recognized.

I waited another ten minutes, then ambled over to the café. Through the window, I could see our mark still alone at his table, but he sat up straighter and had mustered a slight grin that almost seemed natural on his meaty puss. Natsumi sat at a table nearby in full view of his, and had her legs crossed. She sipped at a tall glass of red wine and was saying something to him that I couldn't make out.

I decided it was time to go inside. I was

happy to see an empty stool available at the bar, since the persistent soreness in my leg made standing still far more tiring than even a long walk. I sat, then ordered a brandy, ice water and a basket of bread.

It wasn't long before Natsumi joined the man at his table. He waved to the sole waiter, who brought them fresh drinks. He was now doing most of the talking, while Natsumi listened with rapt attention. When I walked past their table on the way to the WC, it sounded as if he was mixing some heavily accented English in with the French.

"Ça doit etre très dur labeur," I heard Natsumi say. That must be really hard work.

The Frenchman's capacity was formidable, but eventually Natsumi's encouragement to continually refill began to have an effect, proven by his own journey to the restroom which involved a noticeable heel to port.

Natsumi checked her lipstick in a tiny round compact taken from her clutch, in almost a caricature of feminine preoccupation. Then she hooked a finger at the waiter, who brought over another round. Back at the table, the Frenchman stared at the drink as if wondering how it got there. Natsumi raised her wine in salutation, and they clinked glasses.

I texted her. "Ready to bug out?"

"Ready," she wrote back.

"Say you need to make a call outside then run for it."

"Not in these boots."

From her hand gestures, it looked like she was telling him to stay put, that she'd be right back. Ten minutes later he was still looking toward the door, but his squared-off shoulders had begun to sag back into their original position.

Knowing how the guy drove, I hoped we hadn't just committed vehicular manslaughter.

When I got back to the flat, Natsumi had already changed into sweatpants and a T-shirt.

"Where did you get that little black number?" I asked. "And the boots?"

"The boots I bought yesterday. I was going to surprise you, which I guess I did. The skirt is one you've seen. I just shortened it with some duct tape. You can use that stuff for anything."

"What did you think of our Frenchman?"

"Don't let Monsieur Arnold hear you say that. He's Alsatian. And damn proud of it."

"Ah."

"He's the full-time caretaker of the Château de Saint Sébastien. He's got a 6,000-square-foot house, a few barns and a lot of little outbuildings, and seventy-five acres, mostly forest and garrigue, to look after."

"Who's the boss?"

"A Spaniard named Fulgenzia Bolaños de Sepúlveda."

"A woman."

"*Si*. A very rich woman who visits her château maybe a dozen times a year, including her big annual event in the spring."

"A social event?"

"More like a business meeting, he thinks, because he clears the furniture out of the biggest room in the house and sets up chairs theater style. He doesn't know what they talk about, because the Madame makes him leave for the week they're there and brings in temporary housekeepers. Wouldn't matter anyway. Christian can't speak a word of Spanish."

"Christian Arnold. Sounds Alsatian. I bet he hasn't been on the job very long."

"Two years. The Madame recruited him off a big farm up in Alsace. He was single, no kids, bored with growing hops, thought it would be romantic to live in Provence. Now he's not bored, since there's so much work to get done, but he's lonely as hell."

"You didn't happen to get his phone

number did you?"

She handed me a damp paper napkin.

"His mobile. Although he might hate me now for ditching him."

"Does the Madame have a Monsieur?"

"Nope. Not that he can determine. He called her *la vieille chatte dingue.* Something like, that crazy old pussy, and I don't mean the feline variety. Though it sounds worse than it is. He actually seemed to like her. Maybe because she's the only company he gets."

"She's not there now, I take it."

"No. And won't be for another few weeks."

By now I was at the computer searching for Fulgenzia Bolaños de Sepúlveda. In America, it's a whole lot easier to track down someone named Horatio Hortence than Bill Smith. Same with Señorita Bolaños de Sepúlveda. There couldn't be that many of them.

I was almost right about that. There were none. At least none that attracted the attention of Google's omniscient bots.

I turned to Natsumi. "I liked the boots. You looked great."

"In a slutty sort of way."

"What was your cover story?" I asked.

"Looking for real estate for my rich parents back in Japan who always dreamed of retiring to Provence. I thought that might wrangle me an invitation to his place, but he didn't bite. In fact, he said he was under strict orders to never let anyone set foot on the property."

"What kind of a guy do you think he is? How safe did you feel with him?"

"He was pretty sweet, all in all. For a rough farmer-type character. Just wicked horny, and who can blame him."

"How would you feel about one more date?" I asked.

"Depends."

I told her my plan. She calls Arnold and apologizes for disappearing on him. Couldn't get off the phone with a neurotic girlfriend until it was too late to call. Would like to see him again, but during the day.

"You want a tour of Aix. Keeps you out among the public. Meanwhile, I'm breaking and entering, seeing what I can dig up at the château."

She poked me gently in the chest.

"Okay, but don't start getting pimp fantasies. A café table is as close as anyone's going to get to this *chatte dingue.*"

Two days later I was walking through the Provençale woods with my smartphone in my hand and pack on my back. I had a new pair of hiking boots and a light rip-resistant jacket designed for the exact purpose they were being put to. I had a compass and a second handheld GPS just in case the phone fell in a stream or had a sudden software glitch.

It was ten in the morning. Natsumi had texted me while I waited in the Opel that she and Christian were having a lovely late breakfast under the plane trees of the Cours Mirabeau. I left the car in a little glade accessed by an unpaved road I'd spotted on my first trip into the hills, and I was now within the confines of the Saint Sébastien estate, as shown by no-trespassing signs posted with great frequency.

The early autumn day was pleasingly on the cool side, though the sun, still close to the horizon, was bright and difficult to block with the rim of my baseball cap. The woods were thick, but frequently opened up on garrigue — treeless spaces filled with local varieties of bramble and dense shrubbery, like kermes oak, juniper and wild thyme. The ground was littered with the pale grey rocks, designed to twist ankles, that seemed ubiquitous around the Mediterranean region. Which meant I spent as much time looking down as I did staring at the smartphone or surveying the landscape around me.

It took about an hour of strenuous hiking before I came on the first man-made landmark, a stone structure enclosing an ancient well once used to water livestock. I fixed it on Google Earth and the smartphone, and created a waypoint on the GPS. The house was about twenty minutes away, assuming the same speed-over-ground. I pressed on.

The blue dot representing me came within theoretical eyeshot of the main house about the same time I actually did. It was a mostly stone dwelling made up of several buildings of different heights cobbled together in an orderly fashion, which I knew from the aerials was in the shape of a U.

There wasn't much in the way of landscaping beyond a few pergolas buried under mounds of roses, honeysuckle and wisteria, and small patio seating areas furnished with heavy iron tables and chairs and teak chaise longues.

I moved through the aromatic air and searched the exterior of the house for a way in other than the front door. I found what I was looking for near the end of a perpendicular leg of the U. There were no little signs alerting the criminal class that this building was equipped with an alarm sys-

tem, as there would be in America, but that
didn't mean there wasn't.

I studied the door frame and those of
nearby windows, but found no telltales, like
brass contacts, blinking motion sensors or
errant narrow gauge wires, not that these
things were usually visible from the outside.

While thus engaged, I didn't notice the
actual domestic defense apparatus walk up
and sniff the small of my back.

I turned to see a *Dogue de Bordeaux,* a
dog the size of a stunted elephant with a
grotesquely wrinkled head about twice that
of a beach ball. I looked at him and he
looked at me for nearly a minute.

"What a beautiful dog," I said in French.
"Would you like a treat?"

I unwrapped and handed him a gooey
energy bar.

He took it and left about a quart of slime
behind, covering my hand and halfway up
my forearm. I petted his gigantic head and
his thin tail began to wag.

"You are a very distinguished gentleman,"
I said, this time in English. "I think maybe
you've been miscast as a ferocious guard
dog. At least, that's what I hope."

As I intensified scratching the furrows
between the big flaps of skin covered in
short, reddish brown fur, he thrust his head

forward, challenging the strength of my hand. The downward Churchillian cast to his face belied what seemed like sheer pleasure at being thus attended to. When I got my other hand into the action, he reared up and lapped a slippery tongue from chin to forehead across my face. I repressed the thought that he probably outweighed me by about forty pounds and could have taken the whole of my head in his mouth.

"You are a total mush, you know that?" I said. "Thank God."

I told him in French to sit and give me his paw. He got the first part, and failure at the second likely meant I didn't use the correct French. I gave a few commands in Spanish, which he took to more readily.

"Eres un perro muy bueno. Muy guapo. ¿Me puedes decir cómo invadir su casa?"

He seemed to like the compliments, but opted not to show me how to break into his house. Though he also did nothing to stop me when I used a glass cutter to remove a piece of windowpane and reach in to unlock a casement window. I patted him on the head once more before pulling myself up to the windowsill and slithering headfirst through the opening. I rolled onto my back and lay there, listening for threatening sounds.

What I got was ten tons of dog when my new friend followed me through the window. The gouges in my arms and chest fortunately missed important veins, but the ballistic force of his weight crashing down made me fear for my ribs.

"Holy crap," I yelled, involuntarily.

My recompense was an aggressive lapping by the bath towel-sized tongue, which I eventually resisted well enough to get back on my feet.

"Man, you are a very persistent doggie."

I don't think he heard this, because he was already prowling around the dark room, his nose to the ground and tail in the air, great baritone sounds emanating from deep in his chest. I realized he'd probably spent no more time in the big house than I had, and was keen on investigating this long withheld prize.

I was in a little library, barely big enough to contain a pair of high-backed stuffed chairs and a love seat. The walls were lined with bookshelves, and books were stacked on a surplus of side tables. A shallow desk made of satin-finished fruitwood had a felt writing pad and a stand with a quill pen. But for the slightly fussy excess of the Provençale aesthetic, it was a nice room. I could live there, assuming broadband access.

I searched the desk and poked around the bookcases for boxes or anything else that might contain papers, mail or documents. The Dogue rejoined me and I asked him if he liked the house. He shook his head, showering me and the environs with stringy saliva, which explained why he hadn't spent much time inside.

We moved on.

A hallway led to other small sitting rooms, more than one would think normal people would need. "I'm tired of sitting in the blue room, Philippe. Let's sit in the pink room tonight."

I searched each one without result. I next came across what I assumed was the principal living room, very large with a half-dozen seating areas. I could see that Madame could create a meaningful meeting space by switching out the furniture. I went back to searching every drawer and shelf and looking behind every picture frame. I wasn't a professional at this by any stretch, and there was no time to check floorboards or tease out hidden panels. But I felt like I was doing the best I could under the circumstances.

The Dogue offered little assistance,

though I started to enjoy the company. He'd disappear on quests of his own, then re-appear, his arrival signaled well in advance by the sound of tiger claws clattering across the floor. I learned to guide him into pressing against my leg, avoiding most of the torrent of slobber. As long as the crushing mass didn't cause a compound fracture of the thighbone, it was a good approach.

We worked our way to a large kitchen and separate eating area with a blocky natural wood table and chairs. Dozens of copper pots, bunches of wild herbs and oversized forks and ladles hung from wrought-iron racks attached to the ceiling. Open shelves screwed into clay-colored plaster walls were crammed with crockery and glass jars filled with grains, rice, pasta and coffee.

I tried to figure out how to say, "Go fetch the secret documents. Good boy," to the Dogue, but he was busy jumping up on the counters and center island seeking targets of opportunity.

It wasn't necessary. A desk built into an alcove directly off the kitchen had a woven basket filled with mail contained by a rubber band. I sat down at the desk and unbound the mail. All but two letters were addressed to Madame Fulgenzia Bolaños de Sepúlveda. These belonged to Domingo

Angel. One was from the *Dirección General de la Policía y de la Guardia Civil,* the other was a plain envelope. The return address was on West 72nd in New York City. Apartment number, but no name.

I put both letters in my pocket and searched the desk. Nothing.

It took an hour to go through the bedrooms upstairs. Then the Dogue and I left the house and went to visit the outbuildings. The first was a huge barn, dark and filled with the stink of abandonment. I didn't even try to mount a search, knowing it would take a full team of crime-scene investigators a week to make a dent in the possible hiding places. And given that the mail was dropped off at the desk, I thought, what was the point? They didn't think they needed to hide anything.

I checked the other building just for the hell of it, and finding nothing of obvious interest, decided to leave. The Dogue walked with me through the forest. Along the way I told him stories — all true — and he seemed to enjoy hearing them.

When we reached the border of the property, he sat down. It didn't seem possible that he was stopped by an invisible fence, given the property's size. Somehow, he just knew. I scratched his gigantic head and

224

thanked him for being such a good host.

"Adiós mi amigo. Gracias por su hospital-
idad."

He seemed to grin as I scrunched around his wrinkly skin a little more. Then I stalked off, focused on the smartphone's GPS, which was busy delivering me back to my car, and subsequently our flat in Aix, and the wise and tender arms of Natsumi Fitzgerald.

CHAPTER 12

I texted Natsumi to tell her I was back in the car on the way to Aix. She wrote back, "Okay."

She was at the flat when I got there.

"How's Christian?" I asked.

"He's beginning to regret never getting that degree in philosophy from the University of Strasbourg."

"Existentialist?"

"I don't think he made it past Socrates. Find anything at the château?"

"Mail."

We opened the official letter from the *Dirección General* first. It was a statement from his pension fund. We did some quick calculations, and estimated the colonel's take-home to be about $125,000 a year. This helped explain Spain's crushing indebtedness to its public-sector employees, but not the château in the woods.

The other letter was far more interesting.

It was a short note printed out on a single piece of paper, in Spanish:

Domingo:
Friends in DC place Rodrigo in Como area. Address has been forwarded to the field. Interpol friend reports the wounding of two terrorists in England.

Joselito

"Rodrigo," she said.

"One of the coordinates is on Lake Como."

"Good thing we have a decent travel budget."

"Should we assume the guys I shot in Surrey are still alive?" I asked.

"We should. No reason not to."

"Are we flying or driving?"

"I booked the car for six months."

"You're becoming aerophobic," she said.

"More autophiliac. I'm an American. We like to drive."

This time we took La Provençale and hurtled across the south of France, crossing over the Italian border in fewer than three hours. La Provençale then turned into the Autostrada dei Fiori, and we noticed an immediate change in the relative condition of the roadway and a gradual evolution of the landscape. Natsumi slept off and on, and I thought about the Caymanian police officer who said, "You Americans think you own the world. But this girl and people like her are gonna take it away from you. One day at a time. They never gonna give up."

What the hell did that mean? Who did they think she was?

Maybe I knew already, but didn't know I knew. This was the type of paradox I often faced as a researcher. The information was there, but not a chain of logic, or a hierarchy of importance between chunks of data. It was rarely a failure of knowledge, but rather imagination. It was an affliction of the age — too much information, not enough wisdom to make sense of it.

What I did have were two names: Rodrigo and Domingo. Men I'd never seen, much less met. And yet evidence of their existence was the only tangible thing we had, though answering nothing. Even the questions felt hidden in shadow.

The so-called "dirty war," between ETA and the *Grupos Antiterroristas de Liberacion,* or GAL — an extra-legal paramilitary group, essentially vigilantes — had ended in 1987. We gave up after page 400 of a Google search trying to connect the GAL with the VG, *Los Vengadores del Guardia.* If it weren't for Professor Preciado-Cotto, I would have assumed the VG was a figment of the imagination of the Latino boys in England.

ETA itself had declared what seemed to be a permanent cessation of violence in 2011. Defanged by successful, and apparently legal, Guardia Civil action in recent years and delegitimized by the loss of public support, even in the Basque Country, there wasn't much of ETA left to make declarations.

So maybe what seemed to make sense wasn't sensible at all.

"Do you think Christian Arnold will make the connection between our date and the house being broken into?" Natsumi asked, the morning after we'd rented a villa in Menaggio on Lake Como in Northern Italy. We were sitting on a balcony looking out over the lake through a scattering of cypress trees.

"Probably."

"So it's another exposure."

"It is, though would he reveal it to the Madame?" I asked. "No reason to. Just fix the window and lie about the mail."

"No other way for her to find out?"

"Not unless Dogues de Bordeaux learn

how to talk."

"I feel a little bad about Christian," she said.

"That's because you're a good person."

"Do you have a plan?"

"Not beyond improvisation."

"I feel like a cat, with about four out of nine lives already cashed in."

"Me, too."

"Any thoughts?" she asked.

"We need to be more careful. The surveillance gear will be here tomorrow. I'm thinking we should switch cars. We can be reasonably sure the men in Madrid never saw your face. I'll have to work a little harder on a disguise. Neither of us speak much Italian, so that's a liability. Eventually, the cops on Grand Cayman will discover the phone tap. And the security company in London will find the video feed. No way to trace that stuff to me, now that I know how to completely obliterate serial numbers. A hard learned lesson. As usual, it's impossible to know what other precautions to take when you don't know who, if anyone, is looking for you, or for what."

"As usual for us."

"That's right."

The house was modest, but tall, with three stories stacked on a relatively small footprint. It was an old stucco affair whose best feature was the third-story balcony. Though not at the high end of villa rentals, the interior was filled with fine art, silk fabrics and vases overflowing with white marguerites. It had plenty of bedrooms for sleeping and electronic gear — along with other standard living accommodations, including an attached two-car garage, added by the current owner, an American from Chicago, naturally. I loved this feature. The rental agent could have posted it as a key benefit — "Keep vehicles and equipment transfers hidden from the prying eyes of neighbors and potential terrorists!"

We were about a half hour's drive north of the city of Como, which was built at the narrow southern tip of the big glacial lake. At first I was struck by how many of the code's coordinates were in congested urban neighborhoods, or resort areas, until I realized if you wanted to escape notice, you go to a place filled with transients, foreigners and temporary residents.

It suited us as well, for many of the same reasons.

The coordinates were unambiguous. The safe house was off on its own, a few miles outside the village of Cardano, and surrounded by cultivated land. It wasn't as much a fortress as the Château de Saint Sébastien, though it also had a long driveway running through stands of tall trees.

I wasn't ready to go down the long driveway just yet; I was more interested in the telephone pole. I spent a few nerve-wracking minutes cracking open the junction box and splicing in a tap, but there was no dial tone. Not surprising given the trend away from permanent landlines.

So I spent the rest of the time mounting a video camera across the street from the driveway. I put the receiver and wireless router about a half mile away in a little ice chest that I covered with branches and brush. Then I drove back to our villa and called up the feed. I'd done this often enough at this point to make it routine. But there was always that moment of tension, fully relieved by seeing the hoped-for image pop up on the screen.

I ran the video stream into an application designed for wildlife trackers that turned on the camera only when detecting movement. Otherwise, it went into standby mode, saving on memory and battery life.

After that, I gladly returned to doing what I earnestly loved to do more than anything in the world. Research.

■ ■ ■

A few hours later I emerged from the vast and labyrinthian immigration, tax and real estate records of New York City.

The apartment building on West 72nd was built in the early twentieth century, and refurbished in 1976 and 2009. It was currently owned by Carrington Realty Holdings, which owned a number of properties in the city, though it was headquartered in Baltimore, Maryland.

Apartment 8G had one bedroom, a living area and eat-in kitchen. The two windows looked out at the building across the street. Riverside Drive and the 72nd Street dog run were only a block and a half away. It had been occupied for five years by the current tenant, Joselito Gorrotxategi. Another Basque.

According to the social media site Linked-In, Joselito was an unmarried Spanish national working for an international corporate security firm called Context, who likely advised their clients to have a corporate name that bore no resemblance to their services. He had a master's degree in forensic accounting from Rutgers, and previous experience with Interpol and the Guardia

Civil. His other interests were hiking, Spanish art — in particular Goya and Velázquez — target shooting and international travel.

His photo on the website showed a handsome, smiling man, about forty years old, in a dark suit and brightly colored tie.

I'd learned a lot, but not enough.

So I placed a call to Ekrem Boyanov, a.k.a. Little Boy, a Bosnian criminal presently living in the South End of Hartford and a friend of mine via the hunt for Florencia's killers.

"Hey, Mr. G!" he said over the phone, using the pseudonym he knew me by, "Long time no hear. I figured you for gangster food."

"No such luck," I said. "I could figure you for the same thing."

"Nobody thinks it a good idea to bump off Bosniaks. We're big on revenge. Start with their grandmothers, then work down from there."

"I've got a little project," I said.

"I'm listening."

I described Joselito Gorrotxategi, where he lived, what he did for a living.

"I need to know everything I can about this guy. Work, play. Habits, good and bad. Friends, family, girlfriends, boyfriends. Cell number. Wiretap his landline, if possible."

"And what do I get?"

"Ten thousand dollars. Flat fee. If you get access to his computer, and we can talk through a hijack, another five."

"Okay. And then you want this guy taking a little swim in the East River?" he asked.

"No. Not now anyway. I don't even want him to know we're looking at him."

"Okay, Mr. G. This we can do. Where you been, anyway?"

"A few places."

I asked about his family and business. He extolled the first and lied about the second. I pretended to believe him, which he knew I didn't, and everybody was happy.

"You need anything else, just let me know," he said.

"I'm good for now. Let me know how you do with Joselito. I'll send you an email address to maintain communications. Once the connection is made, give me your bank account, and the bank's routing number, and I'll wire the money."

"Not a problem, Mr. G. I know you're good for your word."

"Don't be too cocky with Joselito. He's got credentials," I said.

"Hey, I can be completely Mr. Subtle, you know that."

"Information is the game here. You might

consider a honey trap."

"I got just the right girl. Wild lady. Do it for thrills, though a little money go a long way," he said.

"Send the bill. And say hello to the crew for me. Something in Bosnian."

"Absolutely, Mr. G. They all remember the fun times."

"And don't kill the mark. Please," I said.

"For you, we don't kill nobody. Unless they get insulting about Muslims. You understand."

"I do. Then all bets are off."

"Nice to hear from you," said Little Boy. "We do some business, eh?"

"We do," I said, and got off the line, feeling that our crouched and anxious covert world had just doubled in size.

The first car showed up five days after that. I'd been alerted by a little ping on my smartphone. I woke up the computer and ran the freshly recorded footage. The camera had clicked on just as the Fiat mini-SUV made the curve into the driveway. I watched until it was out of sight and the camera clicked off again.

I stuffed a handful of prosciutto and taleggio into a wad of bread from the platter Natsumi had just put out for lunch, kissed her, told her the chase was on and ran to the garage. I put the laptop on the passenger seat and drove like an Italian to the target house. Meaning I wasted little time getting there.

When I was a few hundred feet from the driveway, I pulled off to the side of the road and waited. I budgeted an hour, the limit of my patience, recognizing the Fiat could leave at any moment, or theoretically, be there for weeks or months.

The hour was almost up when the smartphone pinged at me again. I looked down at the computer and saw the Fiat coming down the drive. I started my Ford Galaxy, a trade for the Opel, and waited to see which way the Fiat was headed. Turned out to be away from me, so I pulled straight out and fell in a comfortable distance behind.

Comfortable until we entered the little village of Menaggio, when the danger of losing the Fiat or being noticed increased considerably. I reminded myself this was likely not my only opportunity, to breathe evenly and keep my foot lightly to the gas pedal.

As we were moving down the *corso,* the village's main street, a van wedged in between me and the Fiat. It was large enough to obscure the other car completely from sight. We stopped at a red light, and I guessed the Fiat was still there, but didn't know for sure until it suddenly made a right-hand turn. I followed, now feeling utterly exposed.

Then the Fiat stopped and I saw its backup lights flash on. It was backing into a parking spot along the street. I was able to get fairly close, waiting as any courteous driver would for the Fiat to nudge its way into the tight spot. When I continued on, I risked a look at the driver, a woman with long dark hair partially contained by a full silk scarf, wearing sunglasses and deep red lipstick.

I took another risk at the stop sign several yards down the street, stopping longer than normal to watch her step out of the vehicle, holding a purse in one hand and smoothing down her skirt with the other. A skirt showing lots of long leg, made even more fetching by a pair of black high-heel shoes.

She walked around the front of the Fiat and onto the sidewalk, moving away from me. I turned the corner and squeezed into a parking spot. I snatched a stack of papers and magazines up off the rear seat, then walked as quickly as I dared back toward the woman's car.

She was nowhere in sight, but neither were

other pedestrians, which suited my purposes. When I was alongside the Fiat, I let the stacks of paper slip out of my grasp, and then with a fumbling motion scattered them all over the sidewalk, off the curb and under the car. With no one nearby offering to help, I squatted alone and started gathering up the papers, which involved at one point reaching under the Fiat's chassis, to which I slapped a magnetic tracking device.

With the papers collected under my arm, I moved down the sidewalk, casually glancing at the storefronts, hoping to catch a glimpse of the young woman, though without success.

I went back to my car and pulled up the tracking app on my phone, confirming it was up and running properly. I put the phone back in my pocket and drove away, spending the rest of the afternoon circling around, staying within a few miles of the Fiat's location. It wasn't until a little after 4:00 that the phone chirped at me, and I saw the green dot moving north away from Menaggio.

I intercepted her soon after as she drove back up into the hills, moving at an angle away from the target house. This time I was able to stay well out of sight while I was in pursuit.

239

The green dot finally came to a permanent halt just within the boundaries of Intignano, another little village.

I took up the rest of the distance and drove by a small villa not unlike our rental, in front of which was parked the Fiat mini-SUV. I noted it was the only vehicle in the parking area.

Then I went home to another email from Eloise Harmon.

Dear Mr. Reinhart:

It is regrettable we have yet to hear from you. Over the intervening days we have acquired security-camera footage that clearly shows your features and your companion's, known to be Natsumi Fitzgerald. We also note you have attempted to erase records attached to your name and Social Security number, which was stolen from the actual David Reinhart, who died several years ago. The banks in Chile that received the disbursements from Grand Cayman are cooperating.

It is only a matter of time before you are located. Our sincere recommendation is for you to immediately contact one of our embassies' legal attachés.

Eloise Harmon

"I guess I'm famous," said Natsumi, reading over my shoulder.

"At least among a few people at the Federal Bureau of Investigation."

"They're seriously after us."

"They are. But still light on leads. Tracing David Reinhart is easy. The connection with Chile is easy — they'd get that from the First Australia Bank. If they had more, they'd share it. The idea is to panic us into making contact."

"Not a chance."

"Also interesting, they want us to contact the legal attachés — basically the FBI's overseas representatives stationed in our embassies — without specifying the country. Shows they believe we're offshore, they just don't know where."

"They can connect me to you if they ask the right people the right questions," she said.

"They can only connect you to a few of my false identities."

"That's a slippery slope. I can sum up your biggest liability: 'Seen with Asian woman.' "

Changing the subject, I told her I'd recruited Little Boy to gather intelligence on the Basque security expert in New York City who'd sent the terse letter to Colonel Angel.

That seemed to please her greatly.

"We need a murderous sociopath on the team," she said. "One with a sense of humor."

"The only kind for me."

CHAPTER 13

The next day, the green dot returned to its spot on the *corso*. I left Natsumi at the villa and drove back into the village, parking in a different spot, and moving down the sidewalk on foot. The shops were the usual trattorias, *pasticcerie, gelaterie,* café bars, grocers, shoe repair, and tourist traps with racks of postcards dragged out onto the sidewalk.

I did the usual haphazard tourist meander, wandering in and out of the shops, saying *buon giorno* a few dozen times, stopping for coffee and gelato. Out on the street, I took a few photographs with the big Nikon hanging conspicuously from my neck. One gentleman offered in sign language to take my picture, which I gratefully agreed to. I wished I had the Italian chops to say, "Know the leggy brunette who drives that Fiat?" But I didn't.

It was getting close to lunchtime, which in

Italy is after one o'clock. I picked a trattoria with a good view of the Fiat and ordered. *"Solamente un primo, per favore. Con vino rosso, locale. Grazie."* I ended up with a dish of risotto mantecato and an icy Lambrusco.

Soon after, I was rewarded by the sight of the tall woman, as well turned out as the day before, emerging from a door sandwiched between two shops. I looked up and saw the sign, Laudomia Zambelli, Avvocato.

She was a lawyer. Or worked for one.

She took off in the Fiat, and I followed her on my smartphone. The green dot barely cleared the village when it came to a stop. I watched to see if it would stick, giving me time to finish my meal and down a double espresso. Then I followed by car, passing the Fiat where it was parked in front of a big *ristorante* with tables pouring out from wide openings onto a canopy-covered patio.

Laudomia, if that was her name, was sitting at one of the outdoor tables with a man about her age, just as finely dressed and attractive, terms I was beginning to think were a given when describing almost any Italian.

I sat where I had a good view of her, setting my camera on the table with the lens pointing in her direction. Once I had her in the viewfinder, I pressed a wireless shutter release that I had in my pocket, firing off a series of photos while looking around at everything but Attorney Zambelli.

I ordered the *primo,* passing on the *secondo.* The dignified server was slightly offended by this, allayed I hoped when I said, in English, that I was on a diet.

It didn't appear the woman and her companion had any such inhibitions, as the courses seemed to come in a continuous flow. I nursed my meal as long as I thought seemly. This also involved drinking a beer, which combined with the wine, surpassed my alcohol tolerance. I left the restaurant and carefully drove to a spot where I could monitor the tracking device.

A good hour later, Laudomia drove back to her office and I had some decisions to make. Since nothing ideal presented itself, I decided to go back home and talk it over with Natsumi.

And regain full sobriety.

"My Mata Hari routine probably won't work on this one," said Natsumi, as we sat on the balcony watching dusk fall.

"Probably not. Nor would the male equivalent. Though it's likely she speaks English, being a lawyer."

"What kind of legal trouble could you get

into without actually getting into trouble?" she asked.

"None that I can think of."

"Lawyers are also born wary and skeptical."

"And thus familiar with background checks. I'd have to use one of the comprehensive identities," I said. "And now with the FBI involved, I can't be sure if they aren't compromised."

"Remember the last person we encountered connected to a safe house promised to send you to hell."

"Noted."

I went back online and found a website for Laudomia Zambelli, Avvocato. I determined, after many trips to the Italian/English dictionary, that she was eager to be your advocate for a very wide range of legal circumstances, though her specialty was real-estate disputes. In fact, whether you were interested in acquiring, selling or managing a property, you could find no more capable or diligent counsel than Avvocato Zambelli. As a closer, she also claimed a good command of English, testifying to the large numbers of people from the U.S. and UK who'd been buying up homes in the region.

I secured her email address and had Jonathan Fortnoy, who used an IP address in London, send her an email:

Signorina Zambelli:
My wife and I would like to purchase a villa on Lake Como and fear being taken advantage of, or causing offense, due to our rather poor Italian and cultural naïveté. While no doubt your real-estate professionals are beyond ethical reproach, we would feel much better having a member of the legal community representing us.
Your website indicates you are fluent in English. If so, may we arrange for an appointment? I would prefer to meet in your offices. I will be in Italy starting tomorrow.
Sincerely,
Jonathan Fortnoy

Things must have been pretty slow around the Zambelli practice, because the reply came very soon after.

Mr. Fortnoy:
Buon giorno.
I would be pleased to meet with you at your convenience. My English, I can assure you, would not be approved by Cambridge or Oxford, but I have never heard complaints from my British clients.

My offices are located at the address at the bottom of this email. Please provide desired times and I am sure one will suit my schedule.

Grazie,
Laudomia Zambelli

I sent her a few dates and times, and she quickly picked one — two days away, four o'clock in the afternoon.

I used the intervening time studying the property at the coordinates in Cardano. Google maps showed it to be a two-story villa with several large outbuildings, surrounded by rolling fields covered with grapevines, so it was likely the main house of a vineyard, though not yet possible to verify. Real-estate comparables put the value at around €3.5 million, assuming I'd guessed the right acreage.

I also pondered the situation with Eloise. The fact was I desperately wanted to know whatever they knew, not just for gauging our immediate danger, but to help clear up all the questions I had about Florencia's gambits, the safe houses, the VG, this guy Rodrigo. I was tired of feeling so resentful of people who could know things simply by walking down the hall and asking, things it could take me months to find out.

But eventually I shook it off and forced myself to wait patiently for the meeting with Laudomia, which came sooner than all that frustration warranted.

One of the ways I burned up the time was to drive with Natsumi down to the city of Como to buy some clothes. It was evident the culture in this part of the world put a very high premium on style and good grooming. Two things I knew less about than I did professional ice hockey, though I had once pretended to be a wealthy American businessman with some success. My strategy then was to throw myself on the mercy of a knowledgeable haberdasher, and I could see no reason to change that approach now.

Natsumi picked the place, even though her knowledge of men's fashion was even less than mine. But I trusted her instincts. We stuck with the decision when the principal outfitter showed his facility with the English language, which he used to succinctly sum up the situation.

"You have important meeting with beautiful Lombardian woman. You need to earn respect. I understand. She think you're English, no difficulty there. I know what to do."

I walked out of there with a dark blue pin-striped suit, with the pinstripes about a quarter inch apart, a white pima cotton shirt with French cuffs and a collar that caressed a yellow tie. Add the contrasting handker-chief stuffed in the jacket pocket and kid glove-soft black boots, and for all my theat-rical deceptions, I'd never felt more in dis-guise.

"You actually looked sort of handsome," said Natsumi. "In a crude, haunted and emaciated sort of way. Very sexy, though."

"I'll need to know which part of that was a compliment."

"The sexy part."

"Do you think I can pass as a citizen of the UK?" I said, in what I hoped was a decent imitation of an Oxbridge accent. "It's been a while since I've lived in En-gland."

"You sound fine to me, but that doesn't mean anything."

"Quite."

"She won't know any better than I do. You'll be fine."

"Brilliant."

"Just don't overdo it."

"Right, then."

As a mild precaution, I parked a few blocks

away from Laudomia's office near the promenade that paralleled the lake, which would later be filled with lovers, friends and families joining in the *passeggiata,* Italy's beloved pre-dinner stroll.

Laudomia buzzed me in the main door and I walked up the stairs to the top, where she waited for me.

"Mr. Fortnoy," she said, offering her hand, a significant gesture in proper Italy where handshakes between men and women are at the woman's discretion. Her grip was firm, but her palm very soft. An inside girl with housekeepers and gardeners, was my immediate thought. Big expense.

In her high heels she was nearly my height. She wore a white silk blouse with fewer buttons than professionally required, somewhat compensated for by the big, chunky stones of her necklace. Her grey skirt was a bit more modest than what I'd seen her wear before. It was made of a material that could have been the lightest possible wool, though only divined through touch.

"Avvocato Zambelli, it is my pleasure to meet you," I said in Italian.

"Si parla Italiano?"

I smiled. "Very poorly, I'm sorry to say. I can ask what something costs, inquire about the check and ask for the WC, but that's about it."

"Well, that's better than many. Please come into my office."

It wasn't a big office, but it felt like I was stepping into an interior decorator's photo shoot. The walls were roughed up and painted the color of dried blood. The desk was ancient, finished in clear high-gloss varnish. On top was a leather desk pad and fountain pen holder. Not a piece of paper in sight. A giant, blue vase sprouted long, green fronds. Fragrant, fresh cut flowers sprang from smaller vessels and competed agreeably with Laudomia's perfume. Original paintings and lithographs covered nearly every square inch of wall space.

At her invitation, I sank into one of the two upholstered chairs, she sank into the other, challenging the marginal modesty of her grey skirt. She raked back some errant brown hair with the tips of her long polished nails and shook her head, herding her coiffure back into loose order.

"So, you have some nervousness about Lake Como real estate," she said.

"Frankly, we're a bit at sea."

She seemed to like this idea. "Of course. You can easily put into the wrong port. Why not hold a steady bearing for the whole journey?"

"Very nautical," I said.

"Every summer my family toured the Adriatic. Even during the wars. My father was a crazy romantic. Do you sail?"

"The British Virgins," I said, grabbing the memory of a brochure at the airport on Tortola that proclaimed the islands the "charter sailing capital of the world."

"Ah."

"We're thinking of a country place, but with a view of the lake," I said. I went on to describe the coordinates of the safe-house villa as closely as I could.

"These are available, though a price range would help me advise you."

"I suppose that matters," I said, as if weary of the subject. "Two to three million euros?"

Her measured response contrasted with the bright spark that suddenly lit in her eyes.

"We might be able to manage a few options," she said, "realizing the market is very competitive."

Yeah, I thought, lots of people like you competing over a shrinking number of people like me.

"We have another place in Southampton, New York, not to mention the London flat, so we'll need a caretaker. I'm sure you have sources along those lines."

She looked ever so pleased to assure me she did. "Mr. Fortnoy, property management is very much a part of our services here. If you wish other referrals, that too can be arranged. Entirely your decision."

"Perhaps you could show me villas under your management similar to what we're looking for. Kill two birds with one stone, so to speak."

She wasn't fazed by the idea. Actually seemed to like it. "That is most possible, Mr. Fortnoy. I simply need to examine the options."

"Please call me Jonathan. I detest formality."

This was a bit risky, since all the Italians I knew revered formality. Though for some reason, she softened around the edges.

"Certainly. You may call me Laudomia, though it's good my parents aren't alive to hear such informality. 'You are such a revolutionary,' they would say. First university educated person in the family and all I heard were lectures on proper behavior," she said, though with a gentle smile and not a trace of rancor.

I almost told her my parents turned my upbringing over to a nanny, but it caught in my throat, as associations with my real parents flooded my brain. So instead, I reached over and gave her hand a little squeeze, then sat back again in my chair.

The air in the elegant office suddenly warmed up a few degrees.

"What would be the best way to contact you?" she asked, her voice a muted rasp.

"Email seems to work. Is that acceptable to you?"

"Of course. And next time you will bring your wife." She wagged her index finger at me. "Most of my deals fall through because the Signore does not properly involve the Signora."

"I never make that mistake, Laudomia. It's the secret to happiness."

"No, Jonathan, avoiding envy and greed is the real secret. If you pardon my presumption."

"Both are true," I said. "So, shall I wait for your email?"

"You shall," she said.

I slapped the armrests of the comfortable chair, then stood up. She escorted me to the door, where we again shook hands. She added her other hand and lingered there a few beats past either Italian or American custom.

"I am certain we will find you and Madame Fortnoy the perfect villa," she said.

"I am certain you will be a fine partner in this worthy pursuit."

"As fine as you want me to be," she said, waiting until I climbed down the stairs to the street before closing the door, pleased with the outcome of the meeting, confused by the collateral implications.

"Do you think I'm an attractive man?" I asked Natsumi when we were back on our lovely balcony.

"The most attractive man in the world to me."

"But on an objective basis, how do I compare to other men?"

"Very favorably," she said.

"I have a bald head with two big scars."

"You're usually wearing a wig or a hat. But even if you weren't, there's something intriguing about a man with scars. Suggests an adventurous past."

"Really. I have a big nose and wear glasses."

"So does Woody Allen. The nose suggests virility and the glasses intelligence."

"You learned a lot getting that psychology degree."

"No need for that. Any woman will tell you the same thing."

"I'm forty-four years old. I've never had

women pay any attention to me."

"I've seen pictures of you before the shooting. No offense, but I could see why. You were fat and balding, which is worse than bald. Bald is hip. Whatever you had left for hair stuck out in every direction. And you dressed like you were still living in your parents' basement. Worse than all that, you were flagrantly happy."

"Okay, I was with you till that last bit."

She looked annoyed in an affectionate way, if that's possible. "Most men project a mostly harmless, but automatic, low-level flirtatiousness. Being the type of kid you were, you never learned how to send out those vibes. Or how to read them coming back at you. Better to be oblivious than constantly rejected. Then you marry this Latina bombshell, essentially winning the romantic lottery, and you really have no incentive whatsoever to attract anyone else.

"When I met you, I didn't see the image you have of yourself. I saw this gaunt, but roughly handsome man with sad, haunted eyes. Someone with a deep intelligence, with a lot to hide, but also a person with a good heart. And by the way," she leaned over and stuck a finger in my breastbone. "You weren't wearing a disguise. I saw the real you."

It's a habit of the researcher's mind to decouple intellect from the sentimental aspects of emotion. So, while my cognitive functions were sorting the data and absorbing an aha moment, my heart was in another part of the building doing a little dance.

"Even if my options have widened, I still only have interest in a single woman," I said. "You."

She slid down a bit in the comfy, low-slung outdoor chair and took a sip of her red wine, which she held with two hands.

"Keep thinking that way, mister. And tell me more about this Italian babe who has designs on you."

CHAPTER 14

Laudomia met us at a café a few doors down from her office. She fussed a bit over Natsumi, basically ignoring me in the process. Both seemed to be pleasantly engaged, so if there were any sub rosa communications going on, it was beyond me.

Natsumi had dressed and acted the part of an upper-crust Englishman's wife, who'd met me when we were both working in New York. Laudomia didn't press us on details and we volunteered nothing more.

She discussed the various options for the tour, which included the villa in Cardano, one of her landscaping and housekeeping clients. She offered to drive us in her Fiat, but I told her we'd rather follow in our own car.

"She's very attractive, if you like long legs and eyelashes, perfect skin and a clear view down the front of her blouse," said Natsumi as we drove along in our Galaxy.

"She's only following native customs. We need to respect that."

The first villa was directly on the lake, sitting above a stone breakwater into which a pair of boathouses were carved. It was three stories high, in yellow stucco with shutters painted a pale blue. There was a separate guesthouse and a huge outdoor dining table under a pergola supported by stone columns.

Natsumi and I undermined our presumed British reserve by passionately praising the property. Laudomia seemed pleased.

"By the way," she said, "this villa is for sale, the next is solely property maintenance."

It took about five minutes to get there. The Fiat tossed up a low cloud of brown dust as we curved up a gravel driveway between rows of grapevines. Back at the café, Laudomia confirmed this was a working vineyard leased out to a neighboring winemaker. The villa itself was now strictly a vacation home, though infrequently used.

As suggested by the blurry image on Google Earth, the villa was two stories high, with a shallow pitched hip roof and a full porch. There were a few cypress, some shrubbery and one big shade tree, and though everything was neatly kept, there was little else in the way of landscaping. I noted this to Laudomia when we got out of the car.

"The owners like rustic," she said with a shrug. "To me, it's just as easy to have something beautiful, but I'm Italian."

"So they're not," I said.

"Spanish. A different attitude. Not wrong."

We followed her into the villa, which reflected the spare and unadorned aesthetic of the outside. Though spotlessly clean and orderly, with very old furniture in well maintained condition, the place lacked any of the effortless elegance and beauty of Laudomia's office, or our rented place in Menaggio.

I noted that as well.

"It would take nothing to fill these spaces with splendor and joy," said Laudomia. "But we do what is asked."

She showed us the living areas and separate servants' quarters. Equally plain, but serviceable.

"Do they have a big family?" Natsumi asked.

"I've only spoken to the gentleman by phone, and he is very private. He calls ahead, usually on short notice, and my people are under strict orders to stay away until he and his wife have left. This is not unusual. Every client has different demands. They were here only last week, so your timing was good."

She asked if we wanted to see the upstairs. I told her to take Natsumi while I had another look around the first floor. It took them about ten minutes to explore the six bedrooms and three baths, which was all the time I needed to place microphones in the kitchen, eating areas and living room, and a nanny cam hidden inside a small, traditional clock that I carried in under my jacket. I put it on a table in the front hall and aimed the lens at the door.

A transmitter inside the clock had enough power to feed both video and audio feeds from the mics to the hidden router outside.

"Okay, then," said Natsumi when they were downstairs again, "are we ready?"

"We are," I said, the full implication understood.

There are less engaging ways to spend the day than surveying Italian lakeside villas. Laudomia proved to be a tireless commentator on the visual feast that surrounded us, managing to demonstrate both a talent for hyperbole and a sincere devotion to her home territory. So it was both an education and a satisfying diversion that concluded at another café, where the women drank Bellinis and I had bitters and soda on the rocks.

We discussed the day, with Laudomia gently moving us toward greater clarity in our villa specifications. Natsumi seemed to enjoy this, so I let her lead the fanciful conversation. I asked again about the various owners, disguising my keen interest, I hoped, in the Spaniards. Laudomia was fairly free with her information, but it was clear she knew little more than what she'd already shared.

We left her promising we'd reconnect in about a week, which we would spend pondering the options.

"I like her," said Natsumi, when we were back in the car heading home. "Loves her country, loves her work, generally loves life. And she gets to do all that living in this place."

"Maybe we should just buy one of those villas and call it a day."

"She's divorced," Natsumi continued, still on the same track.

"Said the guy sponged off her and ran around with the local tramps. Her words. Her parents were very religious, so she had to wait until they were gone to go through with it. The husband threatened to kill her if she left him, another hurdle. So she had another guy, known around town to be connected to certain elements, pay a call on the husband. She hears he's now living somewhere outside Naples, but isn't sure."

"You can learn a lot in ten minutes," I said.

"She likes being single, but I think she's a little lonely. She's having a small get-together this Friday evening and wants us to come. I said yes. I hope that's okay."

"If she hasn't included any real Brits. I'll be found out in a half second."

"Oh, dear. Hadn't thought of that."

"Quite."

When we got back to our villa, an email was waiting for me from Evelyn: "Call me." So I did.

"I have some disturbing news," she said. "Damien Brandt, Florencia's comptroller, was found dead. He'd been tortured. I don't know how and I don't want to know."

"Really."

"Bruce Finger said that the day before it happened, two men approached him in the agency parking lot asking about Damien. Said they were very threatening."

Bruce was the old friend of Evelyn's who had agreed to take over Florencia's agency after she was killed, which he'd hoped was on a temporary basis.

"Have the cops told you anything?" I said.

"They haven't. Arthur, I can't take much more of this."

"I know. I'm terribly sorry."

"I think we might have to close the agency. Bruce is terrified and none of the employees want to come to work."

"Let's do it. We can sell the book of business. In pieces if we have to."

It was quiet on the line for a few moments. "Because the agency's contaminated, is that what you're saying?" she asked, in the low tones she would sometimes use when we were kids. It signaled she wanted a full and honest answer.

"Yes. It's worse than I thought."

"I can't do this on my own," she said. "I'm frightened."

I felt a burst of heat somewhere around my midsection. As with Evelyn's tone of voice, I knew what it meant. Deep distress.

"I'm sorry. We'll fix that."

"How?" she asked.

"I don't know yet, but I will. Do you have any vacation time coming to you?"

"That's not a reassuring thing to say."

"Do you?"

"Yes. About ten years' worth."

"I'm thinking Australia."

"Arthur, talk to me."

"It's really hard to work things out when I'm all tangled up in worry. If you disappeared for a while, it would help a lot."

"Disappear? Sure," she said. "It's the family business."

"You're only in this situation because of me. I feel really bad about that. But to get you out of it, you need to sort of go along."

"This is ridiculous."

"Do you have a passport?"

"I do."

"Don't tell anyone where you're going. Don't make any in-country reservations from the States. Fly to Melbourne. When you get there, I'll have a bank account, with a debit card, waiting for you. Before you get to the bank, use cash to rent a car and stay in a hotel. Have fun. Take a lot of pictures. Read some trashy books. Pick up lonely millionaires."

"I'm way past that."

"If you need more money along the way, just let me know and I'll restock. You can use our existing phone and email connection, but monitor both closely. They will probably change every once in a while."

"Do you have any idea how many patients I have?" she asked. "How many appointments and tests that are scheduled?"

266

"There are other cardiologists. There's only one Evelyn. I can't lose you. Not because of me, that's for sure."

She was quiet again before she spoke. "We really didn't know Florencia, did we?"

"No, we didn't," I said.

"I still love the Florencia we knew."

"Me, too. Whatever else she was doesn't change a thing."

"Okay. But what do I do with the agency?" she asked.

"Have Bruce bring in a business broker. Let everyone work from home. Hang in there and check our email account."

"I do it every day, Arthur. Actually, every hour."

After we disconnected, I went back to the computer and spent the next few hours setting up a secure mailbox — as secure as I could make it — and wrote the retired FBI agent Shelly Gross. The email was from Alex Rimes, the fake identity I used when contacting Shelly.

Mr. Gross:
I hope you are well. I assume you are still angry about how our last engagement turned out. I fully understand and apologize for exploiting you the way I did. I made you feel like a sap, and no man likes

that one bit.

Nevertheless, there are much bigger issues afoot I hope transcend these minor discords.

I have valuable information relating to several homicides, financial fraud, criminal enterprises and international terrorism.

I know the FBI is interested in what I can tell them, since they appear uncomfortably interested in me.

Can we talk?

Best,
Alex Rimes

P.S. I could use a favor.

Two days later my smartphone yelped at me. A van was pulling into the driveway of the Spaniards' villa in Cardano. I yelled to Natsumi, then clicked out of Google and into the video application, switching immediately over to the nanny cam. Everything would be recorded at the highest possible fidelity, but I couldn't help staring intently at the screen.

"What, what?" said Natsumi, bursting into the equipment room.

"Van at the Spaniards' house. Minutes away from show time."

She grabbed a chair and pulled it close to the screen.

"This is a little creepy, but I sort of like it."

"It's totally creepy, and I love it," she said.

It took longer than I thought it would for the door to open. When it finally did, it was only because a crowbar had been used to pry it open. In walked four men I'd never seen before. One was maybe late thirties, with close-cropped dark hair and a rough complexion. Two were younger, probably twenties. The fourth was much older, with grey hair and a fleshier face. They were dressed in regular street clothes, though they moved as if informed by intense training and experience: nasty little rifles pointing in opposite directions, eyes squinting down the sights, jaws set and shoulders bunched.

In a few seconds, they were off-camera. It was many minutes later that I heard the Spanish equivalent of "Clear!" repeated frequently as they moved through the house.

After that, I saw them move in and out of the villa, carrying black canvas bags slung over their shoulders. Gear and supplies.

It was easily an hour before one of them spoke, clearly in a phone conversation, with long pauses between words. In Castilian Spanish.

"Villa secured. Yes. Preparing the area and

taking positions. Probably an hour at most. Yes. Do you have more intelligence on the target? Okay, understood. We're good on logistics. Maybe you could send over some sexy women." He laughed. "Okay, central command gets first pick, we get the discards. I understand."

At that point, conversation broke out among all four of them. The first speaker giving commands, allocating living quarters, setting watches and mess rotations, reminding everyone to keep weapons clean and operational, respectful questions from the troops about timing and duration, none answered — all the patter you'd expect to hear from a combat operation in the field.

"Who are those guys?" Natsumi asked.

"Spaniards. Probably military. That's all I know."

"No uniforms?"

"Special forces? Operating under cover in a foreign country? I think. My only reference point is *Guns of Navarone.*"

The conversations dwindled down to talk of sports, women and music celebrities, the great universal themes.

"Theories?" Natsumi asked.

"It's an ambush."

"That's what I was thinking. I should've just said it, damn."

"I believe you."

"Who's getting ambushed?"

I turned in my chair and looked at her.

"The safe-house people, I assume," I said. "Interesting dilemma for us."

"Oh, no. Laudomia."

My mind launched into creating scenarios, each of which ended in some form of disaster, whether for our project, or much worse, for us and those of innocent people. I jumped out of my chair and stalked around the room, a proven way to accelerate the thought process. Natsumi sat and watched me.

"She was just there a few days ago," I said. "I doubt she'll be back again that soon."

"But what about cleaning people? Gardeners?"

"I know."

"We have a line into the safe-house people. We could warn them."

"People who want to kill us? Who already tried to kill me? The ones in the house might be our best friends."

I sat back down at the computer and stared at the real-time view of the front door. No one came in or went out.

"Warn them. The ones in the house," she said.

"They might want to kill us, too."

271

"Who doesn't want to kill us?"

"The astronomer, Mirabella McPherson. She had contrary designs."

That caused her to run a hand down my back and give me a thumbs-up.

"We'll always have Spottsworthy."

I had an idea. Urgency prevented me from sharing it with Natsumi. I just held up a finger while I dialed Laudomia, and she nodded with understanding.

"Buon giorno," I said, when she answered. "We're having strange thoughts."

"Strange thoughts are far more interesting than everyday thoughts."

"We like the Spaniards' vineyard. The other villas are all so beautifully decorated and cultivated. The vineyard is unadorned. A blank canvas upon which we can paint our own unique vision. In keeping with Lombardian aesthetics, of course. For that, we would seek your counsel."

"You know it's not for sale."

"Yes, but things can suddenly be for sale if the right price is suggested," I said.

"Interesting."

"Do you know when they'll be back in Como?" I asked. "I'd love a chance to speak with them directly."

"No idea. But they were only just here a few weeks ago, so it will be a while."

"Of course. But it's so disappointing. Is there a phone number or email address?"

"There are, Signore, but giving them out would violate confidentiality."

"Okay — then would you mind contacting the gentleman and giving him my number? Then it's up to him."

"That I can do," she said, taking down the number.

I thanked her, hung up and filled in Natsumi.

"So the boys in the villa didn't contact her," she said. "Do we know what that means?"

"They're counting on surprise. Or they don't know she exists. Or something else."

"Maybe we should listen to the recordings again. Might learn more."

"That's it," I said, jumping out of my seat again. "Of course."

"What's it?"

I retrieved a fresh CD off a stack and stuck it in the computer. Then I opened the audio files from the hidden mics and downloaded the men's conversations.

"Ah," said Natsumi, as she watched me work, "if they find out the villa's bugged, they'll assume the ambush is blown."

"And not knowing anything else, they'll most likely get out of there in a hurry."

"Great idea, only how do we deliver the CD?"

"Very carefully."

It was about an hour away from nightfall. I used that time studying the villa with Google Earth and aligning the satellite images with the GPS on my smartphone. Natsumi was off on a separate mission, which she completed more quickly than I thought she would.

"It's a pretty boomy boom box," she said, setting it down on a table. "The guy at the store was mortified when I tried it out. Lady Gaga at full volume."

I had about an hour's worth of recordings, which I looped to fill the CD to capacity. I took the player outside and had Natsumi tell me via cell phone how far I could get from the house before the voices became inaudible. I counted the number of paces on the way back.

I put on my all-black outfit, and rigged up a connection from the audio feeds in the villa to my smartphone so I could listen on earphones. There was very little of substance being spoken, but at least I'd know the mood inside the house.

Natsumi drove me to Cardano. I knew she was nervous about the plan, but it was the best I could come up with on short notice.

On the way, we decided on codes from the phone, either voice or text, that would give her my status, and a short list of if/then scenarios.

"If you're dead, I might do a little improvising," she said.

"That's why we push decision-making down to the field."

She took me to a point on the map about a hundred yards from the villa entrance. From there, it was relatively easy to follow the GPS on the smartphone through the grapevines. It was a nearly moonless night, and I couldn't risk a flashlight, so the greatest danger was running into something or falling in a hole. That and the armed-to-the-teeth paramilitary in the villa over the hill.

I slowed my movement to a near crawl and made irregular footfalls, vaguely remembering that was a good idea in this situation. I made a mental note to study Native American tracking skills.

I was still out of range, based on our volume test, when I ran out of grapevines. The villa was dark and the chatter picked up by the mics was restrained and banal. I had no way of knowing if they'd posted a watch, but I had to assume so. I stared into the darkness and willed my pupils to let in maximum light. Which must be possible, because I saw the shape of an outbuilding emerge from the gloom. It was about twenty yards from where I stood and well within the volume range. I walked back into the grapevines, texted Natsumi an "okay so far" code, and moved to where the little building was between me and the villa.

Judging as well as I could in the dark, it seemed as if I'd have about thirty seconds of full exposure if I just ran for it, factoring in my run, which was more like an awkward lope.

I thought about it for about that long, then loped.

The ground was covered in something resembling grass, close-cropped, so the sound was minimal. I knelt in front of the outbuilding, turned on the boom box, pushed the play button and loped back into the grapevines.

Seconds later the voice of one of the Spaniards opened up into the night. I realized some of my precautions were way over-engineered. The voices seemed thunderously loud, and I had the worthless thought that I should have built in some delay. I was nearly at the grapevines when the world around me lit up, a brilliant beam coming from a forty-five degree angle.

"Fermati o sparo!" a man yelled. "Stop or I'll shoot!"

I ran faster and he shot.

The rounds chewed up the ground all around me, but hit nothing but soil. Once I crossed into the vineyard, I put every bit of energy I had into getting as deep into those rows of grapevines as I could. I heard more yelling, but the shooting stopped.

Through my headphones, I could hear the other men in the villa scramble, the leader yelling out orders and the others acknowledging them and muttering barely audible curses.

Seconds that felt like minutes later, all I could hear was the recording of their conversations echoing through the darkness. I pictured them standing over the boom box trying to process what they were listening to. Then suddenly all sound ceased.

I called Natsumi and gave her a one word code in a loud whisper. She yelled back the appropriate response and I clicked off the phone.

The next sound was something like the spatter of raindrops, followed a millisecond later by the roar of gunfire. I dove to the ground as hundreds of rounds from automatic rifles mowed down the grape trellises. Dirt, wood chips and grapevine debris sprayed across my back. Voices in Italian and Spanish rose between the gun bursts.

Then it stopped again. I waited, listening intently. When it seemed quiet for a reasonable amount of time, I stood up and continued running. I stopped every few minutes and listened, but heard nothing. In my mind, I saw the leader commanding the team to pack up everything, destroy all evidence of their presence, and load the van. I wondered if they'd search for the mics, or go with expedience and just get the hell out of there.

I made it to the road, and right on cue, Natsumi drove up and I dove into the Ford. Before I had the door closed she was hurtling down the winding road.

"I heard guns," she said, a trifle louder than necessary.

"I'm okay. Just a little close for comfort."

"Will they chase us?"

"They only have one vehicle. Need to get it loaded. I'm actually surprised they fired their weapons. Not very professional."

"Spooked by the CD?" she asked.

"I think so. Who wouldn't be?"

"Better professionals."

She slowed down to the standard Italian suicide speed, though it wasn't long before we were back at our own villa on the lake.

We went immediately to the computer to view the footage from the nanny cam, which had a poor, but adequate audio function.

I went to real time. Predictably, there was a lot of yelling and hustling in and out the door. We could see one of the men with his rifle at the ready; the others had theirs slung over the shoulder. There was little talk about the hows and whys of the boom box, conjecture presumably overwhelmed by the urgency of the moment.

It took about a half hour and they were gone. That was less time needed to properly scrub the place, but they likely didn't care at this point.

When the clamor subsided, Natsumi and I re-engaged with each other.

"That was really brilliant and really scary," said Natsumi.

"I didn't know what else to do."

"Are you sure you're okay?" she asked.

"My bum leg is killing me. I really can't run."

"I should have done it. I'm a smaller target and I run like a deer."

"You're probably right. It's just hard for me to put you in danger."

"Too late for that. Next time we discuss it."

"Okay. Meanwhile," I said, eager to

change the subject, "we got those guys out of there and still have the mics and cameras in place."

"So we stick here for now."

"Of course. We have a dinner party to go to."

CHAPTER 15

I felt a strange sense of exhilaration the night of Laudomia's party. I knew from a study I once did of a drug designed to dampen the effects of adrenaline overload that a near-death experience, or equally triumphant moment, can have lingering, often euphoric effects. This can translate into grandiose, potentially self-destructive behavior by the victims of this syndrome. In my case, it presented as a particularly loud tie.

"You're going to wear that?" Natsumi asked.

These were the only words ever spoken by Natsumi that I'd also heard from Florencia. Leading me to think it was gender-based.

"I shouldn't?"

"Well, not necessarily."

"It's pure silk," I said. "Famously woven right here in Como."

"Was I there when you bought it?"

"Not exactly."

"It's very bold and lovely," she said, straightening the knot. "I'm sorry if I sounded less than entranced."

I had nothing to criticize about Natsumi's wardrobe — a tightly fitted black thing and toeless high heels. Not that I ever would anyway. She looked like a million bucks and I told her so.

"Thank you. And no worries about the tie, black goes with everything," she said.

What had seemed an attractive, yet relatively common dwelling in the stark daylight, Laudomia's home had become a romantic fantasy at night. Giant candles lined the driveway and the stone walk up to the door. A classical concerto seeped out in low volume from speakers hidden in the darkness. Aromas — mostly from flowers, furniture oil and cooking smells — clung heavily to the soft evening air. Laudomia strutted like a runway model out the front door, long lush hair flowing over her shoulders, and breasts swinging freely under a floral silk blouse. She greeted us, kissing both cheeks and enveloping our senses in clouds of perfume.

"It is so lovely to have you here," she said, holding and swinging our right hands.

"Come, come and meet my friends."

They were primarily Italians, most of whom had a ready command of English, a Frenchman who didn't, an American couple from Rhode Island, a pair of gay German men, and miraculously, no Brits.

Relief filled my heart. Natsumi must have had a similar reaction, because she lit up the rooms with effervescent conversation and feminine charm.

I wondered what was going on inside my mind. This was an ongoing preoccupation, understandably, given that a bullet had gone through it. The brain is the only object in the universe capable of examining itself. In my case, a researcher's brain, one that could experience the world while simultaneously recording the experience.

I concluded that as I healed, I also evolved. Not necessarily yielding an improved version, though interesting new sensations were emerging, mostly emotional. The original me was a very steady lad. Essentially cheerful, but reserved, contained in easy contentment. I'd heard of mood swings, but never experienced them myself. Now, it seemed as if a protean emotional palette was growing in me, aspects of which would spring up with little notice or warning.

I watched Natsumi navigate Laudomia's

plush home, wineglass in hand, her back straight and her face lit with calm amusement. I was on the verge of approaching her to say something sentimental, when Laudomia took me by the arm.

"I have emailed the Señor, Jonathan," she said, "and copied you, asking him to contact you directly if he wants to have a conversation."

"Very good of you. Thank you."

"In the meantime, Roger and Dottie Hardgill, the Newport people, would love to speak with you about their place, the one with the big pergola."

Roger was a tidy little guy of about seventy, with dyed-black hair and a squint. Dottie's plastic surgeon had managed to give her face a permanent cast of startled alarm. It occurred to me that nothing is more damaging to your appearance than excess money in the absence of good sense.

It only took a few minutes to learn that selling the place was Roger's idea, leaving Dottie either bewildered or bereft, it was hard to tell by looking. For Roger, it was simply a smart financial bet, sell high in Italy, buy low in Cape Coral, Florida.

"A house is a house," he said. "You know what I'm saying?"

"Como is drenched in thousands of years

of culture and history," said Dottie. "Cape Coral was a swamp until the 1960s."

"Dottie's got a degree in anthropology from the University of Michigan," said Roger, with some pride. "I got to drop out of high school to keep my family full of losers from starving to death."

"More the victims of structural, societal disadvantage," said Dottie, "anthropologically speaking."

"See what I mean?" said Roger.

Natsumi demonstrated more of her social skills by extracting us from the conversation with no loss of good will on the part of the Hardgills. I promised to keep their property in mind, and he slapped my shoulder as we deftly slipped away.

"A face is a face," Natsumi whispered. "You know what I'm saying?"

The rest of the evening coasted effortlessly through a few rounds of limoncello, from which we both demurred, a spontaneous late-night *passeggiata* around the neighborhood, and lots of *abbracci e baci* before we all embarked for home.

"Do you think I'm behaving normally?" I asked Natsumi, as we drove over the curvy, up-and-down Lombardy roads.

"I don't know what normal is anymore," she said.

285

"You'll tell me if you observe anything odd. I mean, odder than the standard odd."

"Yes."

"I did suffer a traumatic brain injury. We don't know what that could ultimately mean."

"Laudomia's given up on stealing you away," she said.

"What makes you say that?"

"You're probably too odd."

I checked all my email addresses when we got back to the villa and found a lot of interesting stuff. Including a message from Shelly Gross, which had come in only minutes before.

> Mr. Rimes:
> I have no reason to trust anything you say, since you have proven, beyond a reasonable doubt, to be a dishonest person. Consequently, no information offered by you could possibly be of any use to me or my former organization.
> I do not wish you the best. Quite the contrary.
>
> S. Gross

I wrote him back.

Shelly:
You're up early. I think all that rancor is giving you insomnia. Let it go. Not worth it. Email this woman and tell her you have a line into David Reinhart:
Eloise.Harmon@fbi.internationaloperations division.gov.

The other interesting message wasn't interesting in what was written, rather in who wrote it.

Mr. Fortnoy:
The villa is not for sale.
                    Rodrigo Mariñelarena

I called to Natsumi and she read over my shoulder.
"You think?" she asked.
"As Nicho Santillian said, they got a lot of Rodrigos."
"Still."
"Still, it's intriguing. And I've got his email address."
I wrote back:

Rodrigo:
The villa is compromised. Selling it makes more sense than blowing it up.
                    Felingham

I'd signed it with the name I'd given Nicho Santillian in Madrid, presumably one he'd passed along to Rodrigo.

"Wow," said Natsumi, before I pushed the send button. "A little risky?"

I turned around and looked at her. "We have to shake the tree. It means some exposure, but we may not get a better chance to crack this thing."

"We know something he doesn't," she said.

"Correct. But I won't send it if you think it's too dangerous."

She looked at me sympathetically. "You're right. Nothing else we've done is terribly dangerous."

"So I'm sending?"

"You're sending."

I hit the button.

The next day I called Little Boy, the Bosniak criminal boss in South Hartford.

"Mr. G, I was getting ready to call you. We learn a bit about Joselito Gorrotxategi. First thing, very hard to spell his name."

"He's Basque. A lot of them have names like that."

"Slick dude. Got a nice place in the City, drive 7 Series Beemer, likes the ladies. At least we know he like the lady we sic on

288

him. Mirsada is getting snuggly, but not yet put in the hook. She say he's big deal forensic accountant, according to him, which could be crap. Tells corporations how to protect assets jumping from country to country. Growth industry for sure. And you're right about the Basque thing. He tell her, don't you call me Spanish, we all descended from Atlantis, or some such bullshit."

"What are the chances of stealing his computer?"

"Chances good, but can take some time. Don't want to rush things and lose Mirsada. I like that girl, even though the wife threaten my balls whenever I look at her."

My sense was Little Boy's wife was more than capable of following through on that threat.

"One other thing," I said. "Somebody hit Damien Brandt, Florencia's former comptroller. It was messy."

"Wasn't me," he said. "Twerp wasn't worth the cost of a bullet."

"I might need some protection. Maybe on fairly short notice. I'm in Northern Italy on Lake Como. Do you have some local boys who could zip up here in a hurry?"

"You bet, Mr. G. Very fierce customers. From the war."

"Good to hear. Stay tuned on that."

We traded well-meant, but pro forma inquiries into the health and welfare of our respective loved ones; he shared his predictions regarding the World Cup, something I knew nothing about, and I repeated my gratitude for his assistance.

"No worries, Mr. G. We like you. And your money, to be honest."

"Honesty is hard to come by these days."

I hung up and shared the half of the conversation Natsumi couldn't hear. She repeated her pleasure at having Little Boy on board, whose troops she'd once spent a fair amount of time feeding, watering and distracting with wide-screen TVs.

"I have to admit, I miss the big Balkan nut-bag," she said.

"I bet he misses you, too. Just don't let him tell Mrs. Boyanov."

"The jealous type?"

"Think sharp knives."

I didn't hear back from Rodrigo, but Laudomia called that afternoon and told me her Spanish client was planning on arriving sometime after six that night. She was surprised.

"As I told you," she said. "It's very unusual for them to return so soon. But who knows about people's lives."

"His name is Rodrigo Mariñelarena, am I right?"

"You are. He must have emailed you."

"He did. Said the villa wasn't for sale. That's it."

"I'll let you know if anything changes," she said, "but I think he means what he says."

"That's fine. We'll be returning to London shortly. Let's stay in touch."

"Absolutely, Signor Fortnoy. I hope to be neighbors soon."

"Ciao," I said, and after hanging up, briefed Natsumi.

"Should we move?" she asked.

"Laudomia doesn't know where we live. She has a phone number and email address, both untraceable. No advantage to leaving yet."

"What else can we do?"

"Stare at the computer."

Which is what I did until about eight that night, when a mic in the rear of the villa picked up sounds, unidentifiable, but not native to an empty house. I set the volume at the highest level and strained to hear. The sounds were moving away from the mic. I turned them all up to the highest volume. The one in a hallway picked up the sounds, now clearly made by a person moving slowly through the house.

For nearly a half hour, I followed him, or her, with my ears, though seeing a form with my mind's eye.

In the dark, the nanny cam was automatically set to infrared, painting the front foyer a ghostly green. As the form moved down the stairs, which landed in the foyer, I put the image on full screen.

The first thing that came into view was the barrel of an automatic weapon, identical or similar to the ones carried by the prior occupants. Then the rest of the man appeared, in profile. He was in civilian clothes, wearing a loose jacket and blue jeans. And a pair of night-vision goggles. He put a phone to his ear.

"All clear," he said in Spanish. "The villa is empty." It was quiet for a moment as the other party spoke. "Yes, I checked everything. You can come in. I'm turning on the lights."

In the sudden glare, the automatic setting on the nanny cam switched to artificial light. I clicked off full screen and went to split screen, so I could view the man while monitoring the camera at the villa's entrance. Moments later, I saw a Range Rover, a Toyota van and a battered Mercedes sedan pull into the driveway.

A moment after that, the man in the foyer took off his goggles and looked almost directly at the nanny cam, so I got a really good view of the handsome face of Nicho Santillian, the concrete salesman and safehouse operator of Madrid.

One of the other men reached out his hand in greeting.

"*Hola,* Rodrigo," he said, adding in Spanish, "the house is ready for you."

CHAPTER 16

Evelyn called later that night to tell me she was in a town called Port Fairy on the southern coast of Victoria, Australia.

"Drove down through a rain forest of eucalyptus trees, then west along the Great Ocean Road. What a beautiful place. I want to thank you, Arthur, for exiling me. Now that I'm here, not sure I want to leave."

"You're welcome. Have you heard from Bruce?"

"As soon as I got settled, I called him with this phone you gave me. He put the agency with a business broker. If we're willing to settle for net worth, comprised of premium income from the book of business, plus investments, plus the building, it's pretty easy to value. The buyers will fold expenses, like back-office and sales teams, into their own operations. Some of our people will lose their jobs, I'm sorry to say, but this is looking much easier than I thought."

"Good. The sooner everything's absorbed into other companies the better."

"It'll be a lot of money, Arthur. And all legal. I wish we could say the same about you."

"Any more about Damien Brandt?" I asked, dodging the subject.

"Not that they're telling me. Bruce thinks it was a professional hit, which means we'll never know."

She asked if I could tell her what I'd been up to. Again, that perfectly reasonable, but nettlesome question.

"We're in Northern Italy. The only thing in the safe-deposit box was a flash drive taped to a postcard. On the drive was a coded message. It took a while, but we cracked it. Turned out to be a list of addresses, mostly in Europe, but also Costa Rica and New York City. We know the people connected to these addresses, the ones we've identified so far, are Spaniards. There's no definitive connection between the assets that were in Florencia's secret account and these people, though we know money was sent from that account to various banks in Chile. All I have are account numbers, no names and no access, so I don't know where it went from there. But I still think there's a connection. At least that's the working hypothesis."

"So I suppose you just can't walk up and ask them," said Evelyn.

"Ah, no."

"Because it would be dangerous."

"Getting killed would not only be a sad occasion, it would make it a lot harder to figure out what's going on."

"Is it that important to know?" she asked. I'd asked myself the same thing, more than once. "Never mind," she said, saving me.

"I know. It is to you."

I waited till the next morning to check the audio and video feeds from the Cardano vineyard. One major difference between this operation and the other was the size of the force. At least three times bigger. They were also much more casual in how they spoke to one another. Respectful to their leaders, the foremost of which was Rodrigo Mariñela-rena, but less formal or military. Among the men, there was more joking and camaraderie. Though I noticed no names were used, and nothing operational was discussed.

Most of them had taken up defensive positions inside the house and around the property. Although two had been dispatched by Rodrigo to do a deep search of the house. So it was inevitable that my number eight mic suddenly blinked off, right after I recorded the words, *"Micrófono,"* followed by a shout, *"Silencio!"*

An hour later, most of the house was silent to my gear, with only the audio in the nanny cam still operating. With the video feed also still online, I could see that the search team had missed it. So far. It wasn't worth much as an audio device, situated where it was in the foyer, but it allowed me to capture the face of anyone who came through the door.

An hour later, the game was over. The team packed up the vehicles and disappeared out into the early morning light.

I was distracted from the loss of my gear by a chime from my computer. It was an email from Shelly Gross.

> Alex:
> Or is it David? Probably neither. You're right to comment on my enmity. It is unprofessional. It is also clear I have underestimated you. Our international people are very keen on having a little chat. It is a matter of national security. This makes your situation far more perilous than anything you faced Stateside. We must talk.
>
> Shelly

I wrote him back: "Call me," and added the number for an untraceable disposable phone. A few minutes later, it rang.

"Hi, Shelly. How're you doing?"

"I'm healthy and still have all my marbles."

"Anyone else on the line?"

"No. You're mine alone. For now."

"Because we have a history," I said.

"That's correct. Let's start with your request. You asked for a favor."

I'd been rehearsing this conversation in my mind since I'd first written him, but still chose my words carefully.

"You know the owner of the insurance agency in Stamford, Connecticut, had been embezzling from its clients."

"Yes. Substantial funds skimmed off large commercial policies."

"And you know how it was laundered and sent offshore."

"We do," he said. "Only by the time we'd tracked it to the bank in the Caymans, the money was gone and the trail ice cold."

"Damien Brandt, one of the principals of the agency during the fraud period, has been killed."

"I know. You think there's a connection with the missing money?"

"Certainly with the scheme itself," I said.

"There's enough there to excite the interest of the wrong kind of people. Don't forget what's happened already."

"Where does your favor fit in?"

"The agency's being busted up and sold off. Brandt wasn't just killed. He was tortured. Somebody wanted information. And maybe they got it. Either way, it proves the agency's employees, in particular the current owner and acting president, are in danger. I want protection for them and any help the Bureau can provide to smooth the sale."

"Why would they want to do that?"

"To save innocent people's lives and move much closer to their larger goal — deep intelligence regarding international terrorism."

"How would that happen?" he asked.

"I'll tell them. When I'm ready. I'm not being coy. I only have half the story. I can't afford to tell what I know and then have your people climbing up my ass and scuttling the project."

The line was quiet for a moment.

"There's a connection between Natsumi Fitzgerald and what happened in Stamford. That's not a threat. It's intel they probably wouldn't want me to share. But you should know."

"Thank you," I said.

"I just have one question for you," he said. "Are you an enemy of the United States?"

Well, there's a first for me, I thought. "No. Though at the moment it feels like the other way around."

"You've left a lot of trace evidence around the Internet. You're very good, but they can do things today you can't imagine. They'll get there eventually."

"Since I'm asking for the unlikely, here's one that's probably impossible," I said, avoiding the subject. "I'd love to know where the banks in Chile sent the money transferred from Grand Cayman."

"Sure," said Shelly. "I'll have the director invite you over for tea so he can thoroughly debrief you."

"If I were they, the Chilean banks would be the track I'd be running down."

"Okay. Thanks for that. So, channels are open? Do I call this phone?"

"I'll send you another number. Sorry for the paranoia, but like you say, they can do things I can't imagine."

"Who the hell are you, anyway?" he asked.

"Beats me," I said, hanging up and emailing Evelyn in Australia, asking her to pick up a disposable phone with international calling capability and FedEx it to our villa.

■ ■ ■ ■

Laudomia texted me and asked if we'd left yet, and if not, could she buy us lunch. She suggested a café on the lake with a view of the village's tiny harbor. I texted back, "Sure. 1:00?"

We spent the rest of the morning clearing out the villa on the lake and packing up the Ford. It felt at that point that we'd stayed too long in one place, especially given all the other activity. I did want to see Laudomia once more, to ask a few questions, so lunch on the way out of town made sense.

I parked a few blocks away and we walked down the Via Castelli. It was a beautiful part of the village, one we hadn't paid much attention to, so I was doubly glad for the diversion.

Even one in the afternoon was early for an Italian lunch, so we had most of the café to ourselves. We picked a table with a good view of the water and sidewalk. Laudomia showed up minutes later, moving and looking like the exemplar of *la bella figura* that she was.

"Buona sera!" we called to each other as she approached the table.

"Perfect choice," said Natsumi.

"Of course it is," she said, sitting in the caned chair I held out for her, "we must have the finest view if I'm to treat."

"You've already been very generous," said Natsumi.

"Nonsense. So did you speak to Señor Mariñelarena?"

"Just an email," which I described. "He has a gift for brevity."

"Not a friendly man, I will agree with that. Unfortunate. All my Spanish friends have such joie de vivre."

"Did you represent him when he bought the vineyard?" I asked.

"Of course. *Hablo seis idiomas, inclusive español.*" Spanish was one of her six languages. "Why all the foreign people love me."

We paused while Laudomia gave orders to the waiter, without consulting us, but, of course, she was treating.

"So the deed is in his name," I said.

"I told you, these things are privileged information. So the *giudici* shouldn't know I told you it's owned by a corporation."

"Really."

"*Si, si,* nothing unusual in that. Tax purposes, maybe? I never ask. My concern is Italian law, and in Italy, such a thing is perfectly legal."

302

"How do you know the corporation is legitimate?" I asked.

She looked a little insulted.

"This is why people need *Avvocati*. We know how to do these things."

"Of course," I said.

The arrival of the *primi* — first course — diverted our attention. Laudomia provided a detailed description of every component, complete with historical references and local sourcing. Everything was delicious, but likely enriched by our surroundings, since everywhere you looked it was achingly beautiful. The rust-colored and muted-gold stucco and red-tiled roof buildings, rows of tables and jaunty umbrellas, palm trees lined up along the glittering lake.

I knew we had to move on, but I understood what my sister meant about Australia — being rendered immobile by scenery.

I was watching the waiter weave his way toward us holding a tray crowded with our *secondi,* when I happened to look past him at a pair of men out on the sidewalk. There was something odd about the way they looked and how they were moving toward us. When they got closer, I had a better look at their faces, which I suddenly saw in the slightly distorted view of the nanny cam.

Rodrigo's men.

They both reached inside the pockets of their long jackets.

I stood up and flipped the table over, umbrella and all. Laudomia yelled, *"Ma che stronzo che sei!"*

I pulled Natsumi to the ground and told her to jump in the lake and swim against the quay. Screams ignited from the other guests. I heard a splash, then the coughing sound of suppressed semiautomatics. Bullets punched through the table. Laudomia was doing the fastest military low crawl you can achieve in a tight skirt. Other tables fell around us.

I rolled clear of the table and saw the men barely ten feet away. One held a gun aimed at our table, the other was drawing a bead on the crawling Laudomia. She looked up and screamed, covering her head. I stood up and yelled. He turned the barrel toward me and shot.

He missed. They both came toward me, taking slower aim with both hands, sighting down the barrel. The screams faded as the guests ran clear. Laudomia disappeared behind an overturned table.

Tires squealed out on the street. An unsuppressed gunshot came from the car as it lurched to a stop. The men whipped around and fired back. The first loud shot from the car was followed by a deafening fusillade that tore into the two men. They were literally blown off their feet. Blood spray filled the air and bullets rattled into the metal railing above the quay. Seconds later all movement had stopped, and the car, a powerful Alfa Romeo, roared away.

The screams only got louder.

I stepped over the dead men, their faces now mostly mashed-up flesh and blood, and called for Laudomia. She didn't answer, but I knew where she was.

I looked around her overturned table and saw her curled up in a ball, her elbows and knees bloodied and speckled with dark gravel from the paved patio.

"It's okay," I said. "They're dead."

I knelt down and asked her if she'd been shot. She gave her head a sharp little shake. I saw that she was crying. I touched her shoulder and said, "You're safe. They're all gone."

Then I left her and ran over to the quay. I leaned over the railing and saw Natsumi gripping the stone wall about twenty feet away, her soaked hair accentuating her beautiful round face. She smiled at me.

I shoved my way through the tables the fleeing guests had jammed against the railing, and dropped to my stomach, reaching down to grab her hand.

"I'm glad you can swim," I said.

"If you count clinging to a wall swimming," she said, as I hauled her up and through the bottom of the railing.

The singsong Italian sirens floated into the air, increasing in volume as they sped toward us.

"How's Laudomia?" she asked.

"In shock. Elbows and knees chewed up. How're you?"

"Wet."

I grabbed a tablecloth off a wait stand and put it over her shoulders. Then, with my arm around her, moved quickly away from the scene, hugging the railing which allowed us to walk behind the café building and into a parking lot. The sound of the sirens, painfully loud, suddenly snapped off. I guided Natsumi across the street and into a narrow alley.

"Run," I said to her.

We made fast time until reaching the end of the alley which opened up on a street that had been closed to car traffic and turned into a promenade. We walked briskly past a few shops and cafés until we came to another cut-through. Again we ran, this time two blocks, at the end of which we stopped so I could check the GPS.

The Ford Galaxy was still a few blocks away, but now we were too far west. We ran back a block and turned right onto a broad street, but luckily it was residential, with little pedestrian activity. We risked a fast walk, and in minutes were at the Ford. Soon after that we were heading south toward the city of Como.

Natsumi dug her bag out of the back of the car. I turned on the heater as she wiggled out of her wet clothes and used a T-shirt in a weak attempt to dry off. I concentrated on driving within Italian speed norms while keeping a constant eye on the rearview mirror.

"What the fuck was that?" she asked, once reasonably clothed.

"A gift of divine luck," I said.

"Not everyone would look at it that way."

"The first two shooters were Rodrigo's boys. We were seconds from being killed."

I explained the sequence of events, including the fortuitous arrival of the Alfa.

"They saved us," she said.

"They did. But probably not on purpose."

"So who were Rodrigo's guys trying to shoot?" she asked.

"All of us, I think. I guess I shook the tree a little harder than I meant to."

"What are we doing now?"

"Changing cars and disappearing into a hotel in Switzerland. I want to stay in the area, but things have to cool off. Including my impatience. It'll get us killed."

She didn't argue with me, just patted my knee. Another way of saying, "you're right, but I understand." I felt a little nauseated and my hands had a slight tremor, as the adrenaline drained away and full awareness of what almost happened settled in.

The severity of the reminder was equal to the importance of the lesson. Anything short of extreme, paranoid vigilance was stupid and reckless. I hoped I'd never have to be reminded again.

CHAPTER 17

When I was about fifteen, I was transferred to a new high school, the consequence of a consolidation in the city where I grew up. It was a new school, still filled with the smell of fresh tile and sheetrock. The preceding schools, three of them, now closed, were local institutions, reflecting the demographics of their neighborhoods. Mine was heartily white middle class. Unadorned, rough-textured, but solid and tolerant of oddballs like me, if only because I wasn't noticed.

One of the other high schools was in a place they liked to call, euphemistically, under-resourced. If you've ever lived in or near a city, big or small, you know what that meant. Fucking tough.

I was used to benign neglect, so I'd never been a target just for existing. For a chubby kid with little sense of physicality, who never played sports — more out of indifference than lack of fitness — moving schools was an unnerving experience.

The kid who had the locker next to me was marginally bigger, but more physically mature, in that he had a scruffy ill-shaved beard and glossy skin. He was also a low-grade sadist, who on the few occasions we stood there at the same time, would slap my locker shut, nearly slamming my fingers in the door. It was such a blatantly cruel and meaningless thing to do, I could barely comprehend it.

When I pointed that out to him, he'd just laugh and say things like, "Fuck you, freak bag."

One day when I was unloading my books, he appeared from nowhere, shoved me into the edge of my locker door in a way that split my lip, then suggested sexual things regarding my mother.

I felt my lip, looked at the blood, then knocked him to the floor with a single wild, ferocious punch.

It cost me a week's suspension. I spent the time deconstructing my father's abandoned stereo components. Never was a penalty more gratefully received.

The kid never taunted me again. Though already absorbed by more important concerns, I took note.

■ ■ ■ ■

We selected the hotel in Castagnola — a village in Switzerland on the Italian border — based on the availability of a balcony overlooking Lake Lugano. I set up the computer gear, but after a quick glance at my various email accounts, we dedicated the bulk of our time sitting on the balcony composing ourselves. I even napped for two hours in the middle of the day, something I hadn't done since recovering from the bullet wounds.

"There is such a thing as nervous exhaustion," said Natsumi, after I woke up and expressed my surprise. "We're not immune from excess adrenaline. It can actually deplete a person's energy."

I was never big on letting down, but she was making a good point. So, for both our sakes, I practiced calm restoration, albeit fitfully, for a whole day.

The next morning I called Laudomia.

"Signor Fortnoy, my God, where did you go?"

"There is no Signor Fortnoy. Or Signora Fortnoy," I told her, though I stuck with the British accent.

"I told the carabinieri everything I know

311

about you."

"It doesn't matter. It's all made up."

"I don't understand."

"The men who tried to kill us worked for Rodrigo Mariñelarena. You need to tell this to the police. They should investigate the villa in Cardano. It was undoubtedly being used for illegal purposes."

"Who are you really?" she asked.

"I can't tell you. I was the one they wanted to kill. You and my wife would have been taken out for good measure. It's unlikely you'll ever hear from Rodrigo again, but I'd get out of town for a couple weeks, just to be on the safe side. Take a vacation. You'll be glad you did."

"He was about to shoot me when you called attention to yourself," she said. "You saved my life."

"Or almost got you killed, depending on how you want to look at it. Though I would like a favor."

"If I can."

"I want everything you have on Rodrigo. Email, phone numbers, signature. And everything on the villa — contracts, deed of sale, and everything pertaining to the corporate owner. Name, address, and whatever official ID was required at the time of sale. I feel that when a client tries to kill you, it invalidates the rules of confidentiality."

"You are chasing this man?" she said.

"In a manner of speaking."

"How do I do this?"

"Scan the documents and make PDFs. But don't use your office scanner. I'm sure there are places where you can pay a per-scan fee. Use cash. Then email me the PDFs. Again, don't use your own computers. Go to an Internet café or library, or whatever you have here in Italy."

"This is so I can claim the documents were stolen from me, if necessary, am I right?"

"You are."

"You are a spy, no?"

"I'm not sure what I am, Laudomia, quite honestly. But if you could do this for me, it would be a good thing."

"I will, for sure. And pray it isn't an evil thing."

Castagnola, appended to the city of Lugano, possessed all the beauty and charm of the Como region in a more compact size. So there were worst places to commit to R&R.

The only extra effort was putting on a reasonably comfortable disguise, which we achieved before crossing the border. Natsumi assumed her Japanese boy persona.

There were no carabinieri or Swiss National Police at the border to greet us, which was fortunate, since there was no easy way of getting around a wanted person description such as, "Caucasian travelling with Asian."

We each took a separate trip into Lugano, but otherwise were content to hang around the hotel, which was only accessible by foot or motor launch. Natsumi read novels from a bookcase well-stocked with English editions, and I did desultory research on the Internet, which for me represented the most soothing form of relaxation.

I ignored my email inboxes, relying on the alerts I'd set up to keep track of the important stuff. That's how I knew Laudomia had come through.

It was an email from internet.paradiso. Subject line: "Documents. A Good Thing." Attached were a dozen separate PDFs.

I clicked on *"Atto,"* Italian for deed. The owner of the vineyard in Cardano was United Aquitania, Inc., and the address was a post office box in New York City. The company was also registered in New York State. There was a U.S. Federal Employer Identification Number, but no other information was required, since the notary who signed the deed had presumably performed the appropriate due diligence on both buyer and seller.

The information contained in the *compromesso* — a contract laying out the deal prior to a vetting of the counterparties and the ultimate closing — offered nothing additional. It looked like the transaction sailed through without a hitch.

Didn't matter. I had what I needed for the next step.

I used one of my most secure email addresses to write the New York Department of State to request a copy of the Certificate of Incorporation registered by United Aquitania. This would give me the name or names of the people doing the incorporating, and their nationality. It would also describe stock ownership and the purpose of the company's business, which could be bullshit, but might provide some insight.

I sent the email and immediately received an automated reply. It said they had my request and I should expect a response in about three to six weeks.

I went out to the balcony where Natsumi was in a lounge chair reading *This Side of Paradise* by F. Scott Fitzgerald.

"Seemed fitting," she said. "Though I gotta tell you, kids in the 1920s were just as self-involved and grandiose as kids are today. They just dressed better and actually talked to each other."

"We need to move again," I said. "Nothing scary. For research purposes, though it's not a bad idea to get a little distance from recent events."

"Where to?"

"Since you've become accustomed to the beautiful and exotic, how about Albany, New York?" I asked.

"Do they speak English?"

"A form of it."

"Great. I'm sick of all these extra vowels."

The JFK airport is not a kind place, nor an easy place to navigate. In some ways, it was stranger to return there than it had been to leapfrog through foreign environments. Though I liked speaking again in our regional vernacular.

"How ya doin'?" said the customs agent rummaging around in our bags.

"Doin' okay."

"Got stuff to declare?"

"Nuthin'."

I'd sent all the electronic gear ahead via FedEx, including equipment sourced in Europe and other far reaches of the world. There was nothing suspect or explosive in our luggage, with the exception of the tie I bought in Como.

We coasted through, and were in a rented Chevy Impala shortly thereafter. We headed into Manhattan where I'd made reservations at the Remsenberg, a tiny boutique hotel on West 45th, on the same block as the old offices of *The New Yorker* and near the Algonquin Hotel. They'd turned the Oak Room, where Dorothy Parker, Alexander Wolcott and the other Roundtable luminaries once set unsurpassable standards for witty repartee, into a breakfast buffet, but I still liked to be in its proximity.

Another appeal was the availability of two rooms with a connecting door. This allowed us to separate the computer array from the sleeping quarters. Not only could Natsumi now sleep with the lights off, she didn't have to listen to me chat with myself, mutter gentle swear words, guffaw, hum jazz riffs, and make other assorted sounds, something I hadn't realized about myself.

"Are you kidding?" said Natsumi. "It's like eavesdropping on a patient with severe DID."

"DID?"

"Dissociative identity disorder. Split personality."

That might have explained how I was able to spend the bulk of my life alone in a home office glued to a computer screen. I kept myself company.

As soon as we were thoroughly settled in, I called Evelyn.

"So, tell me you're in Kazakhstan," she said.

"West 45th Street."

"As in New York City?"

"Yup."

"That's wonderful."

"I've been working on getting you protection, so you might be able to come home fairly soon."

"Take your time. I spent the whole day at the Twelve Apostles yesterday. Gigantic stone pillars off the Southern Coast. Been dodging kangaroos and emu. Everything's backwards and upside down. I feel like I'm marooned on another planet."

"Have you heard from Bruce?" I asked.

"He sent me the agreement with the broker, and a valuation. How should I get it to you?"

I gave her a secure route.

"What's the bottom line?" I asked.

"Eight million. After taxes, fees and commissions."

"How long?"

"A month, max," she said. "Unless due diligence turns up another nasty surprise."

"Excellent. How's Bruce holding up?"

"Better now that he's back on St. John's with a security team hanging around with him and his wife. Everyone else is working from home and things are running fine. Maybe better."

"Give me a computer and a broadband ISP and I will move the world."

After sleeping off the jet lag and getting fully organized in our new rooms, we took a field trip to the Upper West Side. Far to the west, on 72nd Street, where Joselito Gorrotxategi lived out his dazzling lifestyle.

It was mostly a wasted effort. The block was lined with apartment buildings and the street with cars lucky enough to snag a spot. No different from hundreds of other city blocks. We looked at the door buzzers, as if that would reveal some grave secret, but learned nothing we didn't already know.

We walked the rest of the way to the park and sat on a bench for a while, looking at the Hudson River. Joggers and dog walkers passed by.

"So what're you going to do next?" Natsumi asked.

"We need to shake the tree again, but frankly, I've lost the stomach for playing bait."

We walked all the way back, from 72nd to 45th, my hands stuck in my pockets, her arm through mine. We talked about everything but recent events, instead pointing out city sights and reminiscing over trips to New York in our pasts and the adventures we had there.

"We came on a field trip in high school," she said. "A rare boyfriend and I peeled off from the group and spent the day drinking beer in delis and kissing between the stacks at the New York Public Library. Since both of us were little, ignored nerds, nobody noticed we'd been gone when the group got back on the bus. A good day."

I had a few tales myself, none so romantic and brash. More involving long gawking moments in museums and art galleries.

"And tourist traps, though I was more concerned about the load-bearing physics of the Empire State Building than the gift shop."

When we got back to the Remsenberg, I made a cup of coffee and went into the computer room to check on things. None of my key mailboxes had seen any recent activity, which is all I normally cared about. But occasionally, I'd check dormant addresses still live since they posed little security risk. One of these had belonged to Kirk Tazman, the mythical executive from Deer Park Underwriters that supposedly managed Florencia's secret account.

There was one email, about three weeks old, from Dominic Etherton, the stern safe-deposit manager from First Australia Bank, Grand Cayman.

Mister Tazman:

It is with a heavy heart I write you, despite great jeopardy to my life, that the confidential information on your account with us has been breached in several egregious ways. I take this as a personal shame, though I was in no way able to prevent it.

On the day you came to withdraw the contents of your safe-deposit box, I was alerted individuals were in the bank asking to engage with an account under the highest level of legal surveillance. At that time, I was instructed by my superior manager, Mr. Sato, to inform both the Royal Cayman Islands Police Service and the American consulate office in George Town.

I did so, though I refused Mr. Sato's demand we confine you and your assistant until the authorities arrived. I believed, and still believe, this would have been an unforgivable betrayal of our bank's and nation's commitment to our valued customers.

I was censured for this by my bank's management, but that was the end of it, until two weeks ago when a Latino man came to my office and told me he had guns pointed at my children and wife and would shoot them if I did not turn over every record relating to your account.

I did as he asked, of course, in full. My bank does not know this happened. Neither do the police. I am telling you because I feel a powerful moral obligation. I am also trusting you not to reveal my transgression, understanding that my family's lives were at stake, and still are, I believe, if this event comes to light.

With the humblest and
sincerest apologies,
Dominic Etherton

CHAPTER 18

The next day we were in a bar not far from our hotel drinking straight vodka with Ekrem "Little Boy" Boyanov. More specifically, Little Boy and Natsumi were drinking straight vodka. I was hard into my third club soda.

Little Boy was, not surprisingly, huge. His head alone probably outweighed Natsumi. Boyish only in his tussled good looks and ready grin, his hands could crush golf balls and had, in fact, mashed a few heads.

"So how's Mirsada doing?" I asked him, after about a half hour of perfunctory pleasantries and expressions of irrevocable devotion and regard.

"She's in good graces, which I take to mean getting laid, which believe me, no problem for Mirsada. The girl loves her work."

"I need her to get Joselito out of his apartment for a hunk of time. Not just a night out. A weekend in Atlantic City, or St. Barths."

"This we can do."

"Thank you," said Natsumi.

"And I could use the help of a good B&E man. A New York City apartment specialist."

"Sure. We do anything for you two nuts," he said.

"We are honored to have you as trusted partners," said Natsumi, with a little Japanese bow.

"See? This is why. Respect."

Before it got too ripe, I called the waiter over and we ordered our meals. With that accomplished, I asked Little Boy what he'd been up to.

"A little of this, a little of that," he said. "Nice business in copper from old buildings. We learn this from you, Mr. G. Metals rule. High-end hookers, still too profitable to let go, though the wife don't like this too much. But what the hell? Girls keep signing up, boys keep looking for business, this is my fault? Otherwise, core interests in boosting general merchandise, cigarettes and booze going good. Very dull but profitable, with little exposure. I don't look for glamour, just reliable ROI, you know what I mean?"

"Yes," I said. "I do."

He downed a full glass of Grey Goose and said, "So, what's the big picture?"

I paused to focus his attention. "Joselito is affiliated with an organization out of Spain who we think are right-wing vigilantes, though we're not sure," I said. "We think they're in a fight with another group, also underground, though we're not sure about that, either."

"Things can get pretty murky with Europeans," said Little Boy.

Having fought in the Balkan War, Little Boy's opinion on that had some standing.

"It turned out we could have used your friends over there," I said, and told him about the attack at the outdoor café.

"Sorry about that, Mr. G. Scary shit, right?"

"Oh, yes," said Natsumi. "And that lake is colder than you think."

"So you want some company now?" he asked.

"Again, not yet. But we might."

"Give the word. We got local representation here in Astoria. Can be in midtown in half hour or less, depending on traffic."

"Thanks, Little Boy," said Natsumi.

"You got it, Mrs. G."

■ ■ ■ ■

We waited until Joselito and Mirsada were well on their way to Clear Waters Resort and Casino in Connecticut, Natsumi's alma mater, before breaking into his apartment. Little Boy's go-to breaking and entering specialist was a soft-spoken guy in a nice suit, with a briefcase, who met me in a restaurant about a block away. It was midday, and the place was filling up with the lunch crowd. We shook hands, but he didn't share his name. I gave him the address and he instructed me to stay put until he called sometime in the next hour. He said when I got to the building, I could just walk in, since the access control system would be disabled. At the apartment, I could also walk right in, but should lock the door on the way out.

"Best break-in is the break-in they don't know about, or can't figure out," he said, then left me.

A half hour later, he called. "Not so easy, not so hard," he said. "Come over anytime."

"How do I pay you?" I asked.

"I invoice Little Boy," he said, "he send you a bill. Central processing."

Everything happened exactly as he said it

326

would, with no sign of tampering, but I wasn't surprised. Little Boy set very high standards.

Joselito's apartment looked as if he'd had some help decorating. The motif was basic Manhattan bachelor of respectable, though not excessive means. Leather couches, lamps with black lampshades and brushed-nickel bases. Art on the walls, none of it Goya or Velázquez. Glass coffee table with a few neatly placed coffee table books, one filled with black and white erotic photography.

His computer, a PC, was in the bedroom. I sat at the desk and surveyed the simple array of keyboard, screen, CPU and external hard drive. The first thing I did was unscrew a little service door on the back of the CPU and stick a compressor mic like the ones I used in Italy inside the housing. I was able to use the smallest possible receiver, since it only had to travel as far as Joselito's own wireless router. Then I turned on the system and inserted a boot disk written for that model computer and operating system.

The boot disk had an application you wouldn't think could be legal, since the first thing it did was tell the computer to boot up the rest of the stealth operating system, giving me complete command of the machine's data, including the keys to the wireless access.

I plugged in an external hard drive with two terabytes of memory and started copying everything — all files, folders, applications, photos, music, videos, movies, along with the operating system itself.

While this went on in the background, I stuck a flash drive in another USB port and downloaded monitoring software, another entirely legal application. Used by corporate security departments, the application lived deep inside the operating system, undetectable, where it could record and transmit everything that happened on the computer. So as Joselito worked, all keystrokes, emails coming in and going out, web pages opened and closed, user names and passwords entered, photos looked at and music played would show up on a dedicated PC back at our hotel rooms, in real time, without Joselito ever knowing a thing.

An hour later I left the apartment with Joselito's cyber life — past, present and future — fully secured.

I was tempted to contact Mr. Etherton at First Australia in Grand Cayman, but there wasn't much more he could tell me, and he was already terrified enough. I had all the same information he'd released to the kidnappers, and since most of it was contrived and no longer of any use, not much could be made of it.

There was only one item of concern, a lockbox account in Delaware the embezzled funds had flowed through on their way to the Caymans. With that account in hand, the right people would be able to follow the money laundering scheme all the way back to Florencia's insurance agency.

"Oh, crap," I said out loud, as an electric jolt of revelation shot through me. "Damien Brandt."

"What?" Natsumi called from the other room.

"I just had what an old client of mine called a 'blinding glimpse of the obvious.' "

She came in the room. "About what?"

"When Brandt was killed I naturally assumed people from the same crowd who murdered Florencia were responsible. That would be bad. This is worse."

She sat down on the bed, and I went on.

"In the letter from Joselito to Domingo he referred to various friends. He's not only a forensic accountant, he used to work for Interpol and the Guardia Civil. Not hard to imagine he's got contacts all over the place with whom he can exchange information."

"Including the FBI?" she asked.

"Why not? Very useful in his work in corporate security, financial branch. Information is the fuel that runs international policing, and national security. He's well positioned to have learned about the Grand Cayman account, and has the skills to trace it all the way back."

I explained he'd have to employ some subterfuge to get by various security systems and confidentiality policies, but if I could do it, a professional like him surely could as well.

"Especially if he's willing to kidnap, torture and murder," said Natsumi.

"Not him personally, I'm willing to bet. He's way too valuable to risk that kind of work. He gets the intel, then the VG sends in the shock troops."

"So what are they after?" she asked.

"The money."

She cocked her head and allowed a little of her Japanese composure to slip from her speech. "In other words," she said, "they're after us. Everybody's *after us.*"

"How often do you get consensus between groups of murderous underground Europeans and the FBI, both domestic and international?"

"You forgot the State of Connecticut and

330

certain elements of organized crime."

"Oh, yeah."

"So what do we do?"

"Call Little Boy, then drive to Albany."

I told Little Boy, on speakerphone so Natsumi could join in, that I'd successfully hijacked Joselito's computer and heaped praise on his B&E guy.

"Runs very successful apartment security company over in Astoria," he said. "You can see why, eh?"

"Quis custodiet ipsos custodes," said Natsumi.

"I need time to go through his data, so there's not much else for you right now, though I'd like to keep Mirsada on the case."

"No problem there, Mr. G. She's havin' a blast. Likes the Basque guy. She'd slit his throat without hesitating, of course, but doesn't mean she can't like him."

"Fair enough," said Natsumi.

The next morning we drove north after rush hour had crested. The day was cool and sunny, and traffic on the Palisades Parkway light to moderate. I enjoyed being back on American roads, though I retained the habit of frequently checking the rearview for maniacal European drivers bearing down from behind.

I was wearing a brown-haired wig, full beard, horn-rimmed glasses and a fake nose. And a three-piece suit. Natsumi was appearing as her own self, since we decided she should stay in the car when I visited the New York Department of State, Division of Corporations, State Records and Uniform Commercial Code.

I'd called ahead the day before and was assured by a Mrs. Blakely that if I presented myself at her office at One Commerce Plaza in Albany, she'd be happy to provide copies of up to six Certificates of Registration per day.

"Only need one, but thank you very much for your help."

"It's what you pay me to do."

One Commerce Plaza was a tall, late-twentieth-century office tower in the shape of an H. Even in a town filled with architecture of little distinction, the building had achieved a remarkable glass-walled blandness.

Natsumi took the car so she could find a coffee shop somewhere to go online while she waited for me. The security guard in the lobby took my name and called Mrs. Blakely, who had to be reminded of the call the day before, but eventually let me come up.

Inside a double set of glass-panel doors was a long, high counter where mostly well-dressed people were bellied up talking to the staff on the other side. At either end were wall-mounted paper trays stuffed with forms. A Take A Number dispenser controlled the queues. It looked like I had about ten people in front of me. I spent the time reading posters with severe warnings and declarations, not a please or thank you in sight.

As a researcher, I'd spent a lot of time in places like this, so I was comfortable with the environment and the people who worked here, which contrary to everyone's assumption, aren't as reflexively hostile as their reputations contend. Mrs. Blakely being a good example.

"Yes, sir," she said, with an eager smile, "I do remember the call well. Once you reminded me."

I wrote the name United Aquitania on a slip of paper and handed it to her. She disappeared into the back and was only gone for a few minutes. She smacked two sheets of paper on the counter.

The name of the registered corporation was United Aquitania.

The address was on Spring Street in Soho, NYC.

The official representative of the corporation who signed the Certificate of Registration was Florencia Zarandona.

Back at the hotel, I committed all my time and attention to Joselito's computer. The effort was well aided by the standard search commands built into Windows 7 and other Microsoft applications.

Within minutes I located my first priority, email correspondence with the address, domingoa@ibaceso.es.

Most of the back and forth concerned financial issues, reporting on the movement of funds, incoming statements, currency exchanges, all mundane and all in prose. No figures, and no mention of specific banks or account numbers, or individual names.

Well, I thought, no kidding. The guy was an expert in corporate financial security. He knew the hazards of email.

But I pressed on, working my way back through both the inbox and the sent folders, until an interesting chain started in Spanish with the subject line, *"investigación americanos."*

Domingo:
Have you received current financials?
Note increased expenses over prior year.
Attributable to increase in eliminations
Stateside. Ten versus five. Copies of
authorizations available on request.

Joselito

Joselito:
Expenses approved. Next for elimination
on the way by courier.

Domingo

There were more of these messages, all
with the same sinister flavor. Then this:

Domingo:
Have received very important information. Please call.

Joselito

Then about a week later:

Domingo:
Have researched Caribbean facility. Will
proceed as discussed.

Joselito

A few days after that:

335

Domingo:
Have determined the path. Will need authorization to use friends for nonstandard research.

Joselito

Joselito:
Authorized.

Domingo

Joselito was off his email for about a week after that, then it looked like he put in a day catching up. Most of the correspondence involved his corporate clients, written in flawless English, if you excuse the dopey business jargon. But then he took up again with Domingo:

Domingo:
Funds in question have been removed by an unauthorized and unidentified party. Checked with my friend, who obtained confirmation. Guidance, please.

Joselito

Part of me took pleasure in seeing my scenario validated, the rest was appalled at what those vapid, innocuous words actually described.

Joselito:
Learn more.

                              Domingo

Domingo:
Friend describes American male and Japanese female working for Rodrigo.

                              Joselito

This pissed off Domingo.

Joselito:
Not working for Rodrigo! Domingo

Domingo:
Apologies. Friend claims otherwise. Please call.

                              Joselito

"Swell," I said to myself.

Domingo:
Friend thanked me for new information. Has returned the favor. Please call.

                              Joselito

The subject line went dormant nearly up to the current time, when one last exchange occurred.

Domingo:

As discussed, have deployed friends to intercept American male and Japanese woman.

Joselito

I called Natsumi into the room and showed her the string.

"They don't know where we are," she said, getting right to the point.

"They don't. But I'm feeling less invisible every day."

"Me, too."

"I'm going to call Shelly. Stick around."

When he answered, I put him on speaker-phone.

"Are we still on truce status?" I asked.

"As far as I'm concerned."

"Can you tell me the Bureau's theory on me?"

"Not without more from you."

I took a deep breath and decided on the spot to put a lot of trust in a guy who had very little trust in me.

"There's a Spanish corporate security expert living in New York named Joselito Gorrotxategi. He's a forensic accountant and a veteran of Interpol and the Guardia Civil in Spain. He's also working for what I believe is an underground element of that

338

same organization called *Los Vengadores del Guardia,* The Guard's Avengers. Probably with the help of your mole, he learned about Florencia Cathcart's Grand Cayman account and traced the laundering scheme back to the agency. Ergo Damien Brandt."

"You can prove all this," he said.

"Don't know. I have all the data on his computer, and I've installed monitoring software and a listening bug. Won't be able to benefit from the last two until Joselito gets back from Connecticut. I think tomorrow."

It took Shelly a few moments to respond.

"Inadmissible," he said.

"Since when did you people care about that? Anyway, I'm asking you not to bust him until things play out a little more. And if possible, put a muzzle on that idiot at the Bureau."

"What else do you have?" he asked.

"Your turn."

He huffed into the phone, but gave me something anyway.

"Natsumi Fitzgerald was in the Cayman Islands with a male Caucasian, medium height, black hair and moustache — probably false — forty to fifty years old. They took possession of material left in a safe-deposit box that the foreign service of the

FBI suspected had links to a European terrorist organization. A couple matching the same description was involved very recently in a shooting in the Lake Como region of Italy, where two members of that organization were killed."

Natsumi took my shirt sleeve and squeezed. I patted her hand.

"What about those Chilean banks?" I asked.

"A pass-through to an account in Madrid is connected to that same organization. Shut down right before we got there, with all the funds withdrawn and untraceable. That's all you get."

"Not the name of the organization?"

He didn't like that.

"There's a very strong opinion around here that you're the male Caucasian. You're clever, but not invincible. Important people are getting very interested in you. You can't imagine the shit storm I'm holding back. I can't protect you when national security is involved."

"*Aquitanos Unidos,*" I said.

More dead air, then, "You piss me off in a very tangible and specific way," he said.

"I know," I said. "Sorry."

He hung up.

"I'm becoming a serious liability," said

Natsumi. "It's the Japanese thing. Can't get away from it. You can slide in and out of these situations without notice because you look like everybody else. You're Mr. Average Western Dude. Unless we can move this operation to Tokyo, I'll always stick out like a sore thumb."

"What are you saying?"

"It would be better for you if we split up," she said.

"No, it wouldn't. It would be the worst thing that ever happened to me."

"Seeing your wife murdered, getting shot in the head and suffering through an agonizing recovery was the worst thing that ever happened to you."

"Okay, it's a tie."

She smiled at me and cupped my chin in her hand.

"I love you, Arthur, but you're not the beat-up mess of a man I first met. You're so much better. You're tougher and more energetic than ninety percent of the men in the world, even if you limp a little and occasionally bump into things. You have the most ferociously brilliant mind I've ever come close to knowing, even if you talk to yourself all the time. You probably have a touch of Obsessive Compulsive Disorder, but nobody's perfect. Though I think you might be perfect for me. I mean, you've saved my life more times than I can count. But now I'm afraid I'm going to lose yours. I couldn't survive that."

She was speaking in her regular, slightly melodious lilt, but her eyes looked watery. It made my chest tighten and throat choke in a very unfamiliar way.

"No," I said, "we end this now and go to ground. We still can, relatively easily. Go to Hawaii, the Big Island. Loads of whites and Asians all mushed up together. Get a little tan, they'll all think you're Polynesian. I'll pack while you get the car. We can fly to the West Coast and figure it out from there."

I jumped up, but she grabbed my shirt and dragged me back down.

"You don't want to do this," she said.

"Oh, yes I do. There is nothing more important in the world to me than you. You're right, I'm OCD. More than a little. And you're my number-one obsession. As long as you'll have me, I will stick to you like epoxy."

"Epoxy? That's a lot stronger than glue," she said.

"Unbreakable."

A tear wandered out of her right eye. She briskly wiped her face with the back of her sleeve.

"I liked the life I had before," she said. "I wasn't unhappy, mostly because I didn't know any better. Looking back, I was mostly asleep. Comfortably, blithely unaware. From the moment I fled into your mad orbit, I've been awake. Wide-eyed aware. Every sense engaged, every nerve attuned. You don't understand. I want this. It's a decision, not a consequence. We have to see this through."

Then she got up and went back into the other room, leaving me and the lump in my throat alone in the near darkness.

CHAPTER 19

Joselito was a hard worker, I had to give him that.

As soon as he was back on the job, his email was filled with correspondence, all relating to his consulting business. Most of it involved nailing employees who were diverting revenue into their personal accounts or pumping up expense reports, or disguising bribes to foreign officials as legitimate fees.

Despite myself, I began to admire Joselito's skills, both investigatory and diplomatic. Many of his quarries were family men and women on trysts, and otherwise competent executives only dabbling in petty corruption, the type that barely warrants mention. In most cases, he sold his clients on shutting down their employees' illicit side projects without further recourse or penalty.

For certain clients, however, he suggested more corporal remedies, though in highly euphemistic terms. If I didn't know Joselito better, I would have missed that interpretation. Likewise, there was nothing in the email record that showed how he executed these assignments, but I eventually found out through the audio bug.

"This is Joselito," he said one evening, in English. There was quiet for a moment, then, "That's right. I have a new gig for you."

Aside from a few naughty chats with Mirsada, this was the first phone call I'd heard.

"Selma Lizaran. No, her husband's the target. He had the chance to make his overdue contribution, with interest. Been dragging his feet. He'll pick up the pace if she comes home from the gym with a few broken ribs and a pair of black eyes." Pause. "No, nothing permanent. Just make sure she knows why. Should make for good dinner-time conversation."

I'd learned how to take control of Joselito's computers by pulling off a similar trick at Florencia's insurance agency after she'd been killed. I'd kept all the secret tunnels into her agency's computers intact, seeing no reason not to.

On an educated whim, I went into Florencia's financial management program and rummaged around the tax records. This took some fortitude, because even a data-wonk like me can be pummeled into submission by pages of Excel documents filled with long columns of double-entry accounting.

I realized, finally, that I was in the wrong application, and I kicked myself when I switched over and found the prize almost immediately, under the heading "Online Tax Filing Numbers, Federal and State."

And there it was. The insurance agency's corporate U.S. Federal Employer Identification Number. The same as United Aquitania.

I brought up the code from the Grand Cayman safe-deposit box and copied the coordinates for the safe house in New York City, then pasted them into the marine navigation program.

The pin landed on United Aquitania's headquarters on Spring Street.

I called to Natsumi in the other room.

"It's dinner time," I said. "I'm thinking Soho."

We left the cab and walked into a cool rainy evening. I trod carefully, still not a hundred percent sure of my balance or the sturdiness of my wounded leg. Natsumi kept a grip on my arm, as she always did.

Spring Street was in transition mode, with people getting home from work uneasily sharing the sidewalk with the early dinner crowd. The first looked grim and eager, the second relieved and optimistic. Natsumi and I were our usual selves, watchful and contained.

I wasn't surprised that the building that housed United Aquitania was impenetrable from the street. A brass plate filled with door buzzers gave away nothing. Looking through the glass outer doors, I could see mailboxes and a broad staircase and little else.

We went across the street to assess video surveillance options, but they were scarce. Unlike the cloistered warrens of a London mews, or the wild countryside around Lake Como, Soho was not a place a regular civilian could implant video cameras unnoticed.

We went back across the street and stood around waiting for someone to enter the building. The wait could have been forever, but fortunately less than an hour later, a very short woman with curly magenta hair wearing a leather jacket and sporting a very large diamond stud in her nose pushed between us and stuck a key in the glass door.

I asked her if she knew the people in the

building. She whipped around with her hand still holding the key in the door and asked me what the fuck I wanted to know for.

"We want to find a fucking friend of ours," said Natsumi. "He's supposed to be working in this building, but we don't see the name of the company."

"What's the company?" the woman asked.

"United Aquitania," said Natsumi.

"Never heard of it. There's somebody on the fifth floor, same as me," said the woman, pointing to an unlabeled buzzer. "No name anywhere, but sometimes they have junk mail lying on the floor outside the door. Being a professional busybody, I notice that it gets cleared away by the next day," she added.

"You ever see anyone coming or going?" I asked.

She looked at me a long time with a flat-faced, steady stare. "You don't have a friend," she said. "You're casing the place."

I had to remind myself we were in New York, a city where bullshit better be gold plated, or forget about it.

"You like money?" Natsumi asked.

"Yeah. I do," said the woman.

Natsumi wrote something on a piece of paper and handed it over. "If you see anyone go in or out of those offices, call this number. If it's true, you get a thousand dollars."

The woman studied the number, then looked up. "How do I know you're good for this?" she asked.

"You don't," said Natsumi, "but why not make the call anyway and see what happens?"

The woman seemed to consider this seriously, and left us after sticking the number in the back pocket of her black denim jeans.

After that, we decided there was nothing left to do but find a restaurant and go eat, just like we were regular people. That we weren't was proven by the dinner conversation.

"You think you'll have to break in?" asked Natsumi, after the hors d'oeuvres arrived.

"I don't know. I think Nose Stud might come through."

"We know nothing about the building, or their offices. Or even if they have offices."

"It could be another shell. An empty address."

"Pretty expensive shell," she said. "A million bucks gets you a studio apartment in this part of town."

"No more than the other safe houses. Florencia had expensive tastes."

"So what do we do now?" Natsumi asked.

"We need to shake the tree again. This time, let's not be standing underneath."

I waited until two in the morning, believing that Joselito would be off his computer and sound asleep. Using the mirroring software, I went into his email and wrote a letter.

Señor Mariñelarena:

I am in possession of information that would be of great value to you. It relates to a substantial amount of money belonging to your organization that was withdrawn from a bank in Grand Cayman. Regaining these funds would go a long way toward replenishing your real estate holdings recently compromised in London, Madrid and Menaggio.

As you can see, I know a great deal about you. I note this only to prove the legitimacy of my offer, and the potential consequences of a refusal. Understand that I could make the same offer to the VG, but I have come to abhor their motives, tactics and philosophy. You are, in a very real sense, the lesser of two evils.

Given the sensitivity of these matters, I will insist we meet face to face here in New York City.

Respond to this message and we will move forward with further arrangements.
Joselito Gorrotxategi

Before letting it go, I attached a subprogram to the email that would route the return message through Joselito's computer, bypassing his inbox, and send it to one of my own.

"Shake, shake, shake," I sang to myself as I hit the send button.

The next morning I got a call from Evelyn, who was still Down Under, but getting antsy.

"I do love it here, Arthur, but I have a cardiology practice to support back in Stamford," she said.

"Any news on the sale of the agency?"

"The buyers are identified. We're in due diligence now. Auditors are crawling all over the books. You can understand why they got out the fine-tooth comb, given what happened. It takes time."

"Like what?"

"Like another month," she said.

"What's your position on Bosniak gangsters?"

I told her as much as I dared about Little Boy and his crew. Evelyn was a hard-nosed woman with a greater commitment to privacy than personal safety. I knew it would be a tough sell, and it was.

"No way."

We argued, in the gentle, mostly good-natured way we always had, for nearly an hour. Then I pulled out my last card.

"Do it for me," I said. "If you're coming home, I'll be constantly worried about your safety and won't be able to concentrate. And that might mean I'll make a mistake that'll get us all killed."

"That's a low blow."

"I know, but it's the truth."

"That's not very reassuring."

"That's not my job right now. What I really want to do is scare the crap out of you so you'll do what I'm asking."

"Okay," she said with a sigh. "What's his name again, Little John? Do I also get Friar Tuck?"

After I got off the phone with her, I called Shelly.

"A new number," he said when he heard my voice. "What do you do, change these things every day?"

"Nearly. Cancel the request for protection for the insurance agency owner. Private services have been retained."

"That's good, because I couldn't get it

anyway. In fact, they're politely asking me to go back to my retirement in Rocky Hill."

"Really."

"I can't tell you anything more because it might compromise their investigation, which would be very bad for me and my pension. My advice to you is to come in. Now that they're serious, there's no way this can end well. New York is a big town, but you can't hide there forever."

How did he know we were in New York? I thought, then hit the end button and yelled to Natsumi that we were moving again. In a hurry.

Shortly after, we were in a hotel overlooking Central Park on the Upper West Side. My first impulse had been to fly to Cleveland or Patagonia, but Natsumi's cooler head prevailed, voting strongly that we'd come too far to abandon everything now. And, ultimately, our safety would rely more on reaching some conclusion to this thing than constantly running around the world.

"We've already talked about this," she said. "If you give up now, it'll eat you to death, and that won't be any fun for either of us."

What I had to chew on, at that moment, was a new reality. Pissed at me as he may have been, Shelly had intentionally sent a clear message — they were tracking us down. There was a vulnerability somewhere in my systems, a breach. One likely suspect was the disposable phone. They couldn't connect it to me directly, but they likely monitored my calls to Shelly, then traced the connection back to the city, maybe even to the repeater closest to the Remsenberg Hotel.

Everything I'd done on the computer since waking up from the coma was either obliterated or backed up on a pair of terabyte hard drives. I could spend a year searching around for digital spies and find nothing. Or, I could simply start all over again.

I told Natsumi my plan, which began with a new disposable phone and a few hours on a park bench verbally phishing for social security numbers from a list of dead people I'd been holding in reserve. This should have been very difficult, but I'd learned all the tricks from a project I once did for an insurance company that was designing identity theft coverage, so it wasn't long before I had three strong numbers gladly provided by grief-addled family members.

Thus armed, I opened a new bank account so I could get a fresh credit card. I used the card to go shopping for a new laptop, wireless access via cell service, external hard drives and a few more disposable phones.

My first online purchase was space in a storage facility in Connecticut, where I sent all my old gear, with the exception of a terabyte drive containing the backed-up files. Bypassing the hotel's wireless access, I imported over a few select files and applications, including the programs monitoring Joselito's computer. I scrubbed all the documents, files and programs with antivirus and antimalware tools, which claimed everything was clean and safe — which I prayed was true, recognizing that the U.S. government could do things a hacker couldn't dream of. Thus occupied, it was more than a day before I checked for Rodrigo's response to Joselito's email. I'd directed it to one of my fresh new email accounts.

Sr. Gorrotxategi:
You interest me. I have heard of you. Perhaps because we travel in the same universe, though within different orbits. We will meet, though you understand security demands a great deal of caution. Preparations will need to be made.

Rodrigo Mariñelarena

I wrote him back:

Sr. Mariñelarena:
Thank you for your prompt and respectful response. I appreciate your caution,
because I am also a very cautious man,
which is why I am still here among the living. However, this is not a matter that will
tolerate a long negotiation. I have other
options and must take the course most
advantageous to my interests. I am sure
you understand.
Joselito Gorrotxategi

The next response was even more prompt
and respectful.

Sr. Gorrotxategi:
I do understand and appreciate the position you are in. You will find I am both a
swift and flexible negotiator. Arrangements
are being made. Please stand by for
further instructions.
Mariñelarena

"You think he's chomped on the bait?"
asked Natsumi, when I showed her the exchange.

"I do. It's not just the money, it's Joselito's apparent operational awareness. That's
got to spook Rodrigo big-time."

"He'll come to New York?"

"I think he will. This is too important to sit on his hands in Europe."

"So what do we do?" she asked.

"Take it to the street."

I spent the next three days playing a homeless guy who'd taken up residence across the street from United Aquitania's building. I had a grocery cart filled with empty bottles and cans, a sleeping bag, long greasy hair and beard and more ratty clothes than the temperature required.

A cardboard sign, next to an open cardboard box, said, THE EMPIRE HAS DESTROYED JEDI KNIGHT RETIREMENT ACCOUNTS. DONATIONS APPRECIATED.

I actually did pretty well with that, bringing in a little more than four hundred dollars during the three-day stint. Made me reconsider past career decisions.

The beat cops checked in with me on the first day, and I told them it was a temporary situation, that I was scheduled to start a program — meaning city-sponsored rehab — any minute now. One of the cops said fine, not believing me, then told me their neighborhood's sidewalk housing statute of limitations was five days. Max.

"Then you know what happens," he said.

"I do," I said, even though I didn't.

Living conditions could have been worse, though I'm not sure how. Cement sidewalks are the coldest and hardest surfaces ever conceived. The sleeping bag, purchased like most of my other homeless gear at the Salvation Army, had most of the stuffing long since beat out of it, so it wasn't much of a mattress.

The best moment was when another homeless person, a woman with a livid face and dirty hands, sat down next to me and offered up a midsized 7UP bottle half filled with straight vodka. I demurred, which gave her no offense.

"That's fine. More for me."

"Though it was a generous offer," I said.

"You bet it was. I got kicked out of this very same place, what, a year ago? So what the fuck?"

"I have three days left."

"Oh. Then they do the thing."

"The thing?" I asked.

She looked at me in semi-bewilderment.

"You new here?"

"I am. Down from Connecticut," I said.

She sniffed and shrugged, as if to say, you don't know nothin' about nothin'.

"What, Greenwich?" she asked.

"Yeah, Greenwich. I got a hedge fund run

358

by Jesuit monks. Those guys aren't a lot of fun, but crazy honest, you know what I mean?"

"You're full of shit," she said.

"I am," I said, "and so are you."

She liked that and tried to get me to take a slurp from the 7UP bottle, but I held my ground.

"So you're like a saint," she said. "Like them Jesuits."

"Yes, I am. What's the thing?"

"You don't want to know," she said, standing up. "But you'll find out."

Even in the daylight, I could see the lights were off on the fifth floor of United Aquitania's building. Through a process of elimination while examining the bank of buzzers, I determined this was the organization's space.

Lying there, staring at the façade across the street, I developed a sympathy for real street people based not on their sad economic or psychiatric situations, but on the sheer boredom of being inert within a world of such compulsive energy. I felt I couldn't look at my smartphone when I was on the sidewalk, for fear I'd either wreck my persona or attract a mugger. Knowing that it was in my pocket, right there eager to be perused, was intensely exquisite torture. All

I could do was call Natsumi using an ear-
piece covered by my scraggly wig and sneak
a look at the touch screen. A homeless guy
seemingly talking to himself was beneath
notice.

"Anything?" she asked.

"No. Any word from Rodrigo?"

I had her monitoring my various email accounts.

"Yup, just about an hour ago," she said,
then read,

Sr. Gorrotxategi:
*"Estaré en Nueva York pronto y le
avisaré en cuanto llegue."*
Mariñelarena

"I think I know what that means," she
said.

"He's coming to New York soon and will
contact Joselito when he gets here," I said.
"Write back to acknowledge receipt of the
message. You look forward to meeting him."

"Okay. How are you feeling?"

"I'd be fine if it weren't for the iPhone
withdrawal. I only check email when I'm in
the john, which is a hard thing to come by
in and of itself. Not a lot of shopkeepers
want you around, and what do you do with
the cart? Can't lose the cart."

"The logistics of homelessness."

"Much more complicated than you'd think. I won't last till next week."

I was just back from one such trip, soon after nightfall, and saw lights on the fifth floor. Timing is everything, I thought, with a curse. I settled back into my spot with a promise that I'd be back in bed with Natsumi before the night was through.

In a mood most foul, I glowered at the building across the street and cursed some more, out loud. Another privilege of the homeless. It felt good, though I noted that for me, a homeless man of a different sort, it was a choice, not often for them.

I was thus engaged when a cab pulled up to the curb in front of me and Rodrigo Mariñelarena stepped out.

CHAPTER 20

Behind Rodrigo were two other men, one of whom I recognized from Madrid. They were all somewhat oversized and seemingly unaffected by the ten-hour transatlantic plane ride. They took stuffed duffel bags out of the trunk, paid the cabbie, crossed the street and were buzzed into the building; and judging by the way the fifth floor lit up, welcomed into United Aquitania headquarters.

I packed up my mobile homestead and pushed it over to an empty lot full of rubble one block from Broadway where I'd located a small tribe of homeless people. I gave them my cart with its full load of redeemable bottles and all the money I'd collected during my stint on Spring Street.

"Where you going, brother?" one of them asked me.

"Got a girl on the Upper West Side. She wants to take me in," I said.

They all nodded and looked at each other, as if similar stories frequently circulated.

"Take a shower first," another said. "Use exfoliate soap. Burn the clothes."

"Don't get fucked up on her stuff the first night," said a woman. "It's a temptation, but you can stretch things out with just a little bit of discipline." She looked at the others staring at her. "Really, no shit."

"Yeah, but bring your kit and plenty of supply. Those girls up there can't source for shit."

"When boosting, think cash and jewelry. Don't get bogged down with shiny knives and forks. Too heavy, no return."

"Husbands. They can show up any time. Fly in from Düsseldorf or some shit."

"They can shoot you, legal."

"Fuck, yeah. What're you? Street trash. Supremely shootable."

"This is really good advice," I said, "thank you."

They liked this.

"Fuckin' right it is."

For the hell of it, I walked by the United Aquitania building before returning to the hotel. The woman Natsumi christened as Nose Stud was coming out the door. I went to stop her, but she dropped her shoulder and swiveled around, executing as neat an escape as any professional running back.

"Wait, you know me," I said.

She stopped and pointed her finger at me.

"I thought that was you with the cart," she said. "You're not smellin' too good."

"United Aquitania has some visitors," I said.

"You still owe me a thousand bucks. I called your lady friend right before I left my apartment."

"Fair enough. Three of them got out of a cab. But there was a light on already."

"Don't know about any three. I'm talking about the woman across the hall from me. I don't know her personally, but tonight, I saw her come out of their offices and then lock the door behind her."

"Anybody else there?"

"I don't know. I kept my head down as I walked by. Way too creepy."

"What does the woman look like?"

"Probably early fifties, tall, broad in the butt, long straight hair, too black to be real, narrow face with a long nose, imperfect skin, likes high-heel boots. Affiliates with the creative class, still hip, but slipping behind. And she knows it."

"Thought you didn't know her," I said.

She handed me a business card: Ella Eveningstar, PhD, Anthropology.

"I teach at Columbia. You can send the check to my office. I hate the cops, by the way. I'm an anarchist. But if they ask about this, are you good or evil?"

"We're good. Not sure yet about the other guys."

She gave me a noncommittal look, and left me at the curb. I walked up to Houston and caught the subway back to the hotel.

That night, I dove into my clandestine version of Joselito's email and wrote to Rodrigo.

Sr. Mariñelarena:

I have given this much thought and believe I have a safe way for us to meet.

Assuming you are here next Saturday, you and only one of your men go to Rockefeller Center and take the elevator to the Top of the Rock, planning to be on the observation deck at twelve noon. I will do the same. We will need to pass through metal detectors, so no guns allowed. If either one of us tries to harm the other, the police stationed on the ground will immediately quarantine the building. There will be no way to escape.

I know you come with honorable intentions, but we both understand the need for precautions.

Gorrotxategi

That evening, I had my reply.

Sr. Gorrotxategi:
I will be there, wearing a red beret. My associate will wear one in white.

Mariñelarena

I wrote back.

Sr. Mariñelarena:
We will be wearing Boston Red Sox baseball caps, a dangerous thing to do in New York, but so rare you will not miss us.

Gorrotxategi

All set, I went to bed, nervous and excited by the escalation of risk. I was awake most of the night running through next steps, but it did little to slack my energy, as my obsessive brain hurtled toward the inevitable.

The next morning I wrote a note and printed it out. I took it to a FedEx office and sent it with a disposable phone to Shelly's home in Rocky Hill, Connecticut.

The note said, "Find a place where they can't listen in."

The morning after that, I got the call.

"So you found a place," I said.

"I did, and no, I won't tell you how."

"How bad is it?"

"It's bad," he said. "They've assigned a dedicated team. Five agents. That's a big commitment given budget pressures."

"How well do you know them?"

"Not very. One or two."

"One of them's a mole. He's in steady contact with Joselito Gorrotxategi, with whom he trades, or maybe only sells, intelligence about United Aquitania. Given the quality of the intel, he's got to be part of that team."

"How do you know this?" he asked.

"I told you. I'm living inside Joselito's computer. Do you know people further up the food chain?"

"I know people who know people. At least I did. They're retired, like me."

"You might want to open up those channels. For all I know, the mole doesn't know he's a mole. Joselito is former Interpol and Guardia Civil. Could easily be seen as a trustworthy source. Though I know for a fact he's dirtier than stink."

"I'll do what I can. You don't know how Byzantine these bureaucracies can be."

"Can I call you?" I asked.

"No. I'll call you."

"Okay, make sure it's good news."

Natsumi and I went out that night. We dressed up and ate at a tiny, expensive and quietly refined restaurant with food that could challenge Provence. After dinner, we strolled the streets of the Upper West Side and Natsumi instructed me on living in the moment.

"Your past is gone and your future has yet to come," she said. "So all you have is the present. I don't think this is very hard to understand."

"It is for people like me. We do the opposite. We obsess over what we've done and grind our guts over what we need to do next."

"So knock it off," she said.

"Okay, as soon as I figure out what Florencia got herself — and us — into, and then what to do about it."

"You'd make a terrible Buddhist."

"I know. My mind is never quiet and I never live here, now. I live here, there and everywhere," I said. "However, I never kill other creatures, even the tiniest annoying bug, unless I absolutely have to, and I believe in the eternal continuum of being."

"You do?"

"Before I was shot in the head, I could run the equations for Einstein's General Theory of Relativity. I remember how it felt when all those numbers fell into place. A breathless sort of dizzying joy, making sense of the universe by embracing that which to our common experience makes no sense at all. If that isn't Buddhist, I don't know what is."

"Now I know why I like you."

Back at the hotel room, I woke up the computer and checked all my email accounts. One from Shelly stood out.

"They know about the computer tap."

"Gotta go," I said to myself.

I tried to visualize the connection between Joselito's computer and mine — the links, routers, IP addresses. Instead, all I saw was a huge dark room filled with computer screens and projected images of New York City, with an overlay of multicolored circuits and communications pathways. All narrowing in on me.

I shut down the wireless broadband access, unplugged the laptop and stuck the external hard drive in my backpack. I searched around the room. Fingerprints, DNA, miscellaneous data everywhere. Printouts and travel documents. Not enough time to wipe clean. I stuffed the backpack with identity documents.

"Natsumi!" I hissed her name.

"What?" she hissed back from the adjoining room.

"Put on your hoody and grab all your passports and drivers' licenses. Get the makeup kit. Leave your smartphone."

I looked around the room one more time. I saw a lot of things hard to leave behind, but it was too late. I went in the other room where Natsumi was putting on her own backpack. Her face was tight, but calm and alert. She hid all that under the hoody.

We were halfway to the elevator when the doors slid open and people in black helmets and baggy equipment-laden vests poured out into the hall. We pressed ourselves against the wall and stared, which was likely the smart thing to do, since any normal person would. One of the men looked at us, put a gloved finger to his lips and shooed us down the hall. We watched as they used small battering rams to smash their way into both our hotel rooms. In the midst of all the urgent commands and crashing around, we slipped through a pair of swinging doors into the utility room that served the maid staff, fed by a service elevator which took us to the laundry room in the basement.

From there, we found the parking garage, and then our rental car. I drove up toward the exit and immediately fell into a long line. I got out of the car and saw the reflections of flashing blue lights. I pulled the car into a parking space and we went on foot to a stairwell that took us up to the street.

The world was filled with police cars, blue and white SWAT-team trucks and ambulances. People were standing around the sidewalk wondering, I'm sure, if it was a theatrical moment or the real thing. One of them was a limousine driver leaning against his black Crown Vic.

"Hey, man," I said to the driver, "this is freaking my wife out. Can you give us a ride out of here?"

The man was short and dark, with unruly black hair and a uniform a size or two too small. I held up a fifty-dollar bill.

"Where to?" he asked.

"Just head downtown and I'll figure it out as we go," I said.

We were well past Columbus Circle before I had the address of a tiny hotel in Tribeca that had vacancies for two connected rooms, room service and broadband access. All within walking distance of Soho.

"So we're not fleeing to Madagascar?" Natsumi whispered in my ear.

"Not yet."

"Good," she said, resting her head on my shoulder.

After getting settled into the new room, I lay down on the bed and Natsumi lay next to me.

"I've never been fingerprinted or labeled by DNA," I said.

"I have."

"I know."

"We're gonna get caught," she said.

I lay there quietly and thought about that.

"No, we're not."

"Oh, good. Nice to hear you say that."

"Though we might get killed."

"That's okay. As long as we go together," she said.

"I was kidding."

"I wasn't."

Natsumi slept while I stared up at the ceiling and took stock.

Our smartphones were back in the other room and the laptop we brought was disconnected from wireless access. As far as I knew, there was no other way to track us electronically.

I'd used a clean ID to secure the room in Tribeca. There was no paper trail to follow. More so the electronic trail, though I'd been scrupulously careful with IP addresses and searchable keywords.

Shelly Gross was another component. Either he'd been reeling us in all along, or truly was operating as a quasi-free agent. In which case, he could go to management with the mole story. Though even that didn't guarantee anything. For all I knew, the mole was an official operative.

Then there was Joselito. An experienced security guy like him was capable of finding the tap and subsequently uncovering my secret communications with Rodrigo Mariñelarena.

He'd know a meeting had been set up between Rodrigo and a fictitious version of himself. Rodrigo, meanwhile, had to be prepared for the possibility of a trap. He couldn't know that the possibility had turned into a sure thing.

My objective had been to squeeze more information out of Rodrigo, not assassinate him. He might well deserve it, but since I really didn't know, I couldn't let that happen.

I waited until Natsumi was awake and ordering coffee to make the call to the Nose Stud anthropologist.

"Ella here."

"Hi, Ella. Did you get the thousand dollars?"

"I did. Cash stuffed in a FedEx envelope. Very interesting."

"Can I ask you a question?"

"How much for the right answer?"

"Is there such a thing as a mercenary anarchist?" I asked.

"You betcha."

"Two fifty. I don't want to be a schmuck. You won't respect me."

"Okay. Ask away."

"Do you know the name of the woman across the hall and where she works?" I asked.

"I think she works out of her apartment, but I see her a lot at the deli down the block. She was really loading up on stuff this morning."

"Thanks for this," I said. "It might save a life."

"Is it worth saving?"

"I don't know."

"You're a strangely persuasive person, even if you do have a lot of crazy shit going on," she said.

"I appreciate the favor."

"It's not a favor if you're paying me. It's a task."

"So you don't mind."

"Of course not. I love crazy shit."

The deli at the end of the block was called Milt and Jerry's, and not a single person working the place could have possibly been named either Milt or Jerry.

There were about five tables crammed in the back, but from there you had a clear view of people coming in to order from the counter. A sign hung on the wall announcing free WiFi, so I took that as an invitation to sit with my new laptop — purchased the day before — long enough to see Ella's neighbor swoop into the place.

I snapped the computer shut and brought it with me to stand in line behind the woman. She was ordering bagels, muffins, sandwiches and coffee. She had a pronounced Spanish accent. The guy behind the counter tried to be friendly. The woman was polite, but not engaged.

"*Gracias,* Clementina," said the deli clerk when he slid a paper bag filled with her order across the counter. She nodded, and while she waited to pay at the cashier, I got a free coffee refill.

I followed her out the door, came up close behind, and said, "*Perdóneme,* Clementina."

She whipped around, alarm in her face.

"I have a message for Rodrigo," I said, in Spanish. "It's extremely important."

"Who are you?"

"Tell him not to meet with Joselito. It's a setup. And stay away from him. It could mean Rodrigo's freedom, or his life."

"Tell me who you are," she said.

I stuck a disposable phone in the bag.

"The number's queued up. Just hit send. Tell him to call from the street. I'm not sure your offices are secure."

I turned and walked away. After crossing the street, I looked back and saw her standing there watching me.

Ten minutes later, the phone chirped.

"Si."

"Explain yourself," said Rodrigo in Spanish.

"She wanted to know who I am," I answered in English. "Remember an outdoor café on the Calle Dulcinea del Toboso?"

"You should be dead."

"You keep trying to achieve that and I keep saving your life. Doesn't seem fair."

"Why would you do that?"

"I'm looking for information, and you can't give it to me if you're dead."

"What do I get back?"

"The same."

"I thought you worked for the VG," he said.

"No, but I might start if you don't co-operate."

"I don't like threats."

"I know a lot about your organization, but you know nothing about me. That should be threatening enough."

For a moment or two, he was quiet on the other end of the line.

"What do you want?"

"A meeting. At a place where we both can feel safe."

"Where would that be?"

"Top of the Rock, 10:00 A.M.," I said, "It's a day before you're supposed to meet Joselito. Consider it a practice run without the hats." Then I hung up.

It was a cool, windy morning. I was with one of Little Boy's Bosniak crew, known to me only as Kresimir, on my way up to the top, open-air observation deck of the GE Building at Rockefeller Center. I was wearing a false moustache and wig. Kresimir came as himself.

It was 9:00 A.M., an hour before our meeting with Rodrigo. I would have been very disappointed if he wasn't already up there.

We'd passed through the metal detectors

377

without a hitch since the Bowie knives we each carried were made of an unbreakable polymer.

There were plenty of people keeping us company on the elevator, and a healthy crowd up on the deck. I quickly spotted Rodrigo with one of his boys, Jueventino. I did a pass around the deck to see if he'd brought another guy along, but saw no one I recognized.

"Welcome to New York," I said, as we approached Rodrigo.

"I want my money back," he said.

"What money?" I asked, artlessly, not knowing what else to say.

"The money you withdrew from the bank in the Cayman Islands. It belongs to me."

"I'm not Joselito."

"I know you're not. You were just pretending to be. You're the man with the Asian woman who is trying to destroy me."

"I'm not. I just want some information."

"We are calling you *El Timador,*" said Rodrigo. "The Trickster. Maybe better *El Tonto,* The Fool."

"Why did Florencia Zarandona establish the Caymans account and why did she have a list of your safe houses?"

His grin faded.

"You killed her, you bastard," he said.

"I didn't kill her."

"How else would you know about the account? You killed her and framed other people so you could take the money. You think we're stupid, Timador?"

"No, but you don't know the facts."

"Give me the money and maybe we'll let you live."

"Give me what I want to know, and maybe I'll give you the money."

"He don't kill her," said Kresimir. "I know for sure."

Rodrigo looked at him.

"There you have it," I said.

"I have nothing more to say to you," said Rodrigo, turning and walking away. Jueventino walked backwards at his side, watching us, until they were nearly to the elevator. I watched them go.

"They don't believe you," said Kresimir.

Frustration nearly choked off my voice. "I probably wouldn't either," I said. "But that can't matter."

And that was when the two large men in matching dark blue windbreakers walked up to us. One of them said, "Take a step and you're both dead."

CHAPTER 21

Kresimir obviously had trouble following directions. He not only took a step, he butted one of the guys in the head and stuck the edge of his hand in the other guy's throat. They both went down.

We walked briskly to the elevator, which had just arrived. Kresimir pulled the last few people out and pushed the button.

"Get back," he told those waiting to board, baring his plastic knife.

We went to the floor below the observation decks and left the elevator. In a few moments, we'd found the stairwell and started down. Ten stories later, we left the stairwell and caught an elevator that served the whole building. We took it down to the parking garage. When the door opened, a security guard was waiting with his gun drawn. Kresimir put his hands up, so I did too.

"Drop the knife," said the guard as he

pulled a radio off his belt.

Kresimir smacked the gun aside and snapped a right jab in the guard's face. Before the guard hit the ground we were walking quickly into the garage. We moved through the rows of cars until we came to a pickup truck. He pulled me down to the floor.

"Take off your jacket. Ticket's in the visor. I'll be in the toolbox. They check, we're goners."

He stood up, unlocked the big, diamond-plate box on the left side of the truck, dropped the keys in my lap and somehow managed to fit himself inside. I got in the cab, stripped off the wig and moustache, and my jacket, and started the truck.

Moments later I was in a line at the exit. The NYPD was checking the vehicles as they went through the gate. When it was my turn, a tall white guy chewing gum twirled his finger at the window. I let it down.

"What's up?" I asked.

He looked at me, then down at a smartphone. Then back at me. I realized he was looking at a photo, or video, zinged over to the cops by the building's security.

"What's in the toolboxes?" he asked.

"Tools?" I said.

"Did you go up to the top?"

"Of what?"

"The building."

"You can do that?"

"Can you unlock the boxes?"

I shook my head.

"Nope. It's a company truck. The boss has the keys."

He looked at me for a longer time than I would have wished for, then stood back from the window, rapped the side of the truck and waved me on.

I drove around the city for about a half hour, looking for any signs of a tail. Satisfied, I went back downtown to the parking garage close to our hotel. Kresimir looked happy to be free.

"Next time I'm in a box, I better be dead."

"You saved my ass. I really appreciate it."

"I know, Mr. G. But with all due respect, I save mine, too."

"They got you on security cam. Better lay low for a while."

"No problem. Little Boy send me back to Bijeljina to visit what's left of my people."

Out in the daylight, I strolled back to the hotel. I walked past the entrance, scanning the street for anything suspicious. I went into a jewelry store and asked if I could borrow their phone.

"Lost mine, and I got to call my wife.

She'll really be worried."

The salesperson led me to a small back office, but stood there while I made the call.

"It's me," I said. "Everything okay?"

"You mean with my mother?"

"I know your mother is in the best of health. Robust you might say."

"So, yeah, things are fine here."

"See you soon."

The saleslady looked confused, but I got out of there and walked across the street to the hotel. Nobody attacked me in the lobby and I made it up to the room. I knocked on the door using our secret door knock and Natsumi let me in.

"How's Rodrigo?"

"Homicidal."

As I threw water on my face and washed off the fake moustache adhesive, I told her what happened at the Top of the Rock.

"Good Lord," she said, following me out to the room where I lay down on the bed. She sat on the edge. "You know Kresimir lost his whole family in the war."

"I did. Little Boy told me he's the only person in the world who scares him."

"Who were they?"

"They weren't FBI. They'd send half an army. We'd never get away."

"Theories?"

"Joselito's goons. He knew we were meeting."

"That's impossible, right?"

I sat up.

"Mariñelarena's blown. If I could find United Aquitania, so could Joselito Gorrotxategi, or the FBI."

"The mole," she said.

"My guess is their rooms in Soho are bugged. No other way they could have known."

"Now what?"

"I sent a note to Clementina to warn Rodrigo, the son-of-abitch who wants to kill me, to get out of Dodge. Then we visit Shelly Gross."

"You know where he lives?"

"I know where he eats dinner."

Crossing the New York border into Connecticut felt like what it was — a homecoming. Except for college and graduate school, and the brief stint in London, I'd spent my whole life in Stamford. Winding along the leafy Merritt Parkway stirred up so many associations you could almost see them blowing around in our wake. It's where Florencia and I lived, where she had her insurance agency. It's where our lives ended. I shared those feelings with Natsumi.

"This is where living in the moment really comes in handy," she said.

I'd timed the trip so we could catch him at a restaurant called the Powder Keg where he ate every night. A man of remarkably consistent habits, I knew he'd be there. The restaurant was in Old Wethersfield, about an hour and a half north of Stamford.

I parked in the lot of a florist shop that was closed, and we walked about a block to the Powder Keg.

As the name suggested, the restaurant's ornamental theme revolved around weapons of destruction, specifically of the American Revolution. Muskets and paintings featuring men in blue and red coats shooting each other covered the walls, and a hefty cannon guarded the entrance. It was paneled in dark wood and lit by lamps with red glass shades.

Shelly was in the bar in his usual booth eating a burger and drinking from a mug of beer. He was watching a basketball game on the TV over the bar, a welcome island of modernity amidst the deep eighteenth-century gloom.

We slid into the booth across from him.

"Hi, Shelly," I said.

"Well, well," he said. "The man who lives dangerously. And Natsumi Fitzgerald, I presume."

Shelly was in his late sixties. Lean and athletic, his face resembled a white-haired fox, not inappropriately.

"Did you report the mole?"

He shook his head. "I asked an old friend of mine how well he knew the agents assigned to the United Aquitania team. He asked me why. I told him one of them might be dirty. He told me he'd do some digging. Five minutes later I was being escorted to the door with a warning to stay out of investigations or face arrest."

"Some friend."

"A friend of the friend, I'm guessing. Anyway, I'm really out for good now. Unless you want me to drive you to headquarters in New Haven so you can turn yourself in."

"Dirty is putting it mildly," I said. "It feels like he's in operational unison with the Vengadores."

Shelly shrugged.

"Maybe they all are. United Aquitania is on the list of terrorist organizations. We'd be in operational unison with Lucifer if it helped with the war on terror."

"Lucifer would be an improvement over these guys," said Natsumi.

"Who are United Aquitania, anyway?" I asked.

"Basque separatists."

"ETA?"

"No. A splinter group. They split off when they thought ETA was getting too soft. Hadn't kept up the appropriate level of killings, bombings and armed robberies. At this point, they're the last of the violent elements. The worst of the worst. That makes it very bad for you."

"Why?"

"The Bureau is certain you're one of them," he said. "Are you?"

"What do you think?"

"No. If I thought you were, you'd have been nabbed a long time ago."

"Actually, they're trying to kill me," I said.

"Not surprising. You stole their money."

"Did you share anything you know with anyone outside the United Aquitania team?" I asked. "Except that one time with your friend?"

"No. I never gave them much to begin with. Didn't trust them. No particular reason, just a gut feeling."

"Smart gut," said Natsumi.

He gestured at her with his beer. "You're supposed to be pretty smart yourself, Ms. Fitzgerald. Why do a stupid thing like take up with this nut case?"

"I like nuts."

"You're not in so deep you can't cut a

good deal with the U.S. Attorney. Cooperate a little. Claim coercion."

"Not a chance."

"I didn't think so, but I'm duty bound to ask."

"Why so open with the information?" I asked, getting attention off Natsumi.

"I've been working on two theories about you," he said. "Sort of a retirement hobby. If one of them is correct, it may be okay to give you a hand. You're a liar and a cheat, but maybe there's a reason for it."

"You want to share your theory?" I asked.

"Nope. I said theories. If the other one turns out to be it, I will definitely spend my remaining years hunting you down."

"Any chance you're being shadowed?" I asked.

"Every chance in the world. I'm sure the phone's bugged and my computer's crawling with spyware."

"We'll just be leaving through the kitchen."

We started to slide out of the booth.

"Before you go," he said. "One question."

We paused, and before I knew what he was doing, he reached up and snatched off my baseball hat. He looked closely at my bald head, then handed back the hat.

"Good luck," he said, and went back to

his burger.

The guys in the kitchen barely reacted when we walked through. They'd seen it plenty of times before. Usually guys out with their girlfriends avoiding a friend of their wives, or drunks ducking AA buddies. A few Latinos put their heads down and tried to look invisible.

Outside, we walked through the backyards of the retail establishments along the street, all installed in former old houses, until we reached the florist and our car.

Then we glided off into the tranquil Connecticut night.

After the deeply paranoid experience of walking through the hotel lobby and stepping into our room, I sat down at the computer, and opened up Joselito's email and started searching.

Earlier I'd read through the whole inbox. This time, I opened up the "deleted" folder. It was empty. Joselito had set the program to make every deletion permanent. Only he should have known nothing in cyber-land is really permanent.

"Sloppy, sloppy," I told Joselito, the corporate security expert.

Moments later I had the delete file open and filled to the brim with emails. I started plugging keywords into the search window, which helped organize the effort. I knew he was vigilant about not using traitorous terms and names, but was he perfect?

Hours went by. The night deepened, then slowly turned to morning. I made coffee and kept going. I fed in names and initials, which yielded nothing new. I wasn't discouraged. I was a researcher. We take a complete lack of results as a sign of encouragement.

After plugging in every name and set of initials I could think of, I sat for a long time trying to relax my mind, to live in the moment, allowing the barriers inside my memory to fall away.

"Eloise," I said aloud, and typed it in.

The email, written in Spanish, was addressed to eharmon@gmail.com.

Eloise:
So nice to connect today after so long. Memories of our work in Madrid are never far from my mind. I should have followed you to DC when you were reassigned. But now we're both here and need to catch up. When are you back in New York?

Best,
Joselito

Bingo. I selected that address and hit the

"From" button. A long list popped up.

> Joselito:
> Feelings are mutual. I regret that reassignment more than anything I've ever done. I hoped I would never see you again, so I wouldn't have to relive the regret. But there you were, standing in that room with all those security wonks and I melted. Damn you beautiful hombre.
>
> > Eloise

This went on for more than a year, with exchanges like this typical:

> Eloise:
> Thank you for last night. It's even better than before.
>
> > Joselito

> Joselito:
> Likewise. Come to DC.
>
> > Eloise

The correspondence took the expected path — more and more ardor ineffectively disguised by fumbling euphemism. Joselito was more circumspect, but his co-conspirator was too addled by passion to contain herself. I felt all the more the voyeur, but I'd stopped feeling bad about that. I just stayed in the moment. A moment that lasted another two hours, during which Natsumi brought in breakfast and a big vat of coffee.

Then the chain took an interesting turn:

Joselito:
Very cool case out of the Caymans. I can tell you all about it tomorrow when we're doing you-know-what. It's very exciting. I love exciting you.

Eloise

Eloise:
Don't forget what I told you. I know about these people. You know what I do. We find that money, we can be together.

Joselito

I felt my face heat up. I must have also been making noises, because Natsumi stuck her head in.

"You're making noises," she said.

"That's what a cyber-hound sounds like when he's after a rabbit."

"Nut case."

Joselito:
Let's talk about this on the phone. I'll call

your cell.

Eloise

The emails stopped after that for about a month, then another came through:

Eloise:
You do your part, I'll do mine. Pick out a house. Anywhere in the world.

Joselito

P.S. — No more emails. Close your account and get a tech to wipe clean your hard drive.

I went to the FBI website and started poking around. The executive directors of each division were listed, along with a description of their backgrounds and types of past service. No Eloise. I used the search box, but nothing came up there. Then I realized I was on the wrong site, and pulled up a satellite site dedicated to the International Operations Division.

Personnel weren't listed, but press releases were, going back a dozen years. That's where I found Eloise.

Eloise Harmon named Special Agent for Liaison with International Division
Director Robert S. Mueller III has named Eloise Harmon Special Agent for Liaison

Affairs with the International Operations Division, reporting to the Assistant Director of that division, Steven Holt. After six years as Legal Attaché assigned to the U.S. Embassy in Madrid, Spain, Ms. Harmon brings back to Washington considerable firsthand knowledge of the challenges and opportunities of the international environment.

"I'm keen on putting to use my experience in Spain in the service of our Legal Attachés across the world. Each faces unique challenges, but all share the need for solid support here in DC, as well as smooth and productive relationships with other international law enforcement agencies."

The release went on to describe her education and steady rise through the ranks of the FBI, most of which took place outside the country — in Spain, but also Latin America.

The last paragraph noted she was born in Chile to an American engineer named Lyle Harmon and a Chilean national, Isabella Morales.

That was it. For the first time in weeks, I felt the surge of adrenaline that came with clarity, with the first intimations of a solution to the problem I faced. I didn't exactly know why, but I knew my own mind, damaged though it was.

"All you bastards who want to kill us," I said out loud. "I'm coming after you."

Natsumi stuck her head in the room again. "What did you just say?"

CHAPTER 22

"I've discovered what's at the center of everything we've been going through since we landed on Grand Cayman," I said to Natsumi, as we lay fully clothed on the bed staring up at the ceiling, a habit I'd transferred to her. "The driving force behind everyone's behavior, behind every action we've observed."

"And that is?"

"Us."

"Oh."

We lay quietly for a while, Natsumi respectfully waiting for me to continue my story.

"As a researcher," I said, "I'm trained to stay removed from my subject — aloof, unbiased, entirely objective. People like me are ill-prepared to consider our own influence on the study's results. Even though Werner Heisenberg, the physicist, taught us long ago that the observer will always have an effect on the observed. We haven't just affected the experiment, we are the experiment."

"We decided on our own to go to Grand Cayman," said Natsumi.

"We did. Does a lab rat know the scientist has placed a tasty pellet at the end of the maze? Does a fruit fly question the ready availability of another sexy fruit fly in a lab container? The lure was set, they knew we'd bite."

"I had a bad feeling about that bank," said Natsumi.

"You were right."

"So what's it all about?"

"The money. I took a little over ten million dollars out of that account. Even by today's greedy standards, that's real money. They didn't know what was in the safe-deposit box, but they assumed it was worth a lot, and so just waited for the lab rat who emptied the liquid accounts to show up sniffing for more. And show up he did."

"What's he going to do now?"

"Tear down the lab."

Finding Eloise Harmon's home address wasn't easy, but not as hard as it should have been. She was, after all, one of the top people in a division of the FBI critical to national security.

She was also on LinkedIn, Facebook and Twitter. And an active supporter of her alma mater's recruitment committee, and a frequent user of her local library, and the editor of her swim club's seasonal newsletter. This exposed, a home address will always squirt out, you can't stop it.

I wrote her a note and sent it by FedEx to her house.

> Ms. Harmon:
> Interesting reading: eharmon@gmail.com
>
>> David Reinhart

I had a few more notes to send. The first to Joselito.

> Sr. Gorrotxategi:
> I want to meet with Domingo Angel here in America. I have information he will consider extremely valuable. I have things to ask in return, but will only deal face-to-face.
>
>> El Timador, the guy who hacked your computer (I know about Eloise)

> Rodrigo:
> I just saved your life once again, while

you continue wanting to take mine. If you harm me you will never see a dime of that money. What is the sense of that?

El Timador

Evelyn:

How are things? Are you happy to be back in Connecticut? How're the Bosniaks? It's likely your phone and online activity are being monitored. Even the disposable is insecure. The return address on this FedEx is fake. I will try to drop you messages, but for the time being, I don't know how you can safely return the favor. But I'll figure it out.

BTW, burn this note and the envelope and sprinkle the ashes in the backyard.

Shelly:

As far as I know, we weren't followed home. But I have to stay off electronic communications. I know the name of that little underground mammal, and it's a juicier bugger than I thought. I need an introduction to Steven Holt, the Assistant Director of the International Operations Division. Nobody below him can be trusted.

"How can he make an introduction if he

can't talk to you or send email?" asked Natsumi, looking over my shoulder.

"Working on that."

I was also working on another venue change. We'd clearly overstayed our welcome in New York City.

After pondering the options, I said to Natsumi, "I'm homesick for Connecticut."

"Stamford?" she asked.

"Litchfield County. As far from other houses as possible."

"Should I start the search?"

"While I pack."

For the second time in recent days, Natsumi and I were traveling up the West Side Highway on the way out of the city and up to Connecticut. We'd cleared out of the hotel and traded our rental car for a Dodge SUV into which we piled all our gear, including some new stuff sourced in New York City, the world's greatest source of all manner of stuff.

Natsumi had come up with a rental in the Connecticut town of Canaan, a low-density farming and vacation community in the far northwest corner of the state, not to be confused with the gold-plated New York City suburb of New Canaan down on the coast.

The property included more than two hundred acres of mixed forest and open uncultivated fields, several outbuildings and a farmhouse built in the mid-nineteenth century in the Empire style, which meant it was big and weird-looking, with a mansard roof and clock tower shooting two extra stories above the three-story building.

"I couldn't find anything more remote," said Natsumi. "In addition to the farm's own acreage, state parks and watershed abut all four sides. The closest neighbor is two miles away, and he's sort of a hermit living inside huge piles of newspapers and second-hand clothing. The agent thought he might be dead in there, in which case the next living person is a breeder of beagles a few miles further out. If you know beagles, you know why."

"My parents loved dogs, but thought it was unfair to keep them in apartments. So I satisfied my dog needs playing with the Pomeranian living happily in the apartment next door."

"My Japanese mother used to say, 'Cats, dogs, what's next, water buffalo?' "

"It's a slippery slope."

The traffic and capacity of the roadways diminished over the next two hours until we were riding over a road that conformed to every rise and fall, twist and turn of the topography.

Our SUV handled the increasing challenges with barely a wobble or sway.

We cracked our windows to let in cool, fresh air slightly tinged with the smell of manure.

Guided by my smartphone's GPS, we eventually came to the head of the narrow, unpaved driveway that ran through stands of mature hardwoods and fluffy hemlocks, then open grassland spotted with conical red cedars, and finally up to the imposing farmhouse facade.

Though a modestly ornamented version of the Empire form, the house still looked like it had broken away from a pre-industrial, upper-class Parisian enclave and wandered off into the wilderness.

"If they'd exiled Napoleon in Litchfield County instead of Saint Helena," said Natsumi.

"Lots of room to spread out."

When Natsumi had rented the place online, she'd clicked on the "Will take as is, just leave the key under the mat," and that's where it was. The front foyer was impressively cavernous, even for a big house. A central staircase swooped up to a second-story balcony. The mahogany railing, stained the color of dark chocolate, was missing approximately every fifth spindle. The walls were painted a deep blue and the plaster ceiling had been haphazardly patched more than once, though nothing was currently falling.

The walls in the living room were covered with an expensive-looking woven material in a color Natsumi called pinky-beige. It was furnished in musty over-built and over-stuffed Victoriana and eclectic salvage. The kitchen was clean and well equipped, all but one wall freshly sheet-rocked, though hooks and shelves screwed into the bare studs were well deployed as open storage.

The rest of the house followed suit, successfully avoiding the confines of a unifying decorative motif. We picked the bedroom with the best bed for sleeping and the biggest one for electronics. The other five were held in reserve.

While Natsumi went out for provisions, I set up the gear, opened a fresh IP relationship and dove out into the web.

One of my graduate professors would describe research as a methodical progression, searching for hidden pathways that would allow you to move along from phase to phase. I hated that idea. To me, there was nothing linear about it. Where he saw chain links, I saw a wild, gnarly bush. There was no gleaming, singular truth at the end of the journey. Only a jumble of approximate facts and assumptions, leading to a set of probabilities.

Not that I couldn't arrive at a workable solution to a problem, a repeatable answer to a question, but I was never free of that queasy element of doubt, that persistent itch of uncertainty.

This frequently drove me back to the roots of the inquiry, where it all began. In this case, it had to be the Basque region of Spain, circa 1960. I opened Google España and started the search with the University of Bilbao. Not surprisingly, the university seethed with political turmoil during this period. Though Basque nationalism was certainly an ingredient, most of the commentary involved the fundamental divide between the fascistic central government and the Marxist underpinnings of the separatists that had persisted since the civil war.

I'd already made the connection between the Zarandonas and the leftist movements at the university. That was public record in the form of speeches and essays in academic journals. Though somewhat bland by the standards of left-wing demagoguery, it was still brave stuff for the times. I was able to add to my records, but nothing new emerged.

I remembered the two professors arrived in Chile in 1968, but realized I'd never linked back to their departure. I dumped all the material I had on their time at Bilbao into a single document, then searched for dates. The spread was 1951 to 1962, but nothing after that. There was a six-year gap.

I went back to my Chilean database. The core reference was an article in the student newspaper of the University of Chile, heralding the arrival of the two distinguished professors. During my original research, I'd picked up the highlights, then zoomed on. This time I read the whole article, and as frequently happens, the most important fact lived in the last paragraph.

"Last May, professors Sylvia and Miguel Zarandona were greeted at the airport by President Allende, Mrs. Zarandona's third cousin. They were then honored with a week's stay as the president's guests, which they were grateful for after the long flight in from Paris."

"Paris?" I said out loud.

Once Google has managed to capture all the information on earth, you will theoretically be able to capture it all as well. Assuming you know every language.

I switched to Google France and started anew. Switching between languages and constantly adjusting for the dialects made me dizzy. And my French fluency was not nearly as strong as my Spanish. Luckily, Natsumi was back at the house, and helped fill in the gaps. After a few hours, we hit it.

The first recorded assembly of ETA was in the French Basque city of Bayonne, in 1962. One of the featured speakers was Miguel Zarandona. A local Marxist newspaper, covering the event, had a photograph of the young Zarandona, his wife and two-year-old son. According to the story, Zarandona had exhorted the gathering, demanding they use all necessary means to overthrow the fascist yoke of Madrid, including armed resistance.

"Not just the mild-mannered professor," said Natsumi.

The militant rhetoric inflamed commentators throughout ETA, until then a strictly political and cultural organization. Whether regarded as a hero or provocateur, all were certain Zarandona could never return to Spain.

So the next task was the ugly slog through census data to find out where they actually ended up. It wasn't until the next day, after a brief sleep, when we saw through reddened eyes the names Miguel and Sylvia Zarandona listed as apartment dwellers living with their son, identified only as "male, age five," in the resort town of Biarritz in 1965.

Then the trail was lost again, and after another day of effort, I put that channel of inquiry on hold.

"Where are you going now?" asked Natsumi.

"To bed."

Which I did, sleeping nearly twelve hours, during which I dreamt of men in dark, baggy clothes and berets, shaking their fists and painting huge, heroic murals of men with rifles and slogans of the revolution. Through all the swirling images and phantasms, my dreaming mind kept coming back to the family portrait of the Zarandonas, their unsmiling, determined pose contrasting oddly with their physical beauty.

Moments before waking the answer was there, until the dream state resolved into full consciousness, and it floated away into the random mist of probabilities.

"How about some fresh air," Natsumi asked me, two days later. Two days spent nonstop in front of the computer.

"Are you suggesting the air in here isn't fresh?"

"I am. And neither are the residents."

"Okay."

I needed to get a finer sense of the layout of the property anyway, so it made for a long and pleasant walk.

"Can you tell me what you've been up to?" she asked.

"Going back to the roots of the matter. I was annoyed at myself for missing that period the Zarandonas spent in France. I feel it means more than it seems, but I can't figure out why. The Basque people were used to moving back and forth between the French and Spanish sides with relative ease, even back then. So it probably didn't feel that much like an exile. But that changed for Zarandona who fouled his nest in Spain by addressing the ETA conference the way he did."

"Then why bolt to Chile?"

Some very wise people I've known insist that purging one's mind of the problem one is facing is the surest route to a solution. So I actually tried to stop thinking about it while we walked, instead trying to focus on the abundant pastoral beauty surrounding us. While it's nearly impossible for me to do this, I often tried anyway.

"Do you ever feel you already know something you're trying to figure out?" I asked Natsumi.

"Of course. Much of what amounts to thought happens at the subconscious level, and the subconscious is often the smartest part of the brain. I like to say the conscious part talks and the subconscious feels. But it's all thought."

"So I need to get in touch with my feelings."

"And what are you feeling?"

"Like a screw-up."

"Besides the time in France, what other things do you feel you've screwed up?"

"The dates. I keep missing time-based correlations, even though they should be the most basic."

"I know why," she said. "You're lightning brain tends to skip over the obvious, with the intention of going back later for more careful deliberation. But you never go back, you just race around from pretty flower to pretty flower like a honey bee on speed. And I mean that nicely, because you're my friend."

We were about three-quarters of the way through our walk when I turned us around and headed back to the house.

"What's up?" she asked.

"1968," I said.

Back at the keyboard, I looked up the first violent exchange between ETA and the Guardia Civil. It was a few miles inside the Spanish border with France, just beyond the city of Irun. A car carrying two ETA leaders was pulled over by two Guardia Civil, based on a tip, it was later suspected, from a Guardia agent inside ETA's inner circle. The two ETA leaders refused to leave their car, causing the Guardias to pull their weapons and demand they do so. From somewhere inside the car a shot was fired that killed the Guardia at the driver's side window. The Guardia on the passenger's side managed to get the door open and drag the passenger out of the car. The Guardia pinned the ETA man to the ground, wrenched his gun from his hand, and began firing at the man driving the car, forcing him to race away, leaving the two adversaries in a wrestling match by the side of the road.

The ETA man managed to overpower the Guardia and get away on foot. The Guardia called in reinforcements, and a few hours later they trapped the ETA man in a barn and summarily executed him.

The Guardia killed that day was Eugenio Angel. The ETA man suspected to be at the wheel of the car was Miguel Zarandona, Florencia's father.

I took my hands off the keyboard and placed a call to Professor Preciado-Cotto.

The next few days were consumed with installing security cameras at strategic locations around the property and inside the house. I eventually had two dozen cameras feeding a program that let me monitor any and all, in whatever combination I wanted, either on the laptop or smartphone. Each camera was also paired with a motion detector, which would set off alarms on the phone and computer.

Anything that moved would be captured on video recorders, and as a backup measure, saved to a data storage service in the cloud.

I kept the Dodge, but rented a Jeep Wrangler equipped with enhanced off-road capabilities and parked it in the woods on an old logging trail that led out to the street from the rear of the property. When I got back to the house, Natsumi was naturally curious.

"Do we have a plan?" she asked.

"No, but we have a few precautions, and the start of a plan."

"What's the end look like?"

"A good Buddhist would allow the future to be whatever the future wants it to be."

"In other words, you don't know."

"I don't."

Back in the computer room, I sat and stared at the main monitor, assessing the balance between security and the need to communicate. I'd always used proxy servers to put up at least a basic layer of anonymity. There were hundreds of these services with accompanying software available on the web. If my purpose had been to hide my web-browsing habits, most would be fine. Hiding from the FBI, and potentially from the NSA, was another story.

But there was another equation to consider — the time it would take for even those high-powered surveillance operations to follow the trail back to me, especially if I daisy-chained multiple proxies, all offshore and fiercely resistant to law enforcement inquiry. I decided that time would be far longer than I needed.

A few hours later, after freshening my knowledge of the proxy landscape, I felt secure enough to send my first email.

Sr. Gorrotxategi:
I am ready to discuss arrangements for meeting with Sr. Domingo Angel. I have

412

chosen a location. We merely need to set a date and time. Obviously, we need to do this first. Please respond within 24 hours, or the offer is withdrawn.

El Timador

I hardly had to wait twenty-four hours. In less than ten minutes I had a reply:

El Timador:
I want to accept your offer, though you may well imagine that securing a visit with Sr. Angel in the U.S. is a tall order. Is there another way this transaction can be achieved?

Joselito

Joselito:
No. I have the means for contacting him directly. If you force me to do so, I will share with him your correspondence with Eloise and Mariñelarena.

El Timador

El Timador:
I understand. Please stand by while I discuss with Domingo.

Joselito

Joselito:

I will make this much easier for you. The information I have will provide the means for the total destruction of United Aquitania. This will achieve his lifelong mission and free me of a mortal threat.

El Timador

El Timador:
And free up their money for your own purposes.

Joselito

Joselito:
Yup.

El Timador

CHAPTER 23

I called Little Boy.

"Hey, Mr. G., what up?"

"Kresimir's an impressive guy."

"Impressive is our specialty."

"How's it going with Evelyn?"

"Nice lady. Very polite. Not as much fun as you two."

"Do me a favor and tell her I'm fine and will contact her as soon as I can."

"Okay. Should she believe you?" he asked.

I thanked him without answering, hung up, and went to tell Natsumi I was going for a ride.

"Where to?"

"Back to Rocky Hill. This time for a little exercise."

I first got to know Shelly Gross by filming his every move and following him around Rocky Hill and Wethersfield. I learned he was one of the most routinized people I ever knew. This methodical nature must have served him well when he led the FBI's organized crime task force in Connecticut. And probably kept him in good mental and physical shape as a retired widower.

So catching him at the gym at four o'clock in the afternoon was a sure thing.

He knew at this point what I looked like without a disguise, but I wore one anyway, in case Eloise had him under surveillance. It was my favorite hippy look, with a long grey wig pulled into a ponytail, droopy moustache and wire-rim glasses.

The gym was called FutureFit, which I took as an unusually honest, yet aspirational name. I signed up for a trial membership at the desk, changed into workout clothes and went looking for Shelly.

I found him on the stationary bike, his eyes fixed on a bank of TVs high up on the opposite wall. I took the bike next to him and started to peddle.

"Hi, Shelly," I said.

He looked over. "You're kidding."

"Nope."

"You look like an old hippy."

"I do?"

"I got your message. I'm going to need a lot more before going to Holt. I'm under strict orders to stay the fuck away."

"I have the mole, and I can prove it."

"Who?"

"I need a deal," I said.

"Ah. The old catch-22. I need something substantial enough to bring to Holt, but anything of substance could give away your bargaining power."

"Something like that."

"Oh, well."

"Isn't the very fact that one of your people is colluding with a violent militant group good enough?"

"Good enough to go to people well below Holt's pay grade. But not Holt."

I noticed the peddling was bothering my bad leg, so I coasted for a while.

"What if we combine that with information which could lead to the destruction of an international terrorist organization?"

"There's no 'we,' and they hear that crap every day. Goes to special agents in charge of routine investigations."

Frustration began to percolate up from somewhere in my midsection.

"I don't believe you," I said.

"Believe what?"

"That there's nothing you can do. You're a highly decorated former field agent. Nothing garners more respect at the Bureau. You got chased away only because the mole wanted you out of there. You've got a moral responsibility here."

"If you want to invoke morality, tell me the name," he said.

"I want to come in, but I can't go to prison."

"No way around that."

"There is if you want there to be."

"It's not my call," he said.

I got down off the bike and moved closer to him. "If you don't help me now, you'll never get another chance. I can't afford the faint of heart."

He stopped peddling and glowered at me. "I'll talk to Holt, but don't blame me if it blows up in your face."

I left him to finish his regimented exercise routine.

An email was waiting for me when I got home.

El Timador:
Domingo has agreed to the meeting. He can be in New York anytime beginning two days from now. He tells me his men saved your life in Menaggio, Italy. Not on purpose. They didn't know who you were. Now that they know, you will never have

another day without the fear of death.

Joselito

Joselito:
This is why we're meeting. Information in return for freedom from fear. A fair trade, I believe. Today is Tuesday. We will meet next Saturday at noon. I will send you the location at 9:00 A.M.

El Timador

"So you're inviting them here," said Natsumi, when I showed her the exchange.
"I am. Should be quite a party."
"A party. What should I wear?"
"Kevlar."

I was usually so engrossed in my web searches, digital escapades and local surveillance that I often ignored the general news media. Not so Natsumi, who listened to public radio nearly 'round the clock. So it was she who told me to click over to *The New York Times* breaking news.

Eloise Harmon, Special Agent for Liaison Affairs with the International Operations Division of the FBI, was gunned down today in her driveway as she left for work at FBI headquarters from her home in

419

Georgetown. The forty-three-year old mother of two, wife of Edward Harmon, a civilian employee of the U.S. Navy, had spent the bulk of her career overseas as an FBI Legal Attaché stationed at U.S. embassies in Latin America and Europe. In these positions, and in recent times as liaison between attachés around the world and Washington, Ms. Harmon was frequently involved in investigations into organized crime, drug and sex trafficking, money laundering and international terrorism. Officials at the FBI, and the Metropolitan Police Department in DC, refused to speculate on possible suspects or motives in the case. The investigation, they said, would take place on a local, national and international level.

I grabbed my disposable cell phone and called Little Boy.

"Mr. G., long time no hear."

"Write this on a piece of paper." I waited for him to get ready. "Harmon was the mole. I know who killed her. The terms of the deal just tightened up."

"Okay," said Little Boy. "Where to?"

I gave him a description of Shelly and when to find him at the Powder Keg Restaurant in Wethersfield, which was only about ten minutes from Little Boy's house in the South End of Hartford.

"Powder Keg? You're kidding. I go there all the time. Like all those guns."

"Send someone who's never been. Have him drop the note on the table and get out of there quick. Shelly's ex-FBI with a dossier on you probably six inches thick. Don't screw with him."

"Screwing with cops another specialty. But I hear you."

I got off the phone and realized that Natsumi was still standing in the room. Never an insistent person, her presence alone told me she needed to talk.

"Hi," I said to her. "What's up?"

"I like being with you. The life that comes with that is not terribly easy. Do you think it will always be like this?"

"Not sure."

She nodded.

"Okay."

"I'm trying to make it better," I said.

"You are?"

"The only way out is through."

"With me."

"With you," I said.

"I know. I just like to hear it once in a while."

"Your wisdom sustains us. Propels us forward."

"I thought it was my cooking," she said.

"That, too."

"Are we going to live through the next
thing?"

"Not sure."

"Less honesty, please," she said.

"Then definitely," I said. "Without a
scratch."

I spent the time leading up to Saturday sitting on a side porch drinking iced tea and
watching birds, squirrels, chipmunks, and at
dusk, the occasional fox, deer and raccoon
move through the wilderness before me.

"You're not on your computer," said Natsumi, after the first day.

"I'm not."

"How come?"

"No need."

"You have the answers?"

"Most of them."

I spent the next hour telling her what I
thought I knew, and what I thought should
happen. She listened without comment,
until I was done, then said, "No wonder
you're out here sitting with the world." She
joined me and we looked at the colorless
moonlit landscape until we both fell asleep,

struck senseless by the deep and restless New England night.

On Saturday at 9:00 A.M., I gave Joselito directions to the Empire house in Canaan and he acknowledged receipt.

Natsumi and I sat on the side porch where we'd spent the night and waited.

"Is there anywhere particular you'd like to live?" I asked her. "I mean for a longer duration. Not just a few weeks in a hotel or rented house."

"What are the parameters? City, country, developed, remote?"

"Has to have broadband access and decent coffee," I said.

"That narrows things considerably. Why do you ask?"

"We could be going there in a hurry."

"And we can stay for a while?" she asked.

"As long as we want."

"Long enough to get a dog?"

"I thought dogs led inexorably to water buffalos."

"They enforce a settled life," said Natsumi. "And I'm thinking warm. Do you know how to sail?"

"No."

"Jimmy Fitzgerald had me on Long Island Sound every weekend in a rattle-trap, twenty-four-foot, wooden sloop. I can sail better than I can walk. I say we get a heavy-displacement, blue water cruiser and bop around the Caribbean. Blend in with the snow birds and beach bums."

"With a dog?"

"Jimmy sailed with a scruffy little mutt. Shit on a piece of Astroturf. Eminently do-able."

"Okay."

"Unless we die in the next few hours," she said.

"Yeah. Then all bets are off."

Around eleven thirty, the motion detector alarm went off on my cell phone. It was tied to one of the cameras on a distant edge of the property. I ran to the computer room as alarms went off at five more locations. The cameras showed men in rough hiking clothes moving through the woods and crossing into the fields holding assault rifles and lugging backpacks, presumably filled with ammunition.

We went back down to the front entrance of the house and waited, glancing compulsively at my smartphone as it fed video images of paramilitary ground troops encroaching on the property from all sides.

"I don't think we have enough cold cuts," said Natsumi, looking over my shoulder. "I was prepared for two."

"No one RSVPs anymore."

"Will they shoot us outright?" she asked.

"We're good until they have the information."

"And how do they get that?"

"They don't."

Another alarm on the smartphone drew my eye to a black Range Rover pulling into the main driveway and rumbling up toward the house. I put my arm around Natsumi's waist and waited.

The Range Rover stopped a few feet away and a tall, thin man, somewhere in his seventies, stepped out. His hair, well receded from his forehead, was dyed black, and his nose was long and sharply defined. He wore sunglasses and a photographer's vest over a red flannel shirt. He looked around the property like a potential buyer assessing the opportunity.

Joselito got out of the driver's seat and walked around the front of the SUV. He was heavier and older than his LinkedIn photo, no surprise there. He was more or less the morphological opposite of Angel — slump-shouldered, pudgy and furtive.

"El Timador," Angel said to me, in English, extending his hand. "You are indeed a clever trickster."

I ignored his hand. "I assume you're in contact with your forces," I said. "Tell them to stand down, or they'll all be killed."

Angel dropped his hand and stepped backwards as if I were radioactive.

"What forces?" he asked.

I showed him a video feed on my smartphone of his men moving through the adjoining forest.

"I have snipers trained on each of your patrols. The guys in the woods have a slight chance of survival, but the ones in the fields will be as good as dead."

"You bluff," he said.

I used my thumb to toggle over to the cell phone and called Little Boy.

"See if you can shoot the hat off the lead guy moving through sector blue."

I turned the phone toward Angel so he could see the result. Little Boy's guy got the hat, but unfortunately took the head with it. Angel took out his phone and told his men to halt their advance.

"You and Joselito are personally in the cross hairs of our two best," I said to Angel as I took two steps back. "If you make the slightest move toward me or Natsumi, a hand gesture will put you in hell before the thought leaves your mind."

The two of them stood still as statues.

"What do you want?" said Angel.

"To end this war," I said.

"Mr. G.," the smartphone squawked at me.

"Yeah."

"We got two more Spanish guys in a car at the main entrance. Say they're here to see you."

"Let them in."

Everyone stood silently as we watched a silver Toyota drive up the gravel driveway to the house. It stopped a few car lengths from Joselito's Range Rover.

Jueventino and Rodrigo stepped out.

They came within a dozen feet and I motioned for them to stop.

"*Hola,* Timador," said Rodrigo.

"*Hola,* Rodrigo. Or is it Nicho?"

Angel took off his sunglasses and glared at the other two men with unalloyed hatred.

"Natsumi Fitzgerald," I said, "meet Nicho Zarandona. Florencia's brother."

"He didn't die of a brain tumor," said Natsumi.

"No. He needs to die with my hands around his neck," said Angel.

Joselito looked at me nervously, as if to say, "Hey, I just brought the guy here."

"See, this is the problem," I said. "You've been trying to kill each other for, I'm guessing, about eighteen years?"

"This man murdered my parents," said Nicho, pointing at Angel.

"Your father killed my brother," said Angel.

"It's not about fascism or Marxism, Basque nationalism or the preservation of the Spanish state," I said. "It's a blood feud between two families."

"Not true," said Nicho, pointing a finger at Angel. "The Vengadores have slaughtered hundreds of Basques over decades, many guilty of nothing more than speaking their hearts. We have only fought his loathsome death squad."

"He's got a point, Domingo," I said. "ETA and Madrid have a hard-won truce. Your former employers are very unhappy with you for threatening that. If my timing holds," I said, looking at the clock on my smartphone, "the FBI will be here in about an hour. They've got a seat warmed up for you two on a plane back to Spain, where the Guardias will be waiting to welcome you home. Sort of."

"You will destroy yourself, and this terrorist," said Joselito, nodding toward Nicho.

"Hell, no," I said. "We'll be long gone. Along with the snipers, who'll melt away as soon as you're in handcuffs."

Angel's bird-like face nearly convulsed with complicated thoughts and feelings. "This cannot happen," he said.

"Don't worry," I said. "I'll send your new address to Señorita Bolaños de Sepúlveda. Though she'll probably have to give up the château. The French share Spain's interest in a peaceful Basque region."

Joselito, a man with impressive instincts, moved away from Angel a few moments before the old Guardia reached inside his vest and pulled out a stubby revolver. The muzzle barely cleared the rough canvas fabric on its way toward Nicho when Angel's head and torso exploded in a red and grey cloud. A second later the sound of concentrated gunfire came from the nearby woods and the Spaniard crumpled to the ground.

Joselito had dropped to his knees with his hands in the air.

"Don't shoot! I'm not armed!" he yelled.

Nicho shoved Joselito's face into the ground and used his own belt to tie his hands. I set the dead colonel's phone next to Joselito's mouth and told him to warn the Vengadores to retreat or face certain death. Satisfied with the results displayed by video on my phone, Natsumi and I ran in the house and grabbed our gear and belongings, packed at dawn that morning, and loaded up the SUV.

Jueventino and Nicho helped.

"I need to talk to you about the money," said Nicho, heaving a hard case filled with video recorders into the SUV.

"You can't have it," I said.

"Why not?"

"I'm giving it back."

"You're giving millions of dollars to insurance companies who don't even know it's missing? That's crazy."

"It's their money," I said. "You get your freedom and a vastly degraded enemy. And what's left of your safe houses. Take it and consider yourself lucky."

I waited until the silver Toyota was far down the driveway before calling Little Boy.

"How're we doing?" I asked.

"Spanish guys all gone," he said. "We got a tail on the Toyota in case they try doubling back. I think we're cool."

"Thanks, Little Boy. I owe you."

"I know you do. The bill's in the mail."

I squatted down next to Joselito.

"The FBI will be here momentarily. I'll make sure you go down for Eloise Harmon's murder. And whatever else they might put together from your computer records. While you wait you can look at Domingo and ask yourself if it was all worth it."

He mumbled something into the gravel, but I didn't bother to hear it.

CHAPTER 24

The sun had barely broken the horizon, and it was already warm enough to sit in the cockpit of our forty-three-foot sloop in nothing but baggy cotton shorts and linen shirts. There was a breeze, of course. There was always a breeze where we sailed. Sometimes it became a serious wind, but usually the velocity fell between a soft caress and enough to sweep Natsumi's dense black hair back from her forehead.

She brought coffee, fresh-baked scones and strawberries up from the galley. The boat was at anchor in a well-protected, palm-lined cove. There were two other boats nearby, a catamaran full of noisy young women and a small monohull crewed by a pair of neighborly gay men who brought us cookies and painkillers the first night we dropped the hook, and toasted us with coffee cups every morning.

When Natsumi was settled, we repeated

the ritual. The guys hoisted their cups and gave us a thumbs-up.

"So, I haven't asked you," said Natsumi. "What was it like to see Florencia's brother."

"I knew he was her brother when I saw the photo of their father in the Marxist newspaper. Dead ringer. Even before that, something about his face got to me. Turned out to be the ghost of Florencia. To nail it down, I called Monsieur Lheureux at the Egretta Garzetta in Saint-Jean-Cap-Ferrat. I asked him to give me the names of the people staying there at the same time as the Zarandonas. Rodrigo Mariñelarena, by birth Nicho Zarandona, and by now a twenty-eight-year-old man, was in the room next to theirs."

"So the brain tumor was a cover."

"Sure. When they fled Chile they left the boy with friends tied to the Pinochet opposition. Best way to keep him safe was to declare him dead. I know this strategy well."

"Where did they go?"

"Costa Rica. Relatively safe and benign place. They start new lives as simple house-cleaners and landscapers, raising Florencia, and keeping their heads down. Meanwhile, Nicho is growing up in Chile and becoming more and more radicalized."

"So what happened?"

"Pinochet gets his ass thrown out of power. Rejoicing sweeps the anti-Pinochet expats and they flood back into the country. The smart thing for the Zarandonas would have been to keep a low profile, but Miguel has some pent-up stories, which he foolishly tells the local media. Domingo Angel caught wind."

"Where's Florencia in all this?" Natsumi asked.

"In the U.S. going to college and grad school. Meeting and saving a math geek from romantic ignominy."

"That math geek being less ignominious than he thinks," said Natsumi.

"The Vengadores assassinate the Zarandonas, and Nicho — already a committed left-wing revolutionary — mounts a mission of revenge. Moves to Spain, changes his name and founds United Aquitania. Aquitania being the ancient Roman name for the Basque region. In a few years, the new gang has killed enough Vengadores to earn a spot on America's list of terrorist organizations. Along the way, Nicho needs funds, so he taps his rich sister in America, who can't possibly afford his demands, and even if she could, would be in violation of anti-terrorism laws. So she cooks up her embezzlement scheme that not only throws off a lot of money, but operates well below regulatory radar. Would have lasted forever if it weren't for some unfortunate luck having nothing to do with the feuding Spaniards."

"You gave back all that insurance money," she said.

"I did. It wasn't ours and we don't need it. With the sale of Florencia's agency, we're up around eight million free and clear."

"If only we were free and clear."

"I'm working on that. Meanwhile, how bad is this?" I asked, looking around the cove.

"Not that bad."

We finished the first course and Natsumi went below to assemble the main event. Halfway through, she presented the puppy at the companionway, and I took him out to the bow to pee on a scrap of Astroturf. He was a mutt of such complicated ancestry that the pound refused to even speculate. So we named him Omni.

"We're going back to the U.S., aren't we?" Natsumi asked when I got back to the cockpit.

"Soon as I figure out how."

She burrowed into me and sighed, and we watched the day go all the way green, white and blue.

The employees of Thorndike Press hope you have enjoyed this Large Print book. All our Thorndike, Wheeler, and Kennebec Large Print titles are designed for easy reading, and all our books are made to last. Other Thorndike Press Large Print books are available at your library, through selected bookstores, or directly from us.

For information about titles, please call:
  (800) 223-1244

or visit our Web site at:
  http://gale.cengage.com/thorndike

To share your comments, please write:
  Publisher
  Thorndike Press
  10 Water St., Suite 310
  Waterville, ME 04901